Praise for *The Swap*

"A beautiful feat of swapped voices. Hilarious! Seriously, truly, fearlessly funny—and I don't want boys to miss it!"

—JON SCIESZKA, *New York Times* bestselling author and founder of the Guys Read literacy initiative

"Bravo, Megan Shull! *The Swap* kept me turning pages way past my bedtime! Hilarious and yet surprisingly touching at the same time, *The Swap* gives us a microscopically close insider's view at the differences (and similarities) between the lives of boys and girls. I don't know how Megan did it, but I'm really glad she did!"

—MEG CABOT, *New York Times* bestselling author of the Princess Diaries series and Allie Finkle's Rules for Girls series

"Funny, honest, and touching, *The Swap* is the perfect book for tweens ready to learn what's going on inside the minds (and bodies) of the opposite gender. Jack and Ellie are such wonderful characters, and those brothers—wow!"

—FRANCES O'ROARK DOWELL, *New York Times* bestselling author of *Dovey Coe* and *The Secret Language of Girls*

"The internal lives of both boy and girl come across as both authentic and heartwarming. . . . Readers curious about how the other half lives will thrill at this view from the far side of the fence." —*Kirkus Reviews*

the SWAP

MEGAN SHULL

KATHERINE TEGEN BOOKS
An Imprint of HarperCollins Publishers

Katherine Tegen Books is an imprint of HarperCollins Publishers.

The Swap
Copyright © 2014 by Megan Shull

Library of Congress Cataloging-in-Publication Data
Shull, Megan.
The swap / Megan Shull. — First edition.
    pages cm
Summary: When seventh-grader Ellie, who is having best-friend problems,
and eighth-grader Jack, who is under tremendous pressure from his father,
switch bodies and lives, they learn a great deal about themselves and the
opposite sex.
 ISBN 978-0-06-231169-6 (hardback)
 [1. Supernatural—Fiction. 2. Self-actualization—Fiction. 3. Interpersonal
relations—Fiction. 4. Middle schools—Fiction. 5. Schools—Fiction. 6. Single-
parent families—Fiction. 7. Brothers—Fiction.] I. Title.
PZ7.S559428Sw 2014   2014001883
[Fic]—dc23   CIP
                                                                   AC

Typography by Erin Fitzsimmons
14 15 16 17 18   CG/RRDH   10 9 8 7 6 5 4 3 2 1
❖
First Edition

For Maggie Doyne and Margaret Riley King

Could a greater miracle take place
than for us to look through each other's
eyes for an instant?
—HENRY DAVID THOREAU

ELLIE

IT'S SUNNY AND IT'S SUMMER and the three of us are sitting on the scratchy cement edge of the Riverside Swim Club pool, dangling our feet into the deep end. And by the three of us, I mean me (Ellie O'Brien), Sassy Gaines (my formerly best friend since forever), and Aspen Bishop (who moved here from California one month ago and apparently has taken my place). If you'd like to picture us, let me tell you this: Sassy and Aspen are side by side, dressed in pop-orange string bikinis with crisscross backs, "matchy-matchy" (as they like to say), long, sleek, and shiny yellow-blond hair framing their faces. They could pass for sisters—perfect features, perfectly straight teeth, pale-pink glossy lips glimmering in the sunshine.

In case you are wondering? My dark-red hair is wet and

slicked back into a ponytail. I have a little bit of sunblock on my nose. I'm wearing my black, front-zip, short-sleeve Roxy Surfer Girl half wetsuit. My mom got it for me. I love it so much.

"So, Ellie?" Sassy flutter kicks her pink toenails, spraying water into the air. "What's going on with that one-piece?" She giggles. "Is that, like, sporty chic?"

They are both looking at me. Leaning back on their arms, smiling.

Aspen raises an eyebrow. "Are you, like, planning on riding some waves in your boy shorts?"

The two of them make the same face and burst out laughing.

I can feel my cheeks getting redder and redder.

"Oh, um, well . . . ," I begin, then stop. I force myself to smile. I feel my heart kind of drop.

Aspen whispers something into Sassy's ear and they both instantly giggle.

"Um, no offense, but—" Sassy stares at me and shakes her head. "We're going into seventh grade! There are some basic rules. Duuuuuhhhhh! Some people seriously need to work on their style."

Aspen chimes in. "Ellie," she begins, pausing to cringe, "not to be rude or anything, but your freckles are, like, *seriously* out of control! Maybe you should think about using just a little bit of foundation or concealer?"

"Totally!" Sassy agrees. "But don't get the cheap cakey

kind that clogs your pores! No. Ewww! That would be gross."

Um, yeah.

Welcome to my life.

More?

Sure—

Sassy: "Um, no offense, but, guys, seriously, wheelie backpacks at the pool is so not okay!"

Aspen: "Not to be rude or anything, but why is that girl looking at me? I mean, sorry I'm hotter than you, okay?"

It doesn't feel good to listen, even when it's not about you. I am getting the worst feeling inside. I stare ahead across the pool and watch The Prince do a backflip off the diving board. The Prince is with a whole mess of other boys, but he's the only one with completely wild dark, wavy hair and tie-dye-blue eyes. He is definitely the only one with six-pack abs.

The Prince (as Sassy calls him) is Jack Malloy, and Jack Malloy is one year older than we are, and Jack Malloy is in eighth grade, and Jack Malloy is pretty much the most popular boy at Thatcher Middle School. He is handsome and mysteriously quiet and good at everything, including but not limited to every sport he plays and/or just looking cute and not saying a word. Yeah. He does that very well too.

Fact: Sassy is in *love* with Jack Malloy. Like, seriously obsessed! And she's *not* shy about letting everyone know it. She went all boy crazy at the beginning of the summer. It's kind of annoying and kind of weird. When The Prince is anywhere near us, she starts acting all different and, like, literally bats her eyelashes and acts suddenly super sweet and super fake. As soon as he's out of hearing range, she goes right back to being the Queen of Mean. This didn't used to bug me as much, but for some reason, ever since Aspen moved here at the beginning of the summer, the mean stuff Sassy says has started getting meaner. She usually blurts something out, then rolls her eyes and laughs really, really loud. "We're just joking, Ellie!" she'll say afterward. "We're just messing around."

As I tell you this, I know it sounds so stupid that I'm even friends with her, that I actually desperately want her to like me again (I do, I really do), but that's Sassy. She is just that type of girl who you just want to like you. Do you know what I mean? You want her to like you and put her big prettiest-girl-in-the-school stamp of approval right across your forehead so everybody else can see—

You are liked!

You are loved!

You are cool!

Sassy Gaines says so!

But it is on this day, today, under the hot summer sun and the blue sky and right here at the pool as the three of us watch—but are pretending not to watch—shirtless six-pack JACK I-have-no-idea-how-hot-I-am MALLOY, that Sassy says this:

"Ellie," she starts. She looks at me, smiling, running her fingers through her loose hair and tossing her head back. "It's not *that* big a deal. There's just an incredibly awkward time in life where your nose is too big for your face, and you happen to be in it."

I feel the tears coming from deep inside, starting in my stomach, charging up my throat. I swallow hard. I swear, I wish right this second that I could just disappear or that I could click my bare ankles like Dorothy from *The Wizard of Oz* and vanish into thin air. I drop my eyes and stare into the crystal-clear water. I imagine myself plunking in feetfirst, holding my breath, sinking, and sitting cross-legged at the bottom—Sassy and I used to do that all the time, in this very pool, for about a billion summers.

Except I don't jump in.

And I don't disappear.

I'm here, and I have the worst feeling wash over me.

"Oh my goooosh, Ellie!" Sassy exclaims, looking me up and down and scrunching up her nose.

I look back at her, like, *what?*

"Ohmygooooooooooooooooooshhhhh!" Both Sassy and Aspen fall back onto their shared beach towel, their faces to the sky, laughing so hard they can barely speak.

"Honestly, Ellie," Sassy cries. "Your—" She stops, she's pointing down. She can't talk, she's giggling so hard.

"Oh my gosh, *stop!*" Aspen wipes the tears coming

out of her eyes, careful to keep her black mascara from smudging.

My whole entire body just feels like it's shutting down. The only thing I want to do is leave. But I can't even get up. I can't even move. I don't say a word. I don't know what to do. I look off in the distance across the crowded pool: The Prince, his blue shorts hanging low on his hips, leaping off the board, effortlessly tucking into a somersault with two and a half twists, a ball of muscle flying through the air, entering the water with barely a splash. A second later he pops back up, whipping his wet dark hair out of his eyes, flashing a quiet smile at his fans. The boys on the side are just going nuts. "Dude! You killed it, man!" I hear one shout.

And I'm thinking how boys are so lucky they don't have to deal with this stuff, when—

"Ellie!" I hear.

I look back at Sassy and brace myself.

"Oh my gosh!" she shrieks. "I have honestly never laughed so hard! I'm dying! *Oh. My. God!*"

I can feel everyone watching now. Even the boys across the pool look up at us.

"Ellie, your legs—" Sassy squeals in an even louder voice, snorting back giggles. Then she finally spits it out, "Orangutan-man legs!"

Wait, what?

I force a smile and glance down. I never really noticed

it before, the soft red hair growing out of my legs. My head just, like, totally becomes hot—

What am I even supposed to say?

I can barely breathe.

I look at Sassy, rolling on her towel in her tiny string bikini, holding her flat stomach as if her muscles hurt from laughing. I sort of fake laugh too. I play along. I mean, what else can I do? That's just how she is. She has that effect on people. When Sassy is talking, she doesn't really care how you feel. She just says rude things to your face and it's sort of an expected fact that for some reason (probably because she is so pretty and popular and she can go up and talk to any boy in the entire school), you sit there and take it.

But inside? Between you and me? Laughing actually makes me feel even worse, because there isn't really anything funny about being insulted by your best friend since kindergarten, who has apparently decided you aren't her best friend anymore, two days before the start of seventh grade.

Nothing really funny about it at all.

2 JACK

"YES, SIR," I SAY.

I'm talking to my father, and this is how you have to talk to my father.

"Yes, sir, what?" he asks.

"Yes, sir, I understand," I answer, trying not to look at him but trying to seem like I am, because you can't really get away with no eye contact when talking with The Captain. I answer with a quick glance but keep my eyes straight ahead, staring through the windshield of the truck into the glare of the oncoming headlights and the pitch-black darkness.

We're on our way to hockey—I play year-round. I'm on the Boston Junior Bruins. I made the team last April. I'm the first eighth grader to ever make the roster, the youngest player in franchise history. It's pretty unbelievable.

Our first game is Monday night. I have a lot to prove. I have to compete for every shift of every game. I can't take a minute off. I don't want anyone to think I haven't earned my spot—that I got here just because of who my brothers are. I always have to prove myself. It's about battling. I go 100 percent, 100 percent of the time. If you really want something, working hard for it shouldn't ever be a problem.

My dad isn't speaking. He hasn't said anything in at least ten miles of driving through the dark. In The Captain's world, this means my answer was not acceptable. *I need to try again.*

"I will be more respectful of your time by being on time?" I say. I try to remember what it is he's been lecturing me about, what he told me I needed to fix. What I did wrong. I honestly don't really know what I did this time. He was in a bad mood before I even tossed my hockey bag in the back of his truck and hopped up into the front seat beside him.

Let me tell you, there's nothing worse than when my dad gives you the silent treatment. Even though it's dark, I feel his eyes on me.

I search my brain for the right words. "I'm sorry?" I try again.

Nothing.

The Captain reaches for the radio and turns it on. He likes classical music. I think it calms him down.

"Jack." My dad finally speaks. "I don't want to hear 'I'm sorry.' It's inexcusable behavior. I won't tolerate it. How many times do I have to tell you? Actions speak louder than words. If you want to be a man, you need to get things done. You need to be accountable." He looks over at me.

What I want to say is: *Nothing I do is ever good enough.* But of course I don't say that. I'm not crazy.

"Jack?" My dad sounds mad. "Jack!" he repeats. "Have you not been listening to anything I've said?"

Exactly! I think to myself but obviously don't say, because I value my life and I don't want my dad to pull the truck over and chew me out for the next fifteen minutes. Instead, I just keep my mouth shut and think about how much fun I had today.

Today was one of the last days of summer, and it was perfect. Me, Owen, Sammy, Demaryius, Dominic, Brayden, Trey—we just chilled at the pool all day and swam and did crazy backflips off the diving board and ate nothing but hot dogs and greasy French fries from the snack bar. The night before, we were all at Owen's for a sleepover and played video games on his sixty-inch flat-screen TV in his man-cave basement paradise.

Now summer is over.

I press my head up against the truck's window and close my eyes. I just try and, like, breathe and not fight with The Captain. Not say the wrong thing at the wrong time. Not screw up.

School is going to start in two days, and if I'm not care-ful my dad might yank me out of Thatcher and make me go to Saint Joe's. Saint Joe's is where all three of my older brothers go, and at Saint Joe's you have to wear a collared dress shirt, a striped necktie, and a navy-blue blazer. No jeans. No girls. *No thanks*. The only reason The Captain is letting me go to Thatcher is because it fits better with my hockey schedule.

No one loves playing hockey as much as I do.

Hockey is the one thing The Captain and I agree on.

Hockey is my life. My brothers and I all play. It's just how it is—we all got handed a stick when we were, like, two years old. As soon as I could walk, I was put up on skates, pulling my dad on the ice with an inner-tube tire around my waist. All three of my brothers have already committed to Boston College.

I've always been the youngest on my team because my dad wants me to work harder and get better and tougher. There's nothing I'd rather do than play hockey the rest of my life. And there is a plan. I write it down every single night (only after I complete exactly two hundred push-ups, two hundred sit-ups, and recite the prayer to St. Sebastian seven times). This is what I do. This is who I am. I write it in the red-covered spiral notebook I keep tucked under my mattress. My mom told me to do it. She said—"If you believe it, you can achieve it." She told me to write down my goals. And I have ever since.

I write the same three things. Every single night.

1. Play for Boston College.
2. Get drafted in the first round of the NHL.
3. Sign an NHL contract.

And you might think it's weird to have a secret note-book filled with the same three sentences written down every day since I was ten years old, but whatever. It's my dream, and I don't really give a crap if anyone thinks I'm weird about it. I've worked my whole life to take the next step. I'm still young. I still have a lot to work on. When I go to bed, I see myself signing my letter of intent to play for Boston College. I see myself getting drafted, slipping an NHL jersey over my head. I see myself doing *every-thing*. In my mind, I've already done it. I just have to go out and do it. Put in the work. Be unstoppable. My dad tells me all the time, "The true test of a man's character is what he does when no one is watching."

3 ELLIE

I'M STANDING ON THE CEMENT steps of the Riverside Sportsplex, my shin guards still on, my pink Thunderbirds soccer bag hanging from my shoulders. I'm sweaty and sticky and my hair is pulled back tight in a ponytail, like I always wear it. I'm standing here waiting for my mom to get me, when Claire walks up. She's smiling, but only for a second.

"Hey," she says to me. "I just want to say, like, I'm really sorry to hear about everything that happened."

"Um, what do you mean?" I ask. I'm looking over Claire's shoulder and watching Sassy and Aspen skipping across the parking lot all the way to Sassy's mom's minivan. We have just finished the first day of tryouts for the Thunderbirds thirteen-and-under indoor travel team. Sassy and Aspen are leaning into each other, arms looped, and shrieking with laughter like they are in on some big joke that none of us are cool enough to possibly ever get. Usually Sassy's mom gives me a ride too. But ever since Sassy's been acting like I don't exist, their car is suddenly "*full*." As in—"Oh, sorry, Ellie, we're, like . . ." Sassy will pause to glance at Aspen, sharing an entire sentence without saying a word—"We're, like, yeah, we're not going straight home."

I turn back to Claire. She has a funny look on her face, and my heart starts to hurt right then. Right that second. It's so weird, isn't it? How your heart can hurt. How your heart sort of knows more than you know.

"Oh, forget it, nothing." Claire looks at me as if she is really embarrassed, like she wasn't supposed to say anything. She quickly tries to change the subject. "Hey, so are you excited for school tomorrow?"

"Wait, what were you going to say?" I spot my mom's car turning into the Sportsplex and try rushing things. "You can tell me," I say. My voice sounds so soft, and in the gap of quietness I force a shaky smile.

"Oh, I guess, like . . . ," Claire starts, but stops herself.

I stand there.

I don't move.

My heart is pounding and my cheeks get really hot.

"Well, um . . . there's no easy way to tell you this." Claire looks at me uncomfortably, as if she's warning me that she is really very sorry for what she's about to say. "I guess you didn't see the thing Sassy wrote on Facebook?"

I shake my head. *I don't have Facebook.*

Neither of us speaks for a few seconds.

I glance over at my mom waving me toward the car and put my finger up as if to say, "One sec."

"She said . . . uh . . ."

"You can tell me, Claire, *please?*" I am practically begging at this point.

"She said, um . . ." Claire pauses and looks around her as if she's scared of Sassy overhearing her, even though Sassy is long gone. "She said, like, you . . ." Claire's voice trails off just as her ride pulls up. She back steps at first, before whirling around toward the car, then right before she opens the door she looks back over her shoulder. "*Sorry,*" she mouths.

"Wait, Claire," I call after her. "What did she—"

But by then it is too late. Claire is already in the car, with the door shut.

Six older boys burst out the front doors of the Sportsplex and practically plow me over because I am completely in the way. And I just stand there for a few seconds, kind of frozen and kind of shocked. I guess that's when it really hits me. Finally. I get it. I've been officially, unofficially, *dropped.*

4
JACK

"SON?"

"Yes, sir?" I pause, my hand on the truck door handle, and turn toward my dad. This is what we always do before The Captain drops me off at practice. I don't know if it's a superstition or just a routine, but I always stop right before I get out of the truck, and listen. My dad is tough. He pushes us. He was a captain in the army, and before that he was an All-American for Boston College, so, I mean, he knows what it takes.

"Go in there and work hard. Give it all you have. No regrets," he tells me.

"No regrets, yes, sir," I say back. We do a nod, and I finally open the door and leap out of the truck.

The Captain rolls down the window on my side and leans toward me. "Win those battles in front of the net," he tells me. "Be strong on your feet. Play a two-way game."

"Yes, sir." I stand at attention outside the truck, my bag slung over my shoulder, my two best sticks in my hand.

"Hard-nosed discipline."

"Yes, sir." I nod. "Thank you, sir."

My dad is big on please and thank you. All Malloy boys are expected to—let me quote—"partake in the basic civility of life." That means please, thank you, yes, sir or yes, ma'am, holding open a door, firm handshakes, and so on.

"Jack?" The Captain calls out.

"Yes, sir?" I look back at him.

"Go get 'em."

It doesn't matter what kind of day I'm having. The second I step into the rink, everything is better. It's magic. The first thing that hits you is the smell. Every rink is different, but they all smell like hockey. You could put a blindfold on me and put me in any rink and I'd know, just from the salty, sweaty scent and the dampness and the cool air that kind of hits you when you walk in the door. BAM! You are at the rink. You have arrived. There's just this feeling of excitement. It's unreal. And when I walk through the doors to the locker room, that hockey smell is stronger than ever. It's always there. It will never go away. I love that smell. I can't explain it, but it's comforting, I guess. Once you get into the locker room you're sheltered from everything. There are no windows. You have no view of the outside world. You're kind of in a shell. The only contact you have is the other guys, your teammates, sharing stories, talking about different things—hockey, music, where guys went out on the weekend, what they did after, who hung out with who, girls, who's hot, who's not. Guys are chirping, everyone is sort of making fun of each other, joking around. Nothing's off-limits. Most of the guys on the Bruins are one or two years older than I am, so they love to pick on me and razz me, and they all call me "Mallsy," or "Malls." I love it. It's like this place that's different than any other. You're just all together, talking about whatever, no distractions.

To an outsider looking in, it might look like a madhouse—eighteen guys, eighteen equipment bags covering almost every space on the floor—but actually there's an order. Every guy knows that order. All the little adjustments to get yourself ready to go: tying your skates just right, lacing 'em up at just the right time, taping your shin pads, taping your stick, folding your socks just the way you like them. It's like tying your shoes—you're so used to it, you just do it. Then when you're all done? Somehow everyone looks the same, and we all head out to the ice.

You walk out of the locker room on the rubber mats, out to the rink, and as soon as you take a step onto the ice, right off the gate, you glide. It's just effortless. That sensation is really the best feeling in the world. You take your second step and your third step and you pick up speed and the cool wind blasts through your face mask and you inhale that first breath of cold air and it gives you a jolt of energy and you want to go faster and faster. You just feel like you can do anything, like you are invincible. Then there's a screeching whistle that brings everyone to a stop, brings you all together, and you get to work.

For the next sixty minutes of my life, everything is almost a trance.

Nothing else matters.

Nothing else exists.

It's like I'm there but I'm not there.

I don't have to think.

The sound track is the steel on your skate cutting into the crisp ice with each stride, the swooshing of the ice when you stop, the puck hitting sticks, the coach directing players, whistles, so much motion, so much activity.

At my best, everything is clicking, everything is right in the world. The puck goes to where I want it to go, my feet move the way I want them to move. It all flows. I just love to be out there. It's what I'm built for. It's what I do best.

After, in the locker room, I sink into my seat, soaked in sweat. Usually there's a high. All the boys feel really good. And as soon as we're off the ice, we're on to the next thing. Nobody's talking hockey anymore. Someone cranks the music, and as we change, we talk about girls and school. We talk about everything but hockey. The guys are always joking and chirping and throwing tape balls in the garbage. And I'm so spent—not just physically, but mentally too, which is kind of awesome, because in the fifteen minutes before I leave and throw my bag in the back of my dad's truck, in those fifteen minutes I have no worries. None. I get my gear off, get dressed, dry my skates, pack up, and laugh with the guys. I do not have a single worry in the world. I'm free.

5 ELLIE

MY MOM DRIVES OUT OF the Sportsplex, and I sit in the front next to her and pretend everything is totally normal and totally fine as I listen to her questions.

"How were tryouts, honey?"

"Did you have fun?"

"Hey, what do you think of sushi takeout for dinner?"

The thing is, there is a big lump in my throat and it's hard to answer because the minute I try to talk, I know my voice is going to give it away. So I sort of nod and shrug my shoulders and look out the window. I manage to hold it together until the second we turn into our driveway.

"Sweetheart," my mom starts, and I feel the tears building up. "What's going on?"

I open up my mouth to answer, but instead of words, only sobs spill out.

She turns toward me. "Oh, honey. Hey, what's wrong? Did something happen at tryouts?"

"No!" I tell her, but now I'm crying so hard she can barely understand me.

"Are you having trouble with your friends?"

"Noooooo!" I lie again, and shake my head. "I'm okay, I'm fine," I sob.

"Oh, Ellie, honey, it doesn't sound like you're fine." My mom takes a deep breath, reaches over, and with her hand moves the hair out of my eyes. "Did someone say something to you?"

"No, just—" I stop for a second. I'm so embarrassed. I try to take a breath, but . . . yeah, I just burst into tears all over again. I get out of the car and shut the door and start walking toward the house.

"Ellie," my mom calls after me.

I turn around and shout, "It's none of your business!"

Talking to my mom this way doesn't make me feel better at all. I go upstairs to my bedroom and, with all my sweaty soccer clothes still on, crawl under my covers and bury my face in my pillow and cry until the pillow is wet and my nose is running. Then, finally, I sleep.

When I wake up, I look in the mirror on the back of my door. My eyes are all puffy and I have the worst head-ache. My hair is messy and wavy, and my stupid freckles are still there. I flop back onto my bed and stare up at the glow-in-the-dark star stickers that are still plastered all over my ceiling from when I was a baby. Can you make a wish on plastic star stickers? I do. I wish I could be someone else, like, confident and strong, and not so worried about what everyone thinks all the time. But who wishes on dumb stickers?

I guess I do.

At the same exact moment I make my pathetic sticker wishes, there's a knock at my door.

"Ellie, honey?"

It's my mom.

I don't answer.

I don't even know what to say.

"Ellie, are you sleeping?"

"No," I say. My voice is muffled, though, because I am talking into my pillow.

She opens the door. "Ellie, sweetheart, what is the matter?"

My mom sits down on my bed right beside me. I feel her hand on my back. "We need to talk. Something happened and you have school tomorrow and you don't want to go to school in this state, right?"

"I don't want to say," I start. "I don't want to say because I know when I tell you, you're just going to tell me I'm stupid."

"Oh, sweetheart, I would *never* tell you you're stupid. You know that."

My mom leans over and kisses me on my head. "I just see you're having a hard time. Come on, let's talk." She climbs under the covers and curls up next to me like she used to do when I was little.

We stay like that for a long time until she finally speaks. Whispers, really. "Ellie, honey, I just want to know what happened. And I want you to be able to talk about it. You'll feel better if you can just get it out. It will help, I promise."

I take a big deep breath. "Are you sure you won't be mad?"

"Mad? Why would I be mad?"

"It's about Sassy," I say.

My mom lets out a long sigh. "So what did she do this time?"

"Mom! Don't say that!"

She looks me right in the eyes. "You can tell me anything. What did she say? I'm really going to just listen, I'm not going to say anything bad about Sassy."

"Promise?"

"Yes. I promise."

"She hates me!" When I hear the words, and how pitiful I sound, it just makes me burst into tears all over again.

"Oh, honey, I don't think she hates you, she's just—"

"She does, she hates me!"

"Sweetheart—" My mom stops for a second and

takes a deep breath. "A lot of times kids say mean things because they feel insecure, and it makes them feel better about themselves when they put other people down."

"Sassy is NOT insecure, Mom!" I turn toward my pillow again. "And whatever, it doesn't matter, because I still have no friends."

"Sassy Gaines is your only friend?" My mom shoves me playfully, and we both kind of smile—even though I'm trying *not* to smile.

"What about Claire, or Mackenzie, or Sammie from soccer?" my mom offers. "What about Kiana? Remember when you used to take riding lessons with her? I love her!"

"Then maybe *you* should be friends with her," I say, sounding pretty bratty.

"What about Annie Hutchinson? Annie is so sweet. I've always wanted you to be friends with her, and I love her mom!"

"Mom, you don't understand. I'm talking about Sassy! I just want Sassy to like me again. I don't know what I did or, like, why—"

My mom studies my face and reaches over to move a clump of sweaty damp hair out of my eyes. We're snuggled up so close, our noses could almost touch.

"Sweetie, how do you see under all that hair?"

"Mom!"

She smiles. "Look, honey," she starts again, "Sassy is fine and everything, but she does have a little bit of a mean streak; she can be cruel, and I see sometimes she's not nice to you, and who the heck wants to hang out with somebody who's not nice to them?"

I don't answer. I feel a tear streaming down my cheek.

"Your job is to figure out who you are and what your limits are. Sometimes you need to draw that line in the sand. I know it's scary to stand up for yourself, but when you do, sweetheart, I'm telling you it feels so good to be strong."

"Mom, please, just stop! You don't understand!"

"Oh, Ellie, honey, there are so many kids at Thatcher you don't know. Your next best friend in the world is out there, but you're so focused on Sassy, you're missing out on—"

"Mom!" I cut her off. "You don't get it."

"Well, maybe I don't."

She gets up off my bed and moves toward the door, stepping over my clothes. "Ellie, please just clean your room, this mess drives me crazy!"

I don't even care about my stupid room. I don't care about anything right now. I have my face planted in my pillow again. The pressure feels good against my head, which is sort of throbbing from crying so much.

My mom is standing in the doorway. "Look, Ellie, you've got to go to school tomorrow, so we've got to figure out how you can get over this and at least feel okay about yourself. And, Ellie?"

"What!" I look up.

"Honey, if you want me to treat you like you are getting older and more mature, then, well, you need to get yourself together and pick up this room and *blah, blah, blah* . . ."

I stare at my mom and pretend I'm listening, but really I'm not.

"Ellie," I hear her say, "why don't you take a nice bath and—"

"Mom, I'm in seventh grade! I'm *not* taking a bath!"

"Well, I take baths and I'm forty-four!"

"Fine! I'll take a bath."

"Good, and put some of those lavender bubbles in there, and just soak. Then get in your pj's, come downstairs, and we'll have a nice dinner."

"Okay," I answer into my pillow again.

"And this weekend—"

"I know! My room." This time I turn and watch her standing with one hand on the doorknob, the other on her hip. She's smiling at me, like she knows something that I don't.

"You'll get through this, honey. You're such a great kid. You can't control the way people are, and we've just got to help you get stronger, so that you can see who your real friends are and—"

"Mom, Sassy is my real friend. You don't understand. It's just—"

My mom cuts me off. "Ellie, all I can say is, *my* friends don't treat me like that."

6

IT'S THE NIGHT BEFORE MY first day of Thatcher, and my brother is blasting slap shots at my head. We are in the basement, or The Cage (that's what we call it), the empty unfinished room down the steep stairs off the kitchen. We are down here practically every night.

The Cage is awesome. My dad put wire up over the windows, flipped over an old wooden table we use as the goal, and he basically lets us destroy the room.

When we were little we used tennis balls down here, but now we're older and the walls are covered with a million marks from the black rubber pucks dinging the white paint. There's nothing in here besides weights, a squat rack, a bench press in the corner, and our old washing machine pushed up against the wall, covered with black polka-dotted puck dents. It's unreal when it's all four of us, but most of the time it's me and Stryker, because we're closer in age and Gunner and Jett are usually away more for hockey.

As far as The Cage goes, with my brothers, they always make me the automatic goalie because one, I'm the only one crazy enough to stand in front of a firing squad, and two, I'm the youngest and that's what happens when you have three older brothers—you don't get much say in the matter. They like to play around, toughen me up.

"You're nails, Jacko!" my brothers tell me when I stop their shots.

It's a compliment. *Nails* is the opposite of soft. And if you're a boy, especially if you're a boy in my family, you do *not* want to be called soft. That's about the worst thing someone can call you.

Tonight I strap everything on—helmet, mask, chest protector, the works—and Stryker starts firing. We don't really talk.

We just go like that forever.

Target practice.

Stryker could snap pucks at me all day and all night. And he does. We stay down in The Cage until we hear The Captain.

"That's enough, boys!" he yells from the top of the stairs.

My dad isn't the type of guy who likes to ask more than once.

I take off my helmet, but Stryker catches me off guard. He fires a puck and—*BAM!* I throw the gloves and drop to the ground, covering my eye with both my hands, pressing my forehead up against the hard cement floor. No, I don't cry. I'm not a girl! You think I want my brothers to harass me for the rest of my life? Malloys don't cry, okay? I'm not saying it doesn't hurt like a . . .

Stryker crouches down next to me. I can feel his breath on my neck.

For a second I think he actually feels bad.

Then he whispers into my ear, "Aww, you gonna die, princess?"

"Screw you," I say, but he can barely hear me, because I can barely speak.

"Don't be a girl," Stryker says, laughing. "Get up!"

If I was a girl, I'd burst into tears.

No way am I going to cry.

We don't quit, and we don't whine.

"Meow," says Stryker. He thinks this is hilarious. "Meow, meeeeeeeeeeeeow. Let's go, Sally!" He's standing over me now. My brothers love to do this. They call me Sally, or Nancy, or Mary, or Pansy, Wuss, or Baby, or Butter—as in you're as soft as butter, or even worse, Butter Baby.

"Come on, Butter Baby! Don't be soft! You're a tough guy. Let's go! Get up!"

I want to elbow his face in, but by the time I stumble to

my feet and stand, Stryker's already upstairs. He's gone. Somehow I make my way up the stairs too. I slip past The Captain (reading the paper), past Stryker, Jett, and Gunner (watching hockey), and hide out in the upstairs bathroom, where I almost puke, it hurts so bad.

"Oh, you're nails, buddy," Stryker yells up after me.

Then I hear him outside the door. "Hey, you okay, bud?"

I don't answer.

"You're gonna rock a nice shiner, Jacko!"

I stay in the bathroom splashing my face with cold water until I can't feel my eye anymore. Pretty quickly it starts getting a little bit swollen and purple. I stare at myself in the mirror for a good long while.

There's no blood.

Nails, I think, and sort of smile. Honestly? I'm kind of proud. I got a black eye, and it's my first, and it won't be my last.

7 ELLIE

AS SOON AS I WAKE up on the first day of school, I begin tearing through my closet trying to find something, anything, to wear that doesn't make me look like I still sleep with my teddy bear (I do). No matter what I try on, I just look in the mirror and think I look dumb. I strip it off and try something else again. But I feel like I look terrible in *everything*. Plus I hear Sassy's voice, a running fashion-commentary in my head:

That yellow shirt? Ughhh, gross! You look like a walking highlighter!

Flared jeans? So. Not. Okay.

Leggings? Leggings are not pants!

When it comes to fashion, I have no clue. I mean, when did this suddenly become such a *huge deal*? Nobody cared about this stuff before we got to Thatcher. I have no idea how you're supposed to look stylish and cool. Before this summer, I never even cared. But now, suddenly, one hour before I am officially in seventh grade, I care. I care, and I *hate* that I care. Do you know what I mean? And did I even mention my hair? No, I think I did not. Not a good situation happening up there.

I finally settle on my favorite T-shirt and jeans, tie my messy, red, crazy hair back into a ponytail, and give up.

Downstairs, my mom is in much too good a mood for the first day of school.

"Morning, sunshine!" she sings.

"I have no clothes!" I say. I sit down at the kitchen table. "Seriously, I have, like, nothing to wear! Can we please, please, pleeeeeeease go shopping? Pretty please?"

"Ellie," says my mom. She's standing by the stove, and I can tell by the way she says my name I'm about to get some sort of lecture. "I'm not going to argue with you this morning, but really, sweetheart, you sound a little bit ridiculous. If you went through all your clothes on your floor, you'd probably find loads of cute outfits you don't even know you have!"

"Oh, forget it," I say.

But she's not done.

"Also, Ellie, if this needing new clothes business is about a certain someone, I don't think you need to change your clothes, I think you need to think about changing your friends."

"Oh my gosh, Mom," I say. "Forget it!"

My mom places a plate full of my favorite homemade waffles with maple syrup and melted butter in front of me. "Let's focus on the positive." Her smile grows. "Can you believe it? Seventh grade!"

I push the plate away. "Whatever. I'm not hungry."

"Don't be silly and don't be rude. Please, Ellie. You need to eat, it's not good to go all day without breakfast. Do you want to take a bagel and eat it on the bus?"

"Sure." I shrug.

My mom sits down at the table across from me. "Your attitude needs a little bit of work," she says, smiling. "Sweetheart, really, I promise you, you are going to make friends today, I just know it, and everything is going to turn out much better than you think."

"Sure, whatever," I answer.

I cannot possibly begin to explain how much I am dreading going back to school today. At the door, before I leave, my mom tucks the bagel into my backpack and gives me a hug. "Honey, really, try to not take everything so seriously." She closes her eyes and takes this huge deep breath. When she opens her eyes, she exhales, cups my cheeks, and kisses my forehead.

"Ellie, I wish you'd realize even a teensy bit how amazing you are." She looks at me like she's so positive. "You can do anything you set your mind to."

I'm standing half inside the door and half outside the door.

My mom reaches out and moves the hair out of my eyes like she always does. "Don't forget soccer, okay? I'll pick you up right after school."

"I'm *not* playing soccer," I announce. I decided this right that second. I already have to see Sassy and Aspen at school. . . . I cannot possibly face having to deal with them at soccer too.

"Nonsense," says my mom. "Ellie, you can't just quit things when the going gets tough. If you want something, you have to work for it. You can't give up. You've always had so much fun at soccer."

"Yeah, well, it's not really fun right now," I say. "And I'm *not* playing. I'm just not!" I turn and start marching down the driveway toward the bus stop.

This does not discourage my mom. She follows me. She follows me right down the driveway in her lavender kimono bathrobe and fluffy bunny slippers.

"Ellie," she calls after me, "I'll pick you up at three by the back near the gym. And I expect you to clean your room this weekend. Seriously, Ellie, I can't even step foot in there. . . .

"And, Ellie!"

I stop and turn back. My mom is holding her cup of coffee in the air as if she's toasting me. I'm pretty sure she's smiling as she hollers out, "You can do it, honey! You so got this!"

8

JACK

IT'S PRACTICALLY A KNOWN FACT—ALMOST a solid rule—that Malloy men do not speak to each other until breakfast. That means that, during our five a.m. bed check (hospital corners, sheets tucked in, perfectly smooth blanket), our three-mile still-dark-out run, our strength and conditioning session in The Cage, more often than not, nobody says a word. It's work. And we do it.

"Effort is a measure of a man," my dad likes to say.

And breakfast? No junk food. No Lucky Charms. No Froot Loops. No Cocoa Puffs. Only whole grains, lean proteins, greens, fruit, and nuts. Welcome to the Malloy training table: fruit, egg-white omelets, oatmeal, and my dad's famous morning smoothie (fish oil, peanut butter, almond milk, spinach, blueberries, wheatgrass, raw eggs, and frozen banana). Yep.

"Food is for fuel and performance, for power, not pleasure. Your body is a temple," says The Captain. "You don't take Pop-Tarts into a temple, do you?"

I would if I could! That's what I wish I had the guts to say back.

The Captain leaves for work right after our room inspection. After six a.m., the four of us are on "honor code." In some ways it's kind of nice. At least I'm not walking around on eggshells, trying not to be yelled at. With my brothers, I can hold my own. I fend for myself.

After I shower and throw on some jeans, a belt, and a blue polo shirt, I head downstairs and make my lunch (peanut butter, grape jelly, banana slices, whole wheat bread #snackofchampions) and join my brothers at the kitchen table. Today is the first day of school, and Gunner, Jett, and Stryker are all grinding my gears. Saint Joe's doesn't start till next week, so they get to eat and go back to sleep. Why Thatcher bothers to have one day of school before the weekend is beyond me. But whatever. It is what it is.

As soon as Jett sits down, he starts chirping at me. "Are you gonna start wheeling today, or are you gonna just stay home all year, playing *Call of Duty* by yourself?"

To my brothers, "wheeling" means getting all the girls that you can.

I drink my green smoothie and eat my oatmeal and take it.

"That tarp is absolutely disgusting," says Stryker.

"Huh?" I say.

"That shirt, it's brutal." Gunner shakes his head, half grinning. "No swag, bro. How can you expect to wheel with that thing on your back? Maybe mix in some style, bud."

Jett chimes in. "Pretty grungy, if you ask me."

All three of them are laughing.

"Whatever, man." I laugh too. You can't give them too much attention or they won't stop.

"Just kidding, little man." Gunner shoots me a wink. "Don't get rattled. You look good, bud. You're rockin' that shiner like a boss!"

"Whatever," I repeat.

Jett takes off his sweaty hat and slams it down on my head. "Dude, cover up that salad, or cut your mop!"

Jett and Gunner share a smile, and they both get this crazy look in their eyes.

I can tell what they're thinking.

"Nobody is touching my hair," I tell them, and I'm *not* kidding. It took me an entire year to grow it out from the last time The Captain made me cut it.

Stryker stands and burps loudly. "Great grub sesh, boys!"

Jett puts the plates in the dishwasher. "Just keep

yourself in check, little man," he tells me. "And don't be a donkey."

Gunner gets up too. "Naptime," he says, yawning, then snaking his arm under my chin and wrapping me in a choke hold. "Be a man, Jacko, and stay out of trouble."

9
ELLIE

AFTER I GET OFF THE bus and step into the Land of Thatcher, things go downhill fast. I am in first period for entirely ten seconds before I have a terrible feeling in my stomach. And it's not, like, butterflies. It's worse. And it's not just that I get the last seat in the back next to Henry Hodges, who is making farting noises. It's more that I catch a look from Sassy (front row, third desk by the windows), dressed in a tight-fitting black spaghetti-strap top, and the look she gives me does not say, "Ellie! Yay! We're in the same class!"

No, if this look could talk it would be more like, "Ewww, nice outfit . . . hahahaha! Not!"

I watch her, and her glittery eye shadow and her black mascara-painted curly eyelashes stare me down. She starts at my sneakers, and I feel her eyes move right up my body until they reach my face, at which time she turns to Aspen, seated (surprise!) next to her, and whispers something. Then the two of them burst out laughing.

I look around the room, first at Ms. González, who is writing something on the board, and then toward the door, still open because the bell hasn't rung yet, and I imagine myself leaping up from my seat and sprinting straight down the almost-empty Thatcher hallway, past all the bright orange lockers, out the emergency exit door. Maybe I could run to the main office, call my mom, beg her to pick me up, beg her to let me homeschool, or just . . . gosh, anything but be here now. Anything but be *me*.

Every class of my day is pretty much a repeated loop of this exact scene. Me walking into class, Sassy (plus whoever she's sitting with who is not me) sneers, rolls her eyes, then bursts out laughing. At lunch, after I wander into the crowded cafeteria looking lost, I am in line with my melted-cheese bagel and my yogurt, almost to the cash register, when I hear her.

Sassy.

I look over my shoulder and see her by the soda machines in the corner, holding court like some sort of celebrity, obviously talking just loud enough for me to hear her.

"No offense," she starts, then pauses to flip back her golden hair, as if she's a famous actress waiting for her gathered audience to turn toward her (they do). Then she says it (drumroll, please): "Gotta love it when people don't even, like, brush their hair! Eww. Embarrassing." (Hahahahaaa!)

Sassy stops again and looks up just long enough for her entire tribe of girls (Aspen by her side) to turn toward me and give me the death stare. "Not to be rude, but seriously, people, sneakers with jeans is *so* not okay. It's hideous!" (Hahahaha!) "Just sayin'!"

In chorus, the one class I absolutely love, Mr. Pratt puts me right next to Sassy. One song in, she leans over, whispering into my ear, "Some people should probably just mouth the words." She pauses for a beat, overwhelmed by giggles. "Off-key much?"

By eighth period, my last period of the day, I have decided I really can't take this anymore. I honestly hate my life. This has actually been the worst week ever. Today is Friday—how am I going to even make it through the weekend to Monday? I already said I'd go to Claire's birthday sleepover. I supposedly have soccer tryouts. I have an entire Sassy Gaines–filled weekend, and I still have one more class with her—gym.

Walking into the girls' locker room, I am secretly praying the universe will strike me down with some sort of awful feverish sickness that forces me to stay in bed all weekend. Chicken pox? Strep throat? Appendicitis? Could I fake getting my period?

Probably not.

In what might be my only good luck so far today, there is an empty bathroom stall. I slip inside, hang my three-thousand-pound backpack from the hook of the flimsy metal door, and fish out my Thatcher-issued blue-and-orange shorts and T-shirt. At least I don't have to change right out in the open, in front of all the other girls.

Gym. I can get through gym, right? I'm faster than Sassy and probably more coordinated than she is. I picture myself accidentally throwing a softball at her face. Then I switch it up—a basketball, a soccer ball, a floor-hockey puck. In each scenario, I will admit to you that I actually picture her with a bloody nose. *Sorry, not sorry.*

And look, have you ever tried to change in one of those tiny bathroom stalls? There's not a lot of space to move around, and I'm literally, like, slipping off my jeans—balancing on top of my shoes, trying to not touch my socks to the gross sticky floor—when I hear Sassy's voice right outside the door.

Right away my heart starts pounding, and I stand frozen in my yellow daisy-speckled underwear, clutching my gym clothes against my chest, staring at my legs, terrified that she might somehow see me. "*Eww, shave your legs!*" I can just hear her say.

With every ounce of quiet I have in me, I step into the Thatcher gym shorts, slip the orange T-shirt over my head, and peer out the thin gap of space between the metal door and the side of the stall. Sassy is with this girl Tori, who I don't really know that well because she's cooler and prettier and just—

Not someone who would ever hang out with me.

The two of them have already changed and are standing in front of the mirror, fixing their hair and makeup. Why? For gym?!! For gym with other girls.

Exactly.

This is what I hear—

Sassy: I can't believe I got put into Mr. Tate's class. He spits when he talks.

Tori: That's just gross!

Sassy: I know, right? Oh, and Ms. Dennison? Apparently she gives, like, a ton of homework. So annoying. Doesn't she know I have a life? Hold this.

Tori: Hold what?

Sassy: My hair thingie. Here. I feel so naked without a hair tie!

Tori: Ohmigod, can I just say I hate you because your hair is sooooo super soft!

Sassy: I know! It's my new hair straightener. [Sassy smiles at herself in the mirror.] What would I do if you weren't in my gym class? And seriously, how are we not going to be in social studies together this year? Who am I going to sit next to and talk to in the middle of class?

Tori: OMG, seriously! Why are you sooooo pretty! You look amaaaazing!

Sassy: Awwwww, thanks, babe. Oh my god, I hope Ellie stops following me around and gets the hint!

Tori: I know, seriously!

Sassy: Like, do I have to walk up to her and say it to her face?

Tori: I know, right?

Sassy: Yeah, like, ummm, hello? Don't talk to me. Don't look at me. Bye!

Tori: Hahahaha. Seriously. Back off.

Sassy: Totes. I mean, not to be rude, but she is just too—

Tori: Babyish?

Sassy: Yes! Totally babyish! She wears such horrid clothes. And her hair? Hello? She's worn the same dumb center-parted ponytail since kindergarten! She doesn't even *own* a blow dryer *or* a flat iron!

Tori: Didn't you tell me she still has, like, her American Girl dolls on her bookcase?

Sassy: Can you say embarrassing!

Tori: Can you even imagine her *talking* to a boy? Ha!

Sassy: I know! Right? Hahahaha! I seriously can't even picture it. It would be so super awk! [They smile into the mirror, purse their lips, and apply hot-pink lip gloss.]

Sassy: Oh. Em. Geeee! That's so hot. Boo, we definitely gotta hang soon! You're going to Claire's tomorrow right?

Tori: Yes!!! Soooo excited! Can. Not. Wait.

Sassy: Chicka-chicka-yeah-yeah. [They high-five.]

Tori: Hopefully a certain *someone* knows she's *not* invited.

Sassy: Stop, no, ewwwww, barf. Don't remind me!

10
JACK

WHEN I STEP ON THE bus I smile, because right away, straight in front of me, I can see that Owen and I are wearing the exact same shirt. Light-blue polos, except he has his collar popped and I don't, because, well, my brothers would never let me forget it. I drop into the seat next to Owen and Sammy, like I've done every year since we met in sixth grade.

Sammy's chirpin' before I even settle into my seat. "Jack, your hair is pretty flowtastic right now, not gonna lie." He smiles big. "And the shiner? Broads love a tough guy. I can only imagine the girls you'll have after you now, stud."

Sammy's crazy.

The three of us are best friends. We hang out together, and except for hockey, we pretty much do everything together. Sammy is pretty cool, pretty laid back, wicked smart. He's the one all the girls like. Owen, he's more quiet and has huge glasses. He's a gamer. He's all about *Call of Duty*, *Halo*, and fantasy football (in that order). Love the kid. We hang out at Owen's a lot because he has all the cool stuff at his house—a sixty-inch flat screen, a PlayStation *and* an Xbox, a Ping-Pong table, and a pool table. Plus, when his mom throws us out for playing video games too long, Owen has a huge yard with a trampoline. And if we get bored, he lives right next to the elementary school with big grassy fields and a basketball court.

The first day of school is crazy. Everyone is pumped to see all the new kids, to see who's changed. As soon as we get off the bus, Sammy starts a running commentary on girls.

"Yo, bro," he says, elbowing me in the gut. "Total smoke show to your right."

I look over at Sassy Gaines.

Most guys in eighth grade think Sassy is the prettiest girl at Thatcher. (Sammy: "She's hot. She's just so hot.") I've never said a word to her in my life. I'll tell you right now, I've got no game. I'm definitely a quiet guy. I am pretty shy when it comes to girls. I guess I'm just pretty shy, period. I have absolutely no idea what to say to them or how to act. I wish I had some sort of instruction book. I wish I could walk right up to a girl and somehow know what to say. In a perfect world? I wouldn't even have to talk.

Sammy elbows me again.

"This is going to be the best year of my life!" he says, eyes wide, staring at this new girl, Aspen Bishop.

"Whatever, Sammy," I say.

"Yo, bro, do you *see* her?"

"Yeah," I say, shaking my head. "I see her."

"Total rocket, right?"

"I guess," I say with a shrug. Sammy is such a ladies' man.

"Come on, man, she's mad hot! I'd marry her on the spot!" Sammy pushes me into Owen and we all bust out laughing. Kid's crazy.

At lunch, we always sit together. Me, Owen, Sammy, Demaryius, Trey, Dominic, and Brayden. We sit at the same table we sat at last year, on the far side of the cafeteria by the guidance office.

Trey is obsessed with the Red Sox.

"Did you see the Sox blow it last night?" he asks.

Brayden laughs. "Don't even get me started, man!"

"Yeah, dude," says Dom. "That bullpen is an absolute disaster."

Sammy jumps in. "Dude, I think *I* could go out there and do a better job closing games for the Sox right now."

"Then we'd *really* be in trouble," teases Trey.

We all love to mess with Sammy. He's just an easy target.

Everyone starts talking at the same time.

"The Pats are so sick, did you see the game last night?" (Brayden)

"Dude, the Pats are absolutely gonna kill it this year." (Demaryius)

"It's not even gonna be close. They're just unstoppable." (Owen)

"Hands down, best defensive line in the league. Not even debatable." (Me)

"I don't know, though, man. Buffalo's new QB looks like a gun!" (Trey)

"Nah, dude. He's overrated." (Dominic)

"Shut up, Dom. Dude's gonna be a legend!" (Trey)

"Yo!" Sammy raises his voice over all of us and awkwardly nods his head toward the seventh graders walking by. "Two words: Sassy. Gaines. Smoke show!"

"That's four words, Sammy," says Owen.

We all burst out laughing.

Owen raises his hand. Like I said, love the kid. "You guys want to come over tomorrow night and have a *Madden* tourney?"

"*Madden*? No!" argues Trey. "Dutes, man!"

"Cool, *Call of Duty*. Whatever. I can kill you all in that too." Owen smiles.

Sammy throws his hand up for a high five. "Yeeeaaah, buddy, I'm in," he says.

"I have to ask my mom," says Trey.

Owen turns to Dominic. "Dom?"

"Yes, sir!"

"Demaryius?"

"Definitely, I'm down."

"Brayden?"

"You know it."

"What about you, Jacko?"

"Absolutely, man. Sounds good."

To be completely honest, I'm kind of surprised at how much I'm not minding eighth grade. The only sort of bad thing so far is this kid Porter Gibson. The kid's just a loudmouth idiot. Owen and I are walking to Mr. Graves's class when Porter crashes into all eighty pounds of Owen, knocking his books to the floor and his glasses straight off his face.

I kneel down and get his stuff. "Dude," I tell Owen, "I'd really like to punch that kid in the face."

"I can brush it off." Owen shrugs.

But I can tell he's rattled. I hand Owen back his glasses.

Porter keeps at it in science. The kid is always being obnoxious in class, always needs attention, always needs someone to be laughing at him. The guy's a joke. Right away he causes problems.

Owen and I are sharing the desk in the front row. "Since there's so much talking," Mr. Graves announces, "we're going to switch seats. So everyone, let's have the girls stand first. And we're going to count off, girl, boy."

Porter kicks the back of my chair. "Hey, Jack," he whispers, "*girls* first!"

I'm not going to lie.

I'm heated.

I sit there for the rest of the class and seriously consider jumping over the desk and punching him in the face.

In the hallway after sixth period, Owen tries to talk me down.

"He's not worth it, Jack," he tells me. "Don't let him get to you."

And look, I'll tell you the truth. I'm not big on fighting. I mean, sure, I fight my brothers all the time. But as far as fighting at school?

No.

My dad would kill me.

I stop to get a drink at the water fountain, and when I turn around I see Porter coming at me in slow motion.

I'm not ready.

"Watch where you're going," he says, slamming into me.

Porter steps right up to me. Eyeball to eyeball. I can smell fish sticks on his breath. He starts poppin' off. "You're such a pretty boy, Malloy. Think a little highly of yourself, don't you? Think you're better?"

"Get out of my face, bro," I answer. I turn. I swear, I

turn and begin to walk away, but Porter pushes me again. This time a little bit harder.

"Don't be such a girl," he says.

I shake my head and start to walk away again. But then he gives me another shove, this time hitting me in the back of my shoulders. I turn around and look right at him.

"What?" he asks. "You gonna call your *mommy* and cry?"

"Step back, dude," I warn him.

"When you do call your mom, bro, tell her to stop texting me," he says with a laugh.

That's it.

I drop my backpack.

"You got the biggest mouth, dude. You want to go right now?" I say. Out of the corner of my eye I see a crowd forming, and I can hear them cheering.

"Fight him! Get 'em, Jack!"

"You wanna go?" I repeat.

"What?" Porter looks scared now. "I was just playin'..."

I don't have an off switch.

"Let's go right now." I grab him by his backpack strap, pull him in, and connect with a right cross. One punch. Porter slams backward into the locker and starts flailing his arms. I'm looking to strike again. I'm looking to knock him out. I pull back my arm and throw a right uppercut that connects with his jaw. He's getting desperate to end the fight. He lunges at me, wrapping his arms around my waist, and tries to take me down, tackling me, but instead he smokes my head against the brick wall.

I feel my nose crack.

Then blood trickling down my chin.

I just roll him and get on top. I drive him into the floor. I don't stop. He's on his back, full throttle trying to get up. I pin him down with my knee, hook one arm around his neck, and pound him with shots. I'm landing some big punches, just blazin' him, until I feel somebody's hand yank me back off him.

"Boys, this is over!" It's Mr. Graves.

For the first time I notice how many people are watching. It's like the entire eighth grade is standing there in a circle around us, staring.

"Okay, people, show's over. Go to class!" says Mr. Graves. Then he turns to me, "Jack, go to the nurse."

I stand there for a second.

My heart is pounding.

I can taste blood.

"Go!" Mr. Graves repeats, sounding mad.

Somehow a wad of paper towel emerges, and Owen hands it to me with a giant grin on his face. Before I leave, I glance down at Porter, still in a heap on the floor, his lip busted. *You think you're gonna knock me out? Not going to happen.*

I watch him for a second and make sure to catch his eye. Then? I shake my head and toss him a smile.

On my way to the nurse's office, my heart is beating like crazy ridiculous. I can't calm down. My body is shaking and my hand is throbbing. By now there's a crowd following me down the stairs. Everyone's hyped.

"Beast mode, bro!" (Brayden)

"Yeeaah, boyyyy! Dominate!" (Trey)

"Dude's a truck, but you smashed him!" (Demaryius)

"You're an assassin, Jacko!" (Dominic)

Sammy throws his arm around my shoulders. "You're an absolute stud! You rocked him, dude. Ground and pound! You had some big shots, man. He felt it!"

By the time I reach the door to the nurse's office, it's just me and Owen in the empty hallway. He hands over my backpack, while I try to keep the blood-soaked paper towel on my nose.

"You're still coming to my house tomorrow night, right?" he asks me.

"Well, I—" I start, and reality sort of sets in. "I'll probably be grounded. I mean, my dad—"

"Oh, man, bro." Owen looks a little worried. "Your dad is going to lose it!"

"Yeah, so . . . ," I start, but it's hard to talk with the blood and my nose.

"Well, call me when you find out, man."

"Yeah, I will," I answer.

"Jacko?"

I glance back.

Owen flashes me the biggest smile.

"Thanks for shutting him up," he says.

11
ELLIE

I DON'T KNOW IF IT'S possible for you to picture me in my flimsy blue Thatcher gym shorts, orange Thatcher T-shirt, and sneakers, walking as fast as I can down the empty hall with tears streaming down my cheeks, but that's what I look like.

I look like a baby.

I look like a ridiculous baby, and I don't care.

I don't care because all that is on my mind is getting out of here, getting home, and never leaving my room again. Ever! I think about all the things I'm going to *not* do as I move through the deserted hallway—

I will not play soccer!

I will not go to Claire's birthday party!

I will never go to another birthday party again. Ever!!!!!!!!

I pass the closed doors of classes in session. I pass two teachers. I blow right by them.

"Miss? Young lady?" one calls out.

But I don't stop.

Apparently, I am suddenly the type of girl who skips class and doesn't listen.

"Ellie. Ellie O'Brien?" Ms. Walker calls out. "Ellie, where are you supposed to be?"

I don't even turn around. I head straight to my locker and struggle to remember my stupid combination before I finally get it open. I jam the rest of my books into my backpack. I am a girl possessed. My face feels hot and my head is pounding and I'm so—

Mad.

So MAD!

I shut the locker and look around, considering my next move. There is only one period left. I look up and down the hall and try to spot a place to hide. *I could just, like, hide out, right? Wait for the bell to ring. Nobody will even know!*

This sounds like such a good idea in my head.

I'm totally going to do this! I think. And there I am, with my backpack weighing down my shoulders, walking in my gym clothes toward the little gap of empty space between the band room and the hallway, when I hear a voice.

"Young lady?"

I can tell without looking.

Ms. Dean.

And by Ms. Dean, I mean the principal of Thatcher.

What made me think this would ever work out? I mean, really? This isn't exactly my lucky day.

I stand in the hallway, surrounded by a million orange lockers, and force a weak smile and act like I'm not skipping class, like I'm not having a nervous breakdown, like I'm not—

Me.

I have never said a word to Ms. Dean in my life. Before today I have never even been late to class, let alone skipped one. "You're such a goody-goody, Ellie!" Sassy likes to say.

I look at Ms. Dean and try to quickly think of the words that should come out of my mouth. But instead, I look down, fidget with the straps of my backpack, and swallow hard.

"Ellie O'Brien, right?"

I look up and manage to nod. I have no idea how she even knows my name.

"And where are you coming from, Ms. O'Brien?"

"Gym," I answer. Right away, my voice is shaky.

"And why aren't you in gym, Ellie?"

For just a split second I consider spilling everything, but something stops me. And that something is that I don't want—on top of everything else awful about this day—to be a tattletale. I can't imagine how happy that would make certain people.

Sassy's voice in my head is mocking me—"*You're such a little suck-up, Ellie.*"

So instead of answering, I just stare back at Ms. Dean with this dumb blank look.

"Ellie, something is obviously upsetting you, and if you don't tell me what it is, then I'm not going to be able to help you."

"Um," I say weakly. Have you ever talked to your principal, alone in the hallway? It's awkward, all right, and I practically jump when Ms. Dean's phone buzzes.

"One second." She turns and holds the phone to her ear. I can't really hear what she says into her phone. Something about a fight. Eighth graders. Something about her office . . .

I stop trying to listen and start remembering how pathetic I must look standing here in my gym clothes. I try to stand up a little taller. I try to not seem like I have just been crying. I take my ponytail out and slip the elastic on my wrist. I'm pretty sure my messy, crazy red hair hanging down around my shoulders doesn't really improve things as I hoped it would.

Get it together, Ellie! I tell myself.

Ms. Dean turns back toward me.

"Ellie, I'm sorry, but I have to run and deal with—" She stops for a second and takes a long deep breath. "I'll tell you what," Ms. Dean begins again. "Why don't you come with me to my office, and you can tell me what is going on."

That's when I blurt it out.

I don't know what makes me say it! As soon as it's out of my mouth, I wish I could catch up to the words and grab them and stuff them back down my throat.

"I have my period!" I say. (I have not gotten my period yet. This was another thing Sassy liked to point out to me all summer. "Ellie!" she'd tease. "Too bad you're not a woman yet!")

Ms. Dean's eyes light up. "Well, I can certainly understand that," she says, smiling like we are totally in on the same girl secret, if you know what I mean, and I don't even know what I mean!

Suddenly I just start talking.

Each thing I say is a bigger lie.

"Yeah, um," I say. "I have the *worst* cramps, and well, uhhh, I have gym and it's like—" I put my hand a little below my stomach, as if I'm suddenly an expert on menstrual cramps. "It *really* hurts," I completely lie.

It gets worse.

Do you think I can just lie and be normal? I can feel the tears gathering in my eyes. I am such a goody-goody. It's true. I stop talking and try and get myself together, but it's too late to stop whatever I started.

"Oh! Cramps are the worst!" Ms. Dean says, like she knows exactly how I feel. Exactly how I would feel if I weren't a big fat liar. "Poor thing!" Ms. Dean looks like she honestly feels really badly for me. "Do you think you can make it through one more hour?"

I nod and wipe the tears and my runny nose with the back of my hand.

"Try and breathe, okay?"

I nod again.

Ms. Dean starts walking down the hall toward the main office and motions for me to follow her.

"Let's see if we can get you a little bit more comfortable," she says. Every so often she glances over and smiles. This only makes me feel worse.

How am I ever going to get out of this?

12
JACK ▶

THE NURSE TAKES ONE LOOK at me and jumps up from her seat behind her desk. I guess it's the blood.

"Holy cats!" she says. "What happened to you?"

She has these crazy, twinkly, bright eyes, a heap of blackish-purple hair knotted on top of her head, and she's wearing leopard-print pajama-looking pants and top, with a stethoscope slung around her neck.

"Wowzers!" The nurse looks at me, eyes wide. "First day of school and we have blood!" She sounds almost excited and hands me a wet washcloth. "Here you go, hon. Come on in and sit down."

I sit down on the cot and take the washcloth off my nose while the nurse bends over and looks real close.

"Hmm," she says, "doesn't look broken . . ." She's, like, an inch away from my face. She smells like flowers. "I don't really think you need stitches, but dang!" She pauses and smiles big. "Rough day, huh?"

I try and sit up straighter on the cot. I can't stop shaking. I have so much adrenaline going through my body.

"Why don't you lie back?" she tells me.

This is a different nurse than last year. I've never seen her before.

"I'm fine," I tell her.

I don't feel fine. I'm suddenly really tired and a little bit woozy. I grip the edge of the cot with my hands and try and steady myself.

"Hey, so are you going to tell me what happened to your eye?" She smiles. "That doesn't look like it's from today."

"Hockey," I answer.

Her eyes light up. "Hockey? Rad!"

Her eyes are this unreal blue. She's kind of a rocket, as Sammy would say. I watch her as she grabs an ice pack out of the mini fridge and trades me for the damp, bloody washcloth.

"Looks like it might hurt a little bit?" she asks.

I shrug, like, No. Big. Deal. It actually does hurt, though. A lot.

The nurse bends down again and looks real close, right into my eyes.

"Is your vision blurry?"

I shake my head.

"How about double?" she asks. "Do you see two of me?" She breaks into a grin.

"No, ma'am," I answer.

"That would be scary, right? Two of me! Yikes!" she jokes. I notice she has a tattoo of a half-naked lady riding a tiger climbing up her neck toward the word FEARLESS inked onto her skin in curvy dark script, almost like graffiti. She doesn't look like any school nurse I've ever seen.

I try not to be so obvious. I'm kind of staring.

"Okay, so the nose?" she asks. "What's the story there?"

"Um." I stop and try and think of what I should say. "I ran into a wall."

"A wall, huh? Must have been a mean wall." She laughs. She has a warm, funny laugh. I squint back at her because my nose is sort of swelling and the ice pack is blocking my view.

"Hon, you *really* need to lie down." She puts her hand on my shoulder and I flinch. "Just lie back, and keep pinching your nose and keep the ice on it, okay?"

"Yes, ma'am," I say.

I slowly lower myself back onto the cot. The pillow feels good. Man! My heart is still pounding. I'm so amped! I lie there and stare up at the square tiles on the ceiling and replay the fight in my head. I replay it like a high-light video on ESPN, sort of how other people would see it, almost like I'm watching myself on YouTube in super slow motion.

Jack Malloy vs. Porter Gibson 660,000 views

Did I win or did I lose? How many punches did I land? I glance down at my mangled red knuckles. I guess I connected with something! He threw a couple of sloppy punches, but he really didn't hit me besides . . . well, besides the wall . . . I think I landed two or three. I'm pretty sure I got the upper hand. Pound for pound, he's bigger. I'm stronger, faster—I went full out! I replay it again and again. Man. I hate it when guys hide. He was scared. He was all talk! When I fight, I'm gonna throw. I'm not going to back down from anyone.

At first I think I'm dreaming. But then I realize it's the nurse.

She's sitting on the edge of the cot now. "So we kind of skipped something epic." She stops and smiles. "Your name?"

"Jack," I tell her, sitting up a little too fast. "Jack Malloy."

"Whoooooooa." She puts her hand on my shoulder again. "Sweetie, relax, you really need to lie back down."

I'm not used to anyone calling me sweetie.

It's weird, but there's something about the nurse that is just, like, really calm and soothing.

"Listen, Jack Malloy," she says, "how about we give your dad a call?"

Honestly? Maybe today is the weirdest, luckiest day of my life, because as soon as the nurse mentions calling my dad? Like, that *exact* same second? Some girl dressed in her gym clothes walks through the door, and she's crying. She's not just crying, she's, like, bawling. I have no idea who this girl is, but let me tell you, I am grateful.

The girl who saves my life has the most beautiful long dark-red hair I have ever seen, green eyes, and a thousand freckles. She's *really* pretty. I'm about to smile at her, in a thank-you-for-saving-my-life kind of way, when out of the corner of my eye I see—

"Mr. Malloy," says Ms. Dean. Her voice is stern.

The girl? Freckles? She glances at me and then quickly looks away, and I watch as she drops her huge book bag, plops down across from me on the other cot, and buries her head in her hands. The nurse moves straight for Freckles, and Ms. Dean walks straight to me.

Ms. Dean is no-nonsense. She's always dressed really fancy and serious looking. For what seems like forever, she just stands there with her arms crossed, looking straight at me. My heart is still racing from the fight and my nose is stuffed up with bloody snot and I suddenly have major knots in my stomach—I have *never* been in trouble before.

"Mr. Malloy," she finally starts. "I understand you had an altercation?"

I don't say anything.

"Well?" she asks. "Is this an accurate statement?"

"Yes, ma'am," I answer softly.

"What was that?"

"Yes, ma'am," I repeat, lifting my eyes to look back at her.

"Jack, I can't tell you how disappointed I am."

More silence.

She lets out a long sigh. "Honestly, Mr. Malloy, what happened is simply unacceptable."

I stare at the floor.

"Yes, ma'am, but he started it when he—" I start to explain, but then I stop. One, because the more I talk the more my nose begins to kill, and two, I just hear my dad's voice booming in my head: "*Actions speak louder than words, Jack.*"

Ms. Dean shakes her head. "I expect more out of you, Jack. You showed extremely poor judgment."

"Yes, ma'am," I answer.

"Everyone at Thatcher looks up to you."

"Yes, ma'am," I say. I have the worst lump in my throat.

"You're an eighth grader, Jack." (Long pause.) "You're an honor student." (Longer pause.) "And quite frankly . . ." She stops and glances up at the clock on the wall. "I'm not looking forward to calling your father."

You know that feeling you have when you're about to cry? I bite down on my bottom lip, to hold it in, to keep it inside.

No hockey.

No sleepovers.

No friends.

No life.

He'll probably yank me out of Thatcher and make me go to Saint Joe's.

"Jack?"

I look up.

"Do you have anything more you'd like to add?"

"No, ma'am," I lie. I know better than to say what I'm thinking, to say how I feel.

"Mr. Malloy, for the time being . . ." Ms. Dean looks at her wristwatch, then back at me. "I'm going to hold off calling your dad. But you and I are going to have a serious discussion on Monday."

For a second, I'm completely relieved. But then it hits me: *Monday will be here soon enough. How much will change, right?*

I watch Ms. Dean turn and leave.

"Whoa, easy does it," I hear the nurse, then I feel her hand on my shoulder. "Just relax," she says. "Lie back."

I do. I fall back.

I give in.

Everything is sort of foggy.

I turn on my side and look over at Freckles.

She does not look happy.

She's got big fat tears trickling down her cheeks.

"Middle school sucks, huh?" I whisper. I smile really gently. She looks so sad.

"My entire life sucks," she answers.

"Yeah?" I say. "I can relate."

"Probably not," she mumbles. "Boys have it so easy."

"Um." I turn my head again toward her. "Have you looked at me?"

Freckles lets out the tiniest smile, but then, just as quickly, the smile fades, almost like she remembered something.

"So what happened to you?" I ask.

She looks so . . . I don't know. Defeated. She doesn't say a word. I move the ice pack away so she can see my messed-up face.

"Want to trade places?" I say.

She almost laughs.

"Yeah," she answers. She says it so softly I can hardly hear her. I watch her close her eyes.

"We could, like, magically trade lives, right?" she says.

I just nod and close my eyes too. "You be me," I whisper. "And I'll be you."

"Holy bananas! Wouldn't that be fun?" I hear the nurse say. "You two could do a swap, a little switcheroo!" She giggles. "Help each other out."

This nurse is kind of crazy cakes, but in a good way.

The room gets really quiet.

The lights go off.

And the last thing I remember is the nurse whispering into the darkness, like she's casting a spell. "See the world through eyes anew, until you learn what's deep and true. Heart and courage to speak and feel, will return you to the home that's real."

I WAKE UP WHEN I hear Ms. Dean's voice over the loudspeaker.

"All buses will be running late today due to sixth-grade orientation. Please remain in your classroom for an additional fifteen minutes before dismissal."

Not a problem, I think. I slowly open my eyes and stare up at the ceiling. Everything is blurry. The lights are dimmed. For just a few seconds, I'm a little confused . . . like, you know—who am I? Where am I? Why do I feel like I got hit by a truck? Then I remember.

I am Ellie.

I am a loser.

I am on the nurse's cot.

I am an escaped gym convict!

I have no friends.

Great.

I do not lift my head. I don't move a single muscle. I lie completely still and replay what happened in the locker room over again. I close my eyes and try to think of something, anything, I did to cause Sassy to suddenly hate me so much. *I don't understand what I did, or why she hates me.* It's so crazy how things can change so quickly. I would do anything to get things back to how they used to be.

I use my hand to wipe the tears that I feel trickling down my cheek. Oh my gosh, my eye feels all tender, and puffy like . . . like I got hit in the face. And my nose. My nose is killing me!

And my head. My head is throbbing. Like I ran into a wall.

At this moment? This very second? It occurs to me that the nurse isn't here.

Where is the nurse?

The room is so still.

It's eerie.

Then I start to remember. I'm not alone.

OMG.

Jack Malloy.

How humiliating! The Prince of Thatcher Middle School saw me crying in my stupid gym clothes! Jack Malloy. Saw. Me. Crying.

Life as I know it is officially over.

I turn my head to glance at The Prince, sleeping, and—

What the—

I close my eyes, then open them and look again.

I'm dreaming, right? I'm dreaming. Of course I am!

When I turn to where Jack is, where The Prince was lying the last time I checked—

It's not him lying over there.

It's *me*.

What happens next is I freak out! I jump up. And this is going to sound absolutely crazy, but I go over to my own body, sleeping on the cot, and poke my arm.

"Hey!" I say. The voice that comes out of my mouth is so raspy and deep! I sound—oh my gosh, I sound like a guy!

"Hey! Get up!" I say.

This has to be a dream, right?

I'm standing beside the cot, looking down at my own body, dressed in the blue Thatcher gym shorts and orange tee, seemingly sound asleep. There's actually a little bit of drool coming out of my mouth. Am I dead?

I must be hallucinating.

I poke again. This time hard. Then I bend down real close and put my lips to my own ear.

"Helloooo!" I say.

Nothing.

So I grab a handful of my loose red hair and yank it. Hard.

I just about faint as my own eyes pop open and stare back.

Face-to-face, one inch away.

It's like I'm looking in a mirror . . .

Only there's no mirror.

I'm looking right at—

ME!

14
JACK

SURE, I'VE HAD MY BELL rung a couple of times. Last year in the playoffs, I got clocked in the head. It's the weirdest feeling. It's like you're in a daze, you know? Sort of like a dream. Like I'm almost hovering above myself, watching everything happen.

That's exactly how I feel when I wake up, all groggy, in the nurse's office, with someone jabbing me in my shoulder.

"Wake up!" I hear my own voice practically yelling in my ear.

"Hey!" I hear myself say. "Helloooo!"

I must be dreaming, right?

I swat away the hand that's poking me.

Chill! I think, slowly opening my eyes.

Holy jeeeeez!

Please don't think I'm insane when I tell you this. I swear to you.

When I open my eyes?

I see *my own face* staring back at me.

For a few seconds I'm sure I look a lot like a little baby playing peek-a-boo. I close my eyes tight, then open them again.

Close. Open!

Close. Open!

Close. Open!

Same result every time . . . my own face is three inches away from me, inspecting me like I'm some sort of full-on freak show.

To make matters worse?

The me standing there? The me I'm staring at?

I'm not looking too good.

Both my eyes are a little bit black, my nose is banged up, and there's a streak of dried blood on my upper lip.

This is some crazy dream! I reach out and touch my cheek. My face jerks back and I hear my own voice let out a squeal. "Ow!"

Okay, this is getting weird. I guarantee you, I've *never* squealed in my life.

Close. Open!

Close. Open!

Close. Open!

"Would you stop doing that!" says the voice—*my voice,*

sounding rattled and much deeper than it does when it's in my own head.

For just a split second, I take a big deep breath and quietly hope that my brothers are going to jump out from behind the nurse's empty desk. "Surprise!" they'll shout. "We're just rippin' you, Jacko!" they'll tell me. "Easy there, bud, settle down!" Only, my brothers aren't here. Nobody is here. Nobody except for—

"Hello?" I say weakly. And by weakly I mean I don't want to actually admit that I'm speaking to what looks like my ghost standing two feet in front of me, and I don't want to tell you the voice that comes out of my mouth sounds like a GIRL!

"What the—" I mutter out loud. Obviously I'm dreaming, right? I'm talking to myself, so you can imagine my surprise when my own body—dressed in *my* light-blue polo shirt and jeans—reaches out, grabs me by the hand, and yanks me up to my feet and toward the full-length mirror hanging from the back of the closed nurse's room door.

15

ELLIE

"LOOK!" I POINT TO THE mirror. The two of us are standing in front of it, side by side, me and Jack. Only, um . . . I don't really know how to say this, because if I say it, if I say it, like, out loud, uhhh, you are going to think I'm—

"What the—" Jack starts, and I watch him staring into the mirror. "This . . . wait, dude, whoa! C'mon, man! This can't possibly be happening. This doesn't make sense!" He grabs me by the shoulder and shakes.

"Stop!" I say. "What are you doing?"

"Are you *real*?" he asks.

I push him back, kind of harder than I meant to, and he stumbles.

"Does that feel real?" I say.

We both turn back toward the mirror, as if the mirror

is going to suddenly change what we see.

What we know.

What is clear as day.

I am in Jack's body, and he is in mine!

16
JACK

"I DON'T GET IT," I say.

Actually, I keep saying it over and over again. "I don't get it. I don't get it."

I'm pacing across the small nurse's room, from one cot to the other, back and forth, like that is somehow going to change things.

Worse, Freckles is starting to cry like a total girl, except—

She's me.

I have never seen myself cry.

This is unreal.

"Freckles!" I say, realizing I don't even know this girl's name. "Dude, you've got to stop crying, you know? You're freaking me out!"

"Yeah, well, your nose is killing me!" she says, snorting

back sobs. "What did you even do to your face?"

I look back at her, I mean—

I look back at *me*. I look pretty banged up. "This is unreal," I say, staring back into the mirror. "It's like I'm living in a movie!"

"We should get someone, right?" Freckles manages to stop the tears long enough to blurt this out. She's looking right at me. "We should, like, go get Ms. Dean, or—"

"No way!" I cut her off. "They'll think we're totally nuts! Who is going to believe this? What would we even tell them?"

"We'll just tell them what happened!" Freckles answers, as if it's all as simple as that.

"Yeah, great." I almost laugh. "We can tell them we fell asleep, and we woke up in each other's bodies?"

Freckles looks mad. "Well? Do you have any better ideas?"

She plops down on the cot. "Oh, my head," she whines.

I hand Freckles my old ice pack and sit down next to her. Honestly? For the first time in my life, I really don't know what to do.

Think, Jack. Think.

When was the last time I remember actually being in my own body?

"That wacky nurse!" I look at her empty desk across the room. "She must have, like—"

"Put some sort of spell on us?" finishes Freckles. She

looks as freaked as I feel. "What are we going to do?" She's crying again. "We have to find the nurse, right?"

"Hey, whoa, whoa, whoa, just breathe, okay? Calm down," I say. Every time I talk, I nearly die. My voice sounds so soft and—*girly*!

I feel dizzy. I flop back on the flimsy mattress. And yeah, if you're thinking this must be weird, it is! I glance down at my—I mean, Freckles's—tight blue gym shorts and puny girlie legs, and look, I'm not going to even say it, like, out loud, but I am in a body that is 100 percent female. Including the upper half and the lower half, and the everything-in-between half!

Oh, god.

I shut my eyes, but only for a second, because the door suddenly opens and in walks the guidance counselor, Ms. Buchanan.

"You kids doing okay? Feeling any better?"

I bolt upright. I say nothing.

"Thank goodness it's Friday, right?" She grins at the two of us sitting next to each other. "Y'all can go now and get your stuff. The bell's going to ring in ten minutes or so, and—" Ms. Buchanan stops. "Ellie, are you okay?"

"Ellie?" Ms. Buchanan repeats, staring at me, which is weird because she's talking to—

Oh.

Freckles elbows me in the gut.

"Oh, um—" I start, my first official conversation as Ellie. "I guess?"

"You guess, huh?" Ms. Buchanan stands in front of us. She crosses her arms and looks down at us both. "*What exactly* was going on in here before I walked in?" she asks, suddenly suspicious.

Ellie jumps up. "Nothing!" she says, sounding totally mortified, except it's my voice and my body that moves across the room and straps on my backpack and looks back at me. I feel a little bit panicked. Where is she going?

"Wait!" I call after Freckles in my new squeaky girl voice, and jump up too.

Ms. Buchanan walks toward the door. "You two get yourselves together. As I said, the bell is about to ring. And leave the door *open*. No funny business. Understood?"

"Yes, ma'am," I answer. "We understand, ma'am."

"Well, thank you, Ellie, I appreciate the respectful tone."

I glance over at Ellie—I mean, me—and notice how much my own eyes look completely relieved when Ms. Buchanan finally leaves.

17
ELLIE

EVEN THOUGH MS. BUCHANAN TOLD us not to close the door, I jump up and shut it, turning the lock just to be safe.

"That was nuts," I say. I don't really know if I'm talking to Jack or talking to myself, but either way, I'm starting to freak out again, and it shows.

"Ellie?" says Jack. "That's your name, right?"

I nod.

"Look," he tells me, "we don't have a lot of time. Pretty soon the bell is going to ring and nothing is going to change here, so let's face it—"

"I'm you," I say, interrupting him.

"Exactly, you are me and I'm you," he says, smiling for the first time. I know this sounds nuts, but I actually feel a little bit more calm when I see myself smiling.

He grins again. "We just have to make it through the weekend, right? Then we'll get back here and find that wacky nurse and—"

"The *weekend*!" I cut him off. "Are you crazy!?"

Jack looks up at the clock. "Dude, come on, do you want to waste time arguing?"

"Fine," I answer. "Go ahead, tell me your great, awesome plan," I say, sounding kind of meaner than I wanted to.

"Okay, first, go home with my dad. He'll be right outside by the gym door in a big pickup truck, and—"

"What color?" I ask.

"What color what?" says Jack.

"The truck?"

"Black," he answers. "Dude, you are asking too many questions. Look, just go with my dad and keep your mouth shut, don't get into it with my brothers, and whatever you do, *don't* tell my dad about the fight, okay?"

"Yeah, okay, whatever," I answer. "I won't tell him."

"No, seriously, Ellie, for real. Promise, okay?" Jack looks really worried. Which means I'm looking at *me* looking really freaked out.

"Okay, okay, I promise," I tell him. "But isn't he going to wonder what happened to your face?"

"Just say it was from Stryker last night in The Cage," answers Jack.

"You were in a *cage* with someone named Stryker?" *Oh god.*

"Stryker's my brother. I have three."

My mouth drops open. "Three brothers!"

"Look, you'll be fine, okay? Just stay in my room. Even if Owen calls, or anyone, just stay home, okay?"

"Okay." I nod.

"My dad, he has, like . . ." He pauses for a moment, then goes on. "He has a certain way about him, so just . . ."

"Yeah?"

"Just say as little as possible."

"Okay," I tell him.

"Well?" he asks.

"Well what?"

"What about me?" he asks. "How am I, or, like—" He stops and looks at me anxiously. "What am I supposed to do?"

I picture my mom waiting in her car by the back of the school. She's probably already even there, waiting with a snack and my soccer gear.

Oh my god, *soccer!*

Sassy!

Everything comes flooding back. I start to panic, and okay, yeah, I can feel the tears gathering in my eyes.

"Look, dude, you seriously have to stop crying!" Jack tells me. "If you're going to be me, you can't be such a GIRL!"

This is so crazy.

"I know this seems unreal," says Jack. He reaches out and grabs my hand. Which is so weird, because I never imagined I'd be holding hands with The Prince of Thatcher on the first day of seventh grade.

Or, I'd *be* The Prince of Thatcher on the first day of seventh grade.

He lets go of my hand and I'm sort of flustered.

"Well? What do I do?" he asks again.

"Uhhh, my mom's picking me up in the back by the gym, and look, number one: do *not* go to soccer, no matter how much my mom says you have to go. Make something up. Just go directly to my room and stay there for the entire weekend!"

"Okay, no soccer," he repeats. "Stay in your room. Got it."

"Yeah, just, like, stay in my room. Please! Promise me that no matter what my mom says, don't go *anywhere*, okay?"

"Okay," he answers. "Chill!"

"*No* soccer," I repeat.

"Okay, no soccer, I get it, you already said that."

"And whatever you do, *no* sleepovers! No birthday parties!"

"Dude!" he says. "Relax! I'm not going to some chick birthday party, okay?"

"Swear?"

"I swear."

Suddenly he looks worried again. "Oh, man . . ."

"What?"

"Hockey . . ." His voice trails off, and for a second I think he might cry too.

"Do *not* under *any* circumstances go to hockey," he tells me.

"Hockey?" I laugh. "I can't even skate."

"Good, yeah, well. Just . . . don't go. Make something up, okay?"

"Sure." I shrug. "No problem."

"Look, Ellie." Jack takes a big deep breath. "We have got to make this work, okay? One weekend, that's two measly days, right? How hard can it be?"

He almost has me convinced.

"How hard can it be?" I repeat.

"So we'll meet by the main office first thing Monday. Deal?" Jack extends my own arm toward me.

"Deal," I say, shaking my own hand.

And, this is embarrassing, but, um, I seriously can't hold it much longer, so I just blurt it out. "Jack, you, I mean we . . . I mean . . . I have to pee."

Jack pushes me toward the small nurse's room bathroom, opens the door, and points to the toilet.

"What do I even do?" I squeal.

"Just go in there and, like . . ." He cringes. "Just, like . . ." He stops and swallows hard. It's pretty obvious he's just as embarrassed as I am.

"Yeah?"

"Grab on, aim, and shake when you're done."

18
JACK

WHEN THE BELL RINGS, I'M not gonna lie—

Freckles has to push me.

"It's now or never!" she tells me, grabbing my new bony-girl wrist and pulling me out the nurse's room doorway. Stepping into the jammed hallway is probably the most petrified feeling I have ever had in my life. It's a madhouse. And it's loud. *So loud.* It seems like every single kid at Thatcher is pushing and shoving and shouting. The two of us stand side by side, our arms brushing, our backs to the lockers, sort of frozen, staring out at the scene.

I grab Ellie's hand for just a second before I realize what it looks like.

Like we're, you know, a couple, holding hands, and I drop it fast.

"Jack! What are you doing?"

"I know, it's just—" I stop. *Just the small fact that I'm a friggin' girl!*

I don't say that out loud, though, because one glance toward Freckles standing in the Thatcher hallway with my banged-up face—black eye, swollen nose—and I can tell she's just as overwhelmed as I am.

"Hey," I say, speaking kind of loud so that she can hear me over the crowd. "Let's move on three, okay?"

Freckles nods.

"Okay," I start. "Ready?"

"Ready," she says.

"One," we both say. "Two . . ." And—

Exactly on three, Sammy appears out of nowhere and throws his arm around Freckles's neck. "'Sup, dude!"

She catches my eye, like, *Could this get any weirder?* Then she glares at Sammy like he's totally crazy.

Really, *we're* the crazy ones!

I nod at her like, you know, *I am you and you are me, remember?* And if that's not enough, I walk behind her and sort of nudge her in the back.

"That's my friend Sammy," I whisper.

Freckles turns to me. "I know who that is!"

Sammy looks around, completely confused. "Um, who *who* is, Jacko?" Then he nods toward me in Freckles's body. "I see the dames are already loving your action, big dog."

Freckles looks back at Sammy in a complete daze.

"Um, dude." Sammy grins. "Are you feeling all right?"

Unreal.

I can't watch any more of this.

I take a step away.

"Monday," I mouth toward Freckles.

19
ELLIE

WHEN WE STEP OUTSIDE THROUGH the back door by the gym entrance, Sammy won't stop talking, and he's *so* gross!

"Duuude, hold up." He smiles at me, then clears his throat and spits out a big green glob of snot that spins through the air and lands on the sidewalk. "Now, *that* was a good horker, bro!"

I look at Sammy Armstrong like he's disgusting, because he is. "Eww!" I say, before I remember that The Prince of Thatcher probably doesn't say *eww*. "I mean, um, uhhh, cool, cool." I try again and give him a little nod like I see boys do.

Sammy grins at me. "Dude, exactly how hard did you hit your head? You're seriously acting weird!"

I glance up and down the back parking area and see if

I can spot my mom or Jack. But I don't see anyone I know, and to make matters worse? Sammy hauls off and slugs me in the arm. Hard.

"Gunner," he says.

"Gunner? What? Someone has a gun?!!!" I look all around and practically drop to the ground.

"Yo!" Sammy starts laughing. "Seriously, you're kind of scaring me, Jacko!" He points to the big black pickup truck. "Your brother? Gunner?

"Helloooo?" He shoves me for emphasis. "Bro's here, broskinator!"

I look toward the big black pickup truck pulled up to the curb. *Brother? I thought Jack said it would be his dad.*

Sammy follows me to the truck. It's huge. The truck, I mean. Like, the kind you practically need a stepladder just to climb up into the seat. The windows are down, and there's country music blaring. I open the door and launch myself up and glance at the kid in the driver's seat, who pretty much looks like an older, even more handsome version of Jack. If that's possible. He's got the same dimples, and big toothy smile, and he's wearing jeans and a gray T-shirt that is just tight enough that his biceps pop out.

He turns to me. "Dang! What happened to you, little man?"

I settle into the front seat. My heart—*Jack's heart*—is absolutely pounding, and my mind's racing for what I'm supposed to say. Something about a cage and nothing about the fight, but before I manage to even get a word out, Sammy takes over. He's wedged himself between me and the door of the truck so there is no way I can close it, even if I want to. *And I want to.*

"Big boy dropped the mitts," announces Sammy. "You should have seen him. He dusted the kid."

"Stud," says Gunner, shooting me a smile.

He starts up the truck, but that doesn't stop Sammy. He just leaps down onto the ground and runs alongside us.

"Jacko," he calls out, "if you are not at Owen's tomorrow night, I will personally deliver you a swift kick in the cashews! And, Jack—"

I turn and look back at Sammy running after the truck. "Stick your hands out the window and squeeze. It feels like boobs!"

Oh my god.

"Try it!" he shouts. He's bent over, laughing.

"Get a load of this guy!" Gunner says, looking back over his shoulder, grinning. "Kid's crazy!"

We pull out of Thatcher onto the main road.

"So, you surprised?" he asks.

"Surprised?" I repeat.

Great. *What am I supposed to be surprised about?*

"El Capitán had a work thing, so it's bro time, little buddy!"

I turn away and stare out the window. *Who the heck is El Capitán?*

Gunner gives me a weird look. "You feeling okay, buddy?"

I nod and quietly pray he can't tell that I'm on the verge of tears.

But it doesn't work.

"C'mon, man, quit being so soft!" he tells me. "Please tell me you aren't crying like a little girl."

That's exactly what I'm doing, I think. I keep myself turned away, looking out the window.

"Take your skirt off, ya big beauty!"

Huh?

"Dude, relax. You stood up for yourself, right?"

I keep quiet.

"Did you win or did you lose?"

I shrug. I have no idea what to say.

He repeats the question. "Did you win or did you lose?"

"Win, I guess." I finally manage an answer.

Gunner's entire face lights up. "Nails, Jacko!" he says, reaching over and squeezing my shoulder.

Nails?

"You took care of your business, little man. Just, you know, there will be some hell to pay. Let's not tell The Captain just yet, okay?"

"The Captain?" I ask.

Apparently I've said something funny. Gunner laughs

and looks at me. "You're sounding a little off, bro. Did you get your bell rung or what?"

I shrug again.

Out of the corner of my eye, I watch Gunner check himself out in the rearview mirror. "Lost about five pounds in sweat today. Good skate this morning with the boys. Grind now, shine later, right?"

He turns the music up. "Nothing better than cruisin' with all windows down, big dog! I can sing as loud and bad as I want." He pauses and grins right at me. "Gonna stop and get my flow chopped. You in?"

"Uhhh, I guess?" I say. I have no idea what he's talking about.

Gunner looks surprised. "Seriously?"

"Sure." I shrug. Whatever I said I would do makes Gunner very happy.

His eyes light up and he reaches over again, grabbing my knee this time and squeezing it hard. "Pumped! Proud of you, man. Holdin' it down. What did the girls think of your eye?"

"Huh?"

"It's a good look, Jacko. Beast mode!"

Boys are so weird!

Jack's brother is kind of funny. He smiles a lot. "Bro," he says. "Pain is nothing compared to what it feels like to quit, right? What did the other dude look like?"

"What other dude?" I say.

Gunner laughs. "The donkey you dusted."

"Um, oh, not too good, I guess." Yes, I'm just making stuff up at this point.

"Did you destroy him?"

"I guess?"

"That-a-boy, little man. Flat-out brawl. Showin' a little grit!" He stretches his arm out toward me and ruffles my—Jack's—thick, messy hair. "Showed some jam, bro!"

I work up the nerve to look over at him again. He's probably sixteen or seventeen, I guess. And he has the same blue eyes as Jack and the same wild dark hair. Gunner catches me looking. It's awkward. "You sure you're okay, little man?"

"Yeah," I manage. "I'm good," I say with a nervous laugh.

I'm not exactly good! I'm riding in a truck with a kid I just met, and I'm in Jack Malloy's body.

20
JACK

AS SOON AS I BUST out the back gym door, I kind of freeze in my tracks. Small problem, right? I forgot to ask Ellie what kind of car I'm supposed to look for.

I stand there and stare out into the bumper-to-bumper line of parents waiting to pick up their kids and just keep thinking, *This has to be a dream . . . tell me this isn't really happening.* But I'm pretty sure it is happening. No, scratch that, I'm positive. First clue? I watch a tall lady with long, wavy fiery-red hair, yoga clothes, and a big beaming smile jump out of a white Volvo, motion to the teacher directing traffic that she'll only be a second, and walk straight for me. She doesn't give me any time to duck the hug. She pulls me in and wraps her arms around me tight. It's awkward, all right—my new face is pressed up against her boobs!

"Day one is in the books, darling!" she whispers into my ear, and it tickles. "You did it!"

It doesn't take a rocket scientist to figure out Red Hair with Yoga Pants is Ellie's mom. First of all, she has milky-white skin and freckles, just like, well—just like Freckles does. Second? She calls me Ellie. Actually, *Ellie honey*. As in, "Ellie, honey, I have the most amazing surprise for you!" When she talks, her whole face smiles, and she doesn't just say "amazing," she says it like this: "Ahhhh-may-ziiiiing!"

Red Hair with Yoga Pants's eyes are big and bright green, and when she hugs me, she smells really good, like . . . I can't describe it because, honestly, I haven't been hugged like that in a really long time. And when she lets go of my new girl arms and my new girl shoulders, she reaches for Ellie's eight-hundred-pound book bag and carries it for me!

Maybe I could get used to this, is what I'm thinking as I slide into the front seat. Red Hair with Yoga Pants shoots me this warm, dazzling smile and hands me a bag of takeout from Chipotle and a Mountain Dew.

"You must be starving," she tells me.

Look, I'm just going to say it. Freckles's mom is unbelievably pretty and not scary and she smells good and she *brought me food*. Not just food, but a grilled chicken burrito with guacamole, salsa, cheese, *and* sour cream!

So what I'm thinking as we pull out of Thatcher is, *this*

might not be so bad after all, right? Maybe I can do this.

I inhale the burrito like I haven't eaten for days. The Captain considers any type of fast food off-limits. Let me put it another way: Chipotle is not on the yes list for the Malloy training table. I'm so hungry I forget that I should probably, like, slow down and not eat like a contestant on *Survivor*. Red Hair with Yoga Pants glances over, smiling. "Wow, you're really devouring that. I guess you're hungry, huh?"

"Yeah," I answer with my mouth full, wiping the sour cream from my chin with the back of my hand and thinking about how The Captain would get so heated if I did that with him. Heck, The Captain does not even let me eat in the truck!

Red Hair with Yoga Pants reaches over and puts her hand on the back of my neck. "Soooo?"

I try not to flinch.

"Soooo," she says again, squeezing this time. "Aren't you dying to know the big ahhhh-may-ziiiiing surprise?"

I make a quick decision: the less I say, the better.

I'll just keep quiet, right?

Wrong.

The more quiet I am, the more questions I get.

She glances at me and smiles big. "What are you thinking about over there?"

"How was your first day?"

"How come you still have your gym clothes on? Do

they give you enough time to change?"

"Are you excited about your classes?"

I keep eating and hope somehow the chewing will excuse the not answering.

Red Hair with Yoga Pants doesn't seem to be too mad. "Well, I'll tell you what. It's fine. You don't have to talk. Just relax."

Okay, thanks, I think silently in my head.

She glances over and shoots me the biggest smile. "And about that surprise? Are you wondering at all?"

"I guess," I say, shrugging my shoulders.

"Well, I'm going to keep you in suspense until after soccer."

"Soccer?" I blurt out, remembering Freckles's instructions.

"Honey, we talked about this. I don't feel good about letting you back out just because of a few bad apples."

Bad apples? What's that even mean? I turn away and press my head up against the glass, just like I do when my dad's lecturing me in the truck.

"Coach Carolyn expects you to be there, Ellie."

A few long seconds go by where neither of us speak.

"Ellie, I'm talking to you." For the first time, Red Hair with Yoga Pants sounds a little bit upset.

"I don't feel well," I say. *It's not exactly a lie*, I think, glancing down at my girlie freckled knees.

"Ellie, seriously, it's not really a choice, okay?" She

shoots me a quick glance. She looks so *not* mad, like the opposite of The Captain. She looks more worried, or concerned, I guess.

"Sweetie, you are going to soccer, and you are going to be fine. Just have fun out there, okay? Don't take everything so seriously!"

I settle back into the seat. I watch her drive.

I don't talk.

"Is it you-know-who?" she finally asks.

"Huh?"

"Are you worried about, you know, She Who Must Not Be Named?"

I look at her like she's crazy. "What?"

"Look, I'm going to tell you the same thing I always tell you, and I know you're sick of it, but it's true. Honey, the more open you can be about your feelings, the better you'll feel."

I nod. But inside? Dude. I am confused.

"Are you worried?" she asks again.

I shrug. Honestly, right now the only thing I am worried about is the fact that I'm a G-I-R-L and Red Hair with Yoga Pants has her hand on my neck again.

We've stopped in front of the Sportsplex. I've been here a million times with Sammy and Owen. Birthday parties. Pickup games. I look at the stairs and the dozens of kids walking in with their soccer gear. I'm pretty sure that this is happening, whether I want it to or not.

Ellie's mom turns to me and hands me a drawstring soccer bag. It's pink.

And look, there's not a big choice here. I take the bag. I take the pink bag and try to force a smile.

"You can do it, honey pie," she says. "You totally got this!"

21
ELLIE

I JUMP DOWN OUT OF the gigantic black truck and follow Gunner down the strip-mall sidewalk because I have no idea what I just agreed to do or where in the world we could possibly be going.

Gunner ruffles my hair again. "Dude, you got some sick flow, bro."

"Huh?" I say.

"Nothin' like a good chop to start the season. Need to shake some things up, right?"

I still have no idea what he's talking about, so I decide the best approach is to just keep saying yes.

"Yeah, um, sure," I say, and nod for emphasis.

Gunner throws his arm around me as we walk side by side. "'Sup, big fella?" He winks. "Feels unreal to be back on the sticks with the boys!"

"Yeah," I repeat, throwing one of those guy nods in again.

"Bro," he starts. "Honestly, I was thinking about growing a mullet. It's making a comeback. Business in the front, party in the back!"

I look at him a little weird again. I can't help it. I like him, but I can't understand a word he is saying. Gunner just keeps his arm around my shoulders. "Tough day, little man. Have to bounce back. Let's get it goin'!"

He shoots me a wink and stops all of a sudden in front of a door, holding it open for me. "After you, Jacko!"

The barber's name is Geno. Geno Anthony DiAngelo, to be exact. The only reason I know this is because I'm so freaked out, I keep my eyes glued straight ahead at the framed barber's license leaning on the counter against the mirror.

I think by accident I agreed to, like—

Get Jack's hair shaved off!

Gulp.

I slink down into the big leather barbershop chair, trembling. Gunner whips out his iPhone and starts filming. "Let's see that shaggy mop, Jacko!" He laughs. "Little bro's flow has got to go!"

Geno the barber looks at me. "The usual?" he asks.

"I, uhhh—"

"Yeah, old-school, Geno," Gunner answers for me, then

looks at me in the mirror. "A fade, right, broski?"

"A fade?" I repeat. I am seriously wondering if boys even speak English.

Gunner turns to Geno the barber. "Big guy's had a rough day," he tells him. "Let's go with number two on top, and number one around those big beauty ears." He laughs and drops into the seat behind me.

It all happens so fast.

Geno the barber moves behind the chair, turns on the electric clippers, and the next thing I know I'm watching in the mirror as huge clumps of Jack's thick, dark, curly, beautiful hair drop off his head. Nobody says a word. Besides the buzzing of the clippers, we sit in total silence.

It doesn't take long.

Seven minutes max.

"Here you go," says Geno the barber, holding up a mirror so I can see the back. There's not really any purpose to that, though. Besides a very minuscule layer of prickly, sandpapery stubble? Jack's hair is—

G-O-N-E.

22
JACK

I AM THREE STEPS INTO the Sportsplex lobby when some girl nearly lays me out with one of those knock-you-down-running-start hugs.

"Girlieeee!" she squeals right into my ear before she finally lets go. "Oh my goooosh! I haven't seen you in for-ever!"

I look back at her like, "Do I know you?" Believe me, I'd remember. I can practically hear Sammy's voice in my head: "SMOKE SHOW!" he'd say.

Smoke Show has long, sun-streaked blond hair, bright blue eyes, and, according to the bubbly script stitched on the upper right side of her hoodie, her name is *Mackenzie*. There's a lot of pink going on—pink-and-white-striped soccer socks, pink shorts, and the hoodie with THUNDER-BIRDS in bold, white, shiny sewn-on letters across the front.

"Girlieeee!" Mackenzie's eyes widen. "We *really* need to make plans to hang! Now that I'm at Mount Saint Mary's, I never see you on the bus! We haven't talked in *so* long! I have *so* much to tell you! You *are* coming tomorrow, right?"

"Tomorrow?" I say. And I'll be honest, I am still absolutely shocked at the sound of the voice I hear coming out of my mouth.

"To Claire's, silly!" Mackenzie laughs.

Yes, I am staring. Really, what do you expect? I can't even talk to girls, let alone talk *like* a girl!

"Ellie! You promise, right? I miss you. I want to hang out with you! You are coming, right?"

I take a deep breath, and before I even have to answer, Mackenzie threads her arm through mine and begins walking, pulling me along past the trophy case and the snack bar. Her eyes light up as she talks. "I'm going to let you off the hook for acting so spacey! Are you nervous?"

Ha. I seriously almost smile. *Nervous? Yeah. You could say that.*

"No worries, girlie! Bus besties, remember? Team No Boobs!"

Huh?

Mackenzie suddenly stops in her tracks, turns, and looks right into my eyes. Man, is she pretty.

"Ellie, you're seeming a little bit, like, not yourself. You would *never* get cut. You're, like, *so* good. You're so fast!"

I manage the slightest smile.

"Don't freak, okay? You're going to make the team!" She sounds so sure. "It's going to be awesome!"

I just stand there like a complete idiot and nod. I *am* nervous, but not because I'm afraid of Freckles's soccer tryouts. It's more because I'm looking over Mackenzie's shoulder at the bright-green turf field and the twenty or so girls who are sitting around stretching, and I realize I have to *change. Change my clothes!*

"Great," I mutter.

"Great what?" asks Mackenzie.

"Oh, uhh, um . . ."

"Ellie." She lowers her voice to a whisper. "You're acting weird. Seriously, are you feeling all right?"

"I'm fine," I lie. I stop and shove my arm down into Freckles's pink bag and fish out her turf shoes, shorts, and jersey. Screw the bathroom. I stand right there in front of everyone and pull on the jersey (pink) and the shorts (pink) right over the gym clothes I'm already wearing. Then I drop down onto the cold cement floor and finish the look with the same pink-and-white-striped socks Mackenzie has on.

"Um, Ellie?" Mackenzie looks confused. "Aren't you, like, gonna, you know, change?"

I look up from tying Freckles's turf shoes tight. "I'm good," I say, standing.

"What's with you, girlie?" She laughs. "Didn't you forget something?"

I glance down. I'm pretty sure girls don't wear a cup.

"Shin guards?" she offers.

"Oh, uhh, yeah, right," I say, embarrassed that I didn't even think of that. I dig them out of Ellie's bag and slip the shin guards into the socks, which makes me think about hockey, which makes me both worried and afraid. I'm the youngest guy on the team. I've never missed a practice in my entire life! I'll just have to pray that Ellie stays put in my room and doesn't screw my career up.

"Hellooooo!" Mackenzie is waving her hand in front of my eyes. "You sure you're okay?" She looks confused. "I can't believe you are seriously nervous about tryouts, Ellie! You're awesomesauce! You're ten times better than, like, almost every girl on the team!" Mackenzie leans in and cups her hand around my ear.

I told you I'm, like, the shyest kid in the entire eighth grade, right? Honestly, I have never been *this close* to a girl in my life.

I swallow hard.

"If you're feeling a little bit stressed . . ." Mackenzie pauses and takes a big, warm breath. "Fake it till you make it, girlie! You got this."

I FOLLOW GUNNER UP THE winding stone path to
the front of the house, but I don't just walk right in. No. I
stand in the entryway, staring at the honey-colored walls
as if I'm a friend or a visitor—before it all comes rushing
back.

I am JACK.

I'm practically bald.

I supposedly live here!

My nose is killing me and my head still hurts.

I watch Gunner hang the keys to the truck on a little
hook and admire himself and his new look in the mirror
by the door. Geno worked his magic on Gunner too, and
now we look scarily the same, like twin marines, minus
the black eye and the busted-up face and the fact that I'm
a girl in Jack's body!

"Geno crushed it, right, bro?"

"Crushed what?"

"Perfection, bud." Gunner thwacks me on the top of my bald head before bounding up the stairs.

"Wait!" I call, disturbingly aware that I'm sounding extremely desperate. "Where are you going?"

Gunner looks back down at me. "Ha ha, love you, bud. Get your rest. Big day tomorrow!"

What I want to do is run after Gunner and wrap my arms around his leg like a two-year-old, clamping on hard and not letting go. What I want is to ask him what exactly he means by "big day," not to mention the more obvious things, like *Where is Jack's room?* and *What am I supposed to do now?*

Instead? I stand alone in the entryway, Jack's bag slung around my shoulder, and steal a quick glance into the mirror. I run my hand over the prickly quarter-inch of hair Geno thankfully left on Jack's head.

Um. Yeah. *He's seriously going to kill me.*

Upstairs, the first door I try is *not* Jack's door. I know this because when I open it, I get a sneaker thrown at my face.

"Let's see that flow show, Jacko!" I hear, and I open the door a little wider.

Brother Number Two is lying on his bed in gray sweat-pants and no shirt, which makes me back away, and fast. "Sorry!" I say.

"Get back in here, you big beauty!"

I open the door just a crack and peek through. This one has to be the oldest. He has Jack's same—I mean, used to be same—wavy, longish, thick dark hair, and he's wearing those Clark Kent–type dark-framed glasses, the kind that make anyone wearing them seem instantly brainy. Plus he's reading, and a guy with a book just looks smart.

"Holy smokes! Shaved your mop! Can't believe you chopped it, bro. You had some sweet locks going. I thought you weren't going to give in? It was about that time, though!" He studies me for a long second, smiling the whole time. "Flow chop, then start growing it for the season. Nice!"

Brother Number Two is unbelievably handsome, and I think I mentioned no shirt? I'm pretty sure my cheeks turn bright red.

"Don't get rattled, bro, it'll grow back." He laughs. "In six months!" Brother Number Two cracks himself up. It's hard not to smile, though, and so I stand in the doorway and I think I honestly kind of almost grin.

"No big deal, little man. The old dome is a bit cooler these days. Still a stud, though." He throws the other sneaker at my head. "What are you waiting for, donkey? Get your butt in here and sit down!"

I step into the room and immediately notice something awful. It smells really bad, like farts and smelly feet.

"Sorry, bro," he says, looking up from his book. "Been rippin' the nastiest bombs all day."

I look all around the room to see if there are any clues as to who the heck I'm even talking to, but besides the bookshelves loaded with a billion gold and silver hockey trophies and medals and three framed, glass-encased jerseys hanging on the wall, it doesn't really look like a teenage boy's room at all. What I mean is, it's not, like, messy. It's actually really, really neat, right down to the fact that Brother Number Two is lying on *top* of his bed, *not* under the covers. The bed is made perfectly. The sheets are flat and smooth and nothing is hanging out over the edge. Everything is tucked in just so and creased and folded over the striped wool blanket. There's not even any stuff on the floor! *My mom would love this kid*, I think, and park my butt on the very edge of the end of the bed.

For a few seconds I just awkwardly sit there in silence while Clark Kent goes back to reading his book in his perfectly tidy room. I wonder what it is I'm actually supposed to be doing.

Then he talks. He doesn't look up from his book, though. "I hear you tangled with some dolt at school," he says.

I nod. At least I know that's true.

He glances up. "Was the dude chirpin' or what?"

"Chirping?" I repeat, and look at him weird.

"Are you kidding me right now?" He shakes his head.

"Well? Did ya pump him?"

"Pump him?" I say, but then I stop, completely confused, and hope he just keeps talking.

"Bud, you're just hilarious." He pauses. "Did you light him up? Did you smoke him?"

"I guess." I repeat the same answer I told Gunner, not exactly sure what I just said I did.

"Not gonna lie, your mug looks a little bit nasty." Brother Number Two laughs, shaking his head. "The Captain is going to be pissed, big dog."

Duhhh! Took me long enough. *The Captain must be Jack's dad.*

"I'm not going to tell him," I blurt out.

He winks. "Good plan, little man."

I flop backward on my small section at the very end of his bed and look up at the ceiling. No fake solar system up there. No free wishes. Just a fan whipping farts and smelly feet around. I close my eyes, just for a second, until I feel a foot kicking me hard in my ribs.

"Oww!" I say. I somehow managed to make Jack's voice squeal.

"Easy, Sally, simmer." He shakes his head.

I look at him, like, *"Who the heck is Sally?"*

"I'll give you this, Jacko, takes some berries to tangle. A little bit grungy, though, to do it in school, bro. Not a good look. C'mon, man, figure it out."

I have no idea what Jack was thinking or why he even

got in a fight or even, gosh, who with!

Brother Number Two nudges me with his foot. "Next time, don't be such a donkey!"

I nod, oddly grateful for the advice that isn't even meant for me.

"Haaa, rookie move, I guess." He closes his book and sits up in bed. I notice he has the same tiny gold pendant hanging from a thin chain around his neck, same as . . .

I slip my hand up and feel around my neck. Same as I do.

"Well?" he says, raising his eyebrows. "Besides the tangle, how was the big first day? Meet any good-looking ladies?"

I look at him, like, "*What are you talking about?*"

But he just breaks into a huge smile. "Handling business as usual, bro. Battled hard and got the W! Throw on a smile, ya big beauty." He kicks me again, harder than before. "My li'l buddy is growin' up so fast."

24
JACK

NO WONDER I HAVE NO game. Girls make absolutely no sense. I come to this conclusion about two seconds after throwing down my bag and sitting on the turf in front of the goal where the rest of the Thunderbirds—and everyone trying to be one—are getting ready for tryouts.

As soon as I do, this bouncy, friendly, smiley girl plops down next to me. "'Sup playa!" she says, sounding a little bit too much like Sammy. "When is your individual?"

"My individual?" I repeat.

"Duuuuh, with Coach?" She laughs. She has a mouthful of braces with fluorescent pink rubber bands framing each tooth.

"Oh, uh, not sure," I answer. At least that's true. I try to glance down at the name sewn on her hoodie.

Her name is Sammie. *Girl Sammie!*

"Relax, dude! You seriously look freaked! She'll probably call us up one by one, right?"

"Sure, yeah, I guess," I say. I look around for the coach. I can't even tell you how much I want to get this over with.

"Wowzers!" Girl Sammie flops back onto the turf and closes her eyes. She's wearing the same pink gear, head to toe. I'm thinking how goofy-funny she is and I'm almost grinning watching her when her eyes pop open and she sits straight up.

"OMG, Ellie, I mean, hopefully, we both make it, in which case"—she grabs my wrist and yanks me toward her—"how excited are you to spend a whole soccer season with me!"

Mostly I'm just hoping you let go of my hand, thanks.

Girl Sammie's smile suddenly dissolves, she lowers her voice. "Incoming!" she says, nodding toward . . .

I look up. Sassy Gaines and that new girl, Aspen, are walking straight toward us, same Thunderbird hoodies, hair pulled back, matching pink headbands. I watch as they stop two feet away, their backs to us, and drop their bags onto the turf. I won't lie. Sassy Gaines is a head turner. You have to work not to stare. When Sassy catches my eye, though, she doesn't smile at me the way she does at school or at the pool all summer. No. She glares.

"Ahem," she says, looking back over her shoulder

directly at me. "Why do people think it's okay to wear their soccer gear *over* their gym clothes?"

Aspen glances back too, scowling with her nose scrunched up. "I know, right? So pathetic!"

Sassy turns to Aspen. "So super awk, when you say something and people think you're talking about them."

"I know, right? If you were talking to *someone*"—Aspen smirks—"you would have said it to *her*."

Sassy starts laughing hysterically. "I was totally just thinking that! We literally thought the *exact* same thing at the *exact* same time!"

"Twins!" they both squeal.

Sassy may be hot, but it's amazing how someone can go from a ten to a two just by opening her mouth. What a clown. I just look at her and shake my head. I mean, if I were in the locker room and one of the guys lipped off to me like that? I'd just throw tape at his head and shut him up. "Easy, buddy," I'd say, and laugh. "That all you got?" That would get the boys going. But I'm not in our locker room and I don't know what the protocol is if you have boobs, so I just keep my head down and fidget with Freckles's pink-striped socks.

Girl Sammie moves closer. "Sorry, Ellie," she says. "It's so not even funny how two-faced people can be."

I shrug. "Girl's a clown," I say under my breath.

"What?"

"Oh, I mean . . ." I stall and try and think hard of

something to say besides what I want to say, which is "I could seriously care less about Sassy Gaines. Girl's a joke, plain and simple."

Don't worry! I don't say that.

I pop up to my feet and start juggling the ball. I haven't played soccer since I was nine. The Captain does not believe in an off-season. It's number four on his list of life maxims: "Success demands singleness of purpose." We play hockey year-round. One hundred games. Even if I wanted to play soccer, I can't. Off-ice training, lifting, working on my shot in The Cage, watching game film. Hockey is a twenty-four-hour, three-hundred-and-sixty-five-day job. The work never stops. My brothers and I train seven days a week. You've always got to be putting in the time. You can always get a lot stronger, tougher, faster.

I kick the ball around for a little bit before I hear the whistle calling us in for a huddle. I don't know why she bothers using her whistle, though. The coach has one of those voices that demands everyone's attention.

"Listen up, ladies," she hollers. She looks more like a small gymnast than a soccer star. She's wearing a black warm-up, zipped all the way up, and a visor with a dark ponytail spilling out the back. And she's smiling.

She waits a few seconds, bringing the shuffling and whispers to a hush. I glance around me and try not to be freaked out by the fact that I'm standing with twenty girls. Twenty-one, including me. My ears tingle and my hands feel sweaty. It's so crazy how much can change in such little time.

"Today and Sunday morning are the two last tryouts before cuts." The coach looks at me. "I'm only keeping ten for indoor. It's going to come down to who is working the hardest—who wants it most! Do you want it?"

"Yeaaaah!" they shriek at the top of their lungs.

Holy jeez, I have to do everything I can to not cover my ears.

Everyone throws their hands in on top of the coach's. "Thunderbirds on three," she says.

I look around as if someone is actually going to be understanding my predicament . . . you know, that I'm not Freckles! I'm *Jack*.

Monday needs to hurry up.

Then, just when it all starts to sink in again? Mackenzie comes out of nowhere and wiggles herself into the huddle right next to me, throwing her arm around my shoulders. We are so close. Her cheek is practically grazing mine. My heart starts beating like a thousand beats per minute.

I mean . . . it's not like I have anything better to do. *Whatever.*

I throw my hand into the pile too.

* * *

Twenty minutes of lunges, squat thrusts, sprints, and military-style warm-ups later? I am not laughing. The Thunderbirds are no joke. I throw myself into Ellie's try-outs like I'm on a mission. I only have one gear. Ask my brothers. We have a lot of heated battles. Doesn't matter what I'm doing. I've played the same way pretty much my whole life. That's just my nature. I'm a competitive guy. I like to win. I hate to lose.

Sassy is chirping at me the whole time. "Some people should save themselves the embarrassment and just quit," she says, talking loud enough for me to hear her.

Gutless.

I will never hit a girl in my life, but between you and me? I'd love to collide Freckles's fist with Sassy's noggin.

The coach calls me over at the start of the scrimmage. I don't come right away. I would have obviously jumped if I heard "Malloy!" or "Mallsy!" The fact that the coach is screaming at me to come over for a good minute is not a good sign. When I finally realize everyone is shouting "Ellie!" and Ellie means *me*, I hustle over to where the coach is standing by the players' box and double over, hands on my knees to catch my breath. I am legit gassed.

These girls can play.

The coach doesn't even really acknowledge me standing there. She clutches her clipboard to her chest. "Let's go, Claire, watch that first touch!" she hollers. "Sassy, pick your head up. You have to see what's around you. Mackenzie, great job supporting the play. Great anticipation, keep it up!" Finally she turns toward me. "Ellie O'Brien!"

"Yes, ma'am," I answer.

She looks surprised. "Yes, ma'am?" she says with a laugh. "How very polite of you, Ellie!"

We sit on the metal bench in the players' box.

"Jeepers, Ellie, you can sit a little closer." She smiles. "I don't have cooties!"

"Sorry, ma'am," I say, and scoot in a little bit.

"So!"

"Yes, ma'am?"

"How was day one?"

"Day one, ma'am?" I repeat, not sure what she means.

"School?" she offers. She looks at me a little strangely. "You okay, Ellie? You're acting a little bit different."

For a few seconds I completely freeze.

I am not okay.

"I'm fine, ma'am," I manage.

She glances down at her notes, then back at me. "You know if something's going on, you can talk to me, right?"

I nod. "Yes, ma'am."

"Look." She sighs. "I have some big decisions to make. I'm only keeping six up front for indoor. Are you ready to play whatever role that's needed?"

The only thing I know for sure is that Ellie told me to

not even *go* to soccer. I try to think.

"Ellie?"

"Yes, ma'am."

The coach looks concerned. "You sure you're okay?"

Actually, I'm pretty sure I am not okay.

"I'm going to be completely honest, Ellie. . . ." She stops and takes this long pause, and I get this totally sinking feeling. "I would say your strength by far is your speed, but your weakness? You need to believe in yourself more! I want to see more of those things that are hard to measure—confidence, risk taking. I need you to take some risks instead of passing off all the time. Attack the goal yourself. And if you lose the ball, what's the worst that can happen? With your speed, you can just run it down and win it back. Show me some determination to put that ball in the goal."

My mind begins to race . . . *Maybe I can help, you know? Maybe I can make Freckles stand out, try to do something to get her noticed.*

"Ellie? Ellie! Are you listening?"

"Oh, yes, ma'am," I say.

"You're an extremely nice kid, Ellie, and sometimes you're *too* nice. You have the speed, the skills. You can be very strong on the ball. You're technically sound. You can dribble. You see the game well. I need you to take the attacking role, be tough up front. It's a confidence thing." She pauses and smiles, eyebrows raised. "You have wheels, Ellie. Let loose out there! Be creative on the ball. Make it fun."

She's so positive and convincing. She's more down-to-earth than any coach I have ever had. For just a second, I completely forget everything. Forget even who I am or where I am or . . .

"Well, what are you waiting for, girl?" She smiles and jumps up. "Get at it!"

25
ELLIE

WHEN I ENTER JACK'S ROOM, I am positive it's Jack's room because there is a license plate on the wall—not a real one, one of those fake ones you get for your seventh birthday—and it says JACK. So yeah, at least I'm sure this is where I'm supposed to be.

It's not a huge room, but it occurs to me right away that it is also not just Jack's room. There's another bed. There is another bed and a thick piece of white tape right down the center of the gray carpet. The two sides of the room are almost identical. Each side has one single bed, one single desk, one bookcase filled with gold and silver trophies, and shiny medals hanging from ribbons.

I stand sort of frozen for a few seconds, only three steps in, suddenly very aware that I should probably take off Jack's smelly sneakers. It's like a museum or something in here. You know, like you're afraid to touch anything? It's so . . . the opposite of my room, which even I will admit is a disaster area. The Prince of Thatcher's room is pretty much the neatest room on earth! There are no layers of dirty, crumpled clothes covering the floor. Nothing is out of place. Not a speck of dirt. Everything is arranged just so. Both beds are made, the blankets smooth, not even one wrinkle.

I walk into the center of the room, and for no other reason other than what else am I supposed to be doing? I walk down the white middle line of tape in my socks, like I'm a gymnast on a balance beam, wobbling and leaping, left foot, right, and when I get to the end? Yeah, I do it. I thrust my hands in the air, all smiles like those Olympic girls do on TV.

Which is when I hear clapping.

Which is when I die of embarrassment.

Which is when I meet Brother Number Three, a little-bit-bigger version of The Prince. Pure muscle. Same dark hair. I can verify the muscle thing because, like Clark Kent next door, Brother Number Three is wearing— surprise! No shirt. Six-pack doesn't describe it for the Malloy brothers. It's more like twelve-pack. They're built like an action heroes come to life. You can see every single tiny muscle popping out. Not an ounce of fat. And I am in the middle of reminding myself not to stare and not to turn bright red from complete you-saw-me-prancing-down-a-white-piece-of-tape-pretending-I'm-an-Olympic-gymnast humiliation when he speaks.

Wait. No. He laughs first, then he shakes his head, *then* he speaks.

"What's up, stud?" he says. "I'm not even going to ask you what you're doing in here, Nancy Pants!"

Thank goodness he is distracted by . . .

"Butter Baby got the flow chopped!"

Without even thinking about it, I know what he means. I lift my hand and run my fingers over the prickly stubble Geno left.

With no warning, Brother Number Three comes straight at me and plants both his hands on top of my head and begins rubbing, as if I'm some lucky Buddha charm.

"Unbelievable!" he says, smiling, and just as quickly I watch that smile melt as Brother Number Three's brain catches up to the fact that my nose is busted up and swollen.

"Wait, that's not from yesterday in The Cage, is it?" He genuinely looks concerned. "Jacko, I am legit sorry if I made your mug that ugly."

"You didn't," I say, surprising myself by how suddenly easy it is to be an expert on all things Jack. "I, um, I got in a—"

"Did you get in a tilt, dude?" he asks, cutting me off.

He looks more excited than if I had told him he had won a million dollars.

"Kind of?" I answer.

"Bro, you either got in a tilly or not, and by the look of it, I'd say you got dusted." Brother Number Three falls back onto his bed, jamming his pillow underneath his neck and folding his arms over his chest.

"I didn't get dusted!" I exclaim. And yeah, it's strange that I am suddenly using words I had no idea existed when I woke up this morning. "I pumped him!" I add in for good measure.

"Okay, easy, bud. Vet move. So you waxed him, don't have to cry like a little baby over it, geesh." He flips over on his bed, his back to me, and curls up with his pillow. "Gonna take a siesta, big dog. Resting up for tomorrow. It's gonna be brutal."

I sit on the very edge of Jack's bed and wonder if I'm going to be arrested if I actually get in it and mess up the perfectly made covers. Also, like, what is all this talk about tomorrow? What does he mean by brutal? My heart begins to pound, and I sit on the bed and copy my mom from this morning, breathing in and exhaling a big, long breath. I do it again and again until—

"Dang, bro, if you're breathing heavy like that, go to the bathroom and handle it."

"Sorry," I whisper.

"Jacko?"

"Yeah?" I answer.

"I was wrong, you were right. I'm stupid, you're smart! I'm ugly, you are good-looking. . . ." He laughs softly. Brother Number Three still has his back to me. "Took one in the melon. Proud of you, bud, and don't worry. I'll keep your little secret—"

For a split second I am like, *Oh my gosh, he knows!* But then, just as fast, I realize what he means.

"I won't tell The Captain, big dog," he says.

"Thanks," I answer.

I sit on the bed for a good long time, long enough to realize that Brother Number Two's name is Stryker—due to the large, gold engraved plaque hanging over his bed that reads STRYKER MALLOY, BANTAM MAJOR AAA SILVER STICK TOURNAMENT MVP.

Stryker. That's a cool name. Fits him, I think as I watch his back rise and fall with his breath.

I glance around the quiet room. Jack's desk doesn't even look like anybody really sits there, except for one framed picture. I pick it up, careful not to make any noise and wake the sleeping teen giant three feet away.

The frame is silver and the photo is definitely Jack, but younger, maybe eleven years old. Next to him—must be his mom. Same dark wavy hair, same bright swimming-pool-blue eyes. She's beautiful.

I hold the frame up closer and read the engraved writing beneath the picture:

MOM. ALWAYS ON MY MIND, FOREVER IN MY HEART, NEVER FORGOTTEN.

I stare at it, and all at once everything around me just turns really dark, and I have the worst feeling wash over me. Jack's mom. She's—

I can't even say it.

She's—

"I miss her too, bud," I hear Stryker whisper into the quiet. "Not a day goes by where I don't miss her too."

26
JACK

AFTER SOCCER, I SLIP INTO the front seat of Freckles's mom's car and try to say as little as humanly possible. To help me achieve this, I move the seat as far back as I can, fold my arms, and stare out the window.

Red Hair with Yoga Pants is barraging me with questions, and in my dad's words, I have not been "acceptably demonstrating that I am listening." I am breaking all of The Captain's rules. I am not squarely facing the speaker, I have not been replying promptly or respectfully, and considering that I'm turned away looking out the window, it's safe to say I am avoiding eye contact—a big no-no with The Captain. But I didn't say I *wasn't* listening. More, I am *half* listening. And by the time we pull out of the Sportsplex, something Freckles's mom says sort of registers. And it's not good.

"Hon, I know you're tired, but Dr. Swenson is doing me a major favor fitting you in."

"Dr. Swenson?" I repeat. This is what I do now, by the way. I just repeat the last thing anyone says. Not exactly a champion strategy, but—

I glance toward Red Hair with Yoga Pants. She turns and looks at me too. "It's totally my fault, hon," she says, taking one hand off the wheel and placing it on my leg. At first I jerk away, but then—I feel the warmth of her hand. I just let it happen. I feel so tired.

"It's my fault, I completely spaced on your medical forms," she goes on, returning her hand to the wheel. "I know this is the last thing in the world you want to do, but you can't even take part in the last tryout on Sunday unless you have a physical."

My throat tightens. "A physical? No!"

"Honestly, Ellie, we're lucky Dr. Swenson squeezed us in on this short notice. We'll get in and out quickly, honey. It will be painless."

I walk into the waiting room. The whole time—every bony, freckle-kneed step—I'm trying to think of some way I can get out of this. I mean, I'm sure you would agree, right? A checkup! A checkup as a *girl*! This is just wrong on so many levels. Freckles's mom stops in front of the row of bright green plastic chairs lining the wall.

"Why don't you sit down, honey, I'll sign us in."

I stay standing. "Please, let's just go," I try.

"Don't be silly, sweetheart, everything is going to be okay." She smiles at me and pushes the sweaty hair out of my eyes. We're standing close. "Take a deep breath."

I drop down hard into a chair.

Oh my gosh. This is—

This is so crazy! I stare at the floor. I'm still wearing Freckles's turf shoes, two pairs of shorts, two shirts, her ridiculous pink-and-white-striped socks, and yes, okay? A bra! (Even though, as far as I can tell, Freckles doesn't exactly need one.) I breathe in slowly, lift my head, and look around. The waiting room is packed, and it kind of smells like throw up. I count three crying babies, one snotty two-year-old, and one little girl crying her eyes out and shaking, she's screaming so loud. "I want to go home!" she is sobbing. "I want to go home!"

Yeah, I think, and look right at her.

Me. Too.

Twenty minutes later I am following a short, wide nurse dressed in green polka-dot scrubs down a rainbow-striped hallway. She stops in front of an open door and points into a small room with one of those examining tables that has the white crunchy paper over it.

"Dr. Swenson will be here in a few minutes," she tells us.

Yes, us. Not to sound like a total soft freaking baby,

but I can't tell you how relieved I am that Freckles's mom got up and walked with me down the hallway too. That doesn't mean I am enjoying this. It just means . . .

God. I don't even know what it means.

Breathe, Jack. Breathe.

I stand against the wall, arms folded, and stare across the room at a huge glossy poster of a gigantic ear. Freckles's mom sits down in the chair by the sink and settles right into a magazine she brought from the waiting room. We are together in complete silence for the longest time until finally I just can't take it.

"I am *not* taking my clothes off!" I blurt out.

She looks up, smiling, eyebrows raised. "Sweetheart, I hardly think you have to take your clothes off. Relax, it's just a well visit."

I let out a long breath.

She gives me a look. "Hey, what's going on?" she asks. Her voice is gentle. "Are you okay, honey?"

"I'm fine," I answer.

"It's been a long day," she says, and smiles softly. "When we get home, you can take a nice bath. How does that sound?"

Bath? I haven't taken a bath since . . . since a long time. I stay standing, staring blankly at the giant ear.

Freckles's mom goes back to reading.

At least there isn't a giant poster of a penis, I think, and I let out a quiet laugh.

She looks up, grinning. "What's gotten into you?" Her eyes widen. "You have some big secret?"

After ten long minutes Dr. Swenson breezes in, smiling like this is the happiest day of her life. "Ellie!" she says. "Please don't tell me you are in seventh grade!"

"I'm in eighth—" I almost say, then catch myself. "Yes, ma'am," I answer.

Dr. Swenson looks a little startled, and it occurs to me only right at this moment that I should probably lose The Captain's required rules of conduct.

"Uh, I mean, yeah," I awkwardly mumble, trying to sound more normal. I throw in a shrug and look back at the doctor. She has smooth chocolate-brown skin and the brightest smile I have ever seen. She's wearing one of those white doctor coats and a stethoscope, which reminds me of the nurse at school, which reminds me of—

"How are you, Ellie?" Dr. Swenson asks.

I shrug again. "Fine."

She glances down at a folder she has open in her hands. "I see you're here for a sports physical. Are you playing soccer this year?"

I nod.

"I hear you are really good," she says.

"I'm pretty decent, I guess," I answer.

The doctor pulls out a stool from under the desk and

sits facing me. "Have you been staying healthy this year?"

Beats me! I hesitate and look over at Freckles's mom.

"She sure has," she answers for me, thank goodness. "Healthy as a horse!"

"Good." Dr. Swenson nods her head. "Any aches and pains bothering you?"

You could say that, I think, but shake my head no.

Dr. Swenson turns to Red Hair with Yoga Pants. "Summer, do you have any questions or concerns?"

Wait, *Summer*? Her name is *Summer*? Like, fall, winter, spring, summer. That's kind of awesome. . . .

"Hmmm. Any questions? Let's see." Summer breaks into a big smile. "Could you get her to clean her room?"

There's a little bit of laughter, then—

"Well, listen," starts Dr. Swenson, sounding suddenly very serious. "When my patients get to be this age, I think they deserve the right to talk to the doctor by themselves—"

Oh, no.

No. Nooooo. Noooooooooooooooo.

"And so, Mom." Dr. Swenson stands. "We're going to kick you out now. Is that okay with you?"

Freckles's mom, or Summer, or Red Hair with Yoga Pants. I watch her stand up. I watch her stand up and smile at me. "Absolutely!" she says.

Alone with Dr. Swenson, it's like time stops. I can hear everything. The buzz of the lights overhead, the ticking of the clock. My heart. *Ellie's heart.* Thumping like crazy.

"So how have you been doing?" asks the doctor. "Is everything going okay at home?"

"Sure," I answer. I look at my feet.

"It's just you and your mom living at home now, right?"

Beats me. I go with a nod. A nod is safe.

"How's that been?" she asks.

"Um, fine, I guess?"

"I know the divorce was rough. Remind me where your dad moved to?"

I keep my mouth shut.

"Seattle?" she asks.

I shrug.

"You don't feel like talking about it, huh?"

"Not really," I answer quickly.

"Oh, Ellie." Dr. Swenson takes a big breath. "I can understand that it must be really tough."

She closes the folder and puts it on the desk. "Today was your first day at Thatcher, right?"

I nod.

"How's that working out? Do you have a lot of friends? Do you have a best friend?"

I picture Owen and Sammy and actually grin when I answer, "Yeah."

"Good! So—" She pauses to flash me a smile and leans forward. "Is there anything you want to talk about with your mom not here?"

I shake my head.

"Sharing your feelings can really help, Ellie."

"I'm fine," I say. *Please, let's just get this over with.*

Dr. Swenson stands and steps toward me. "Okay, I'll tell you what. Let me take a quick listen to your heart and lungs and make sure everything is healthy."

As long as you don't make me turn my head and cough, we're good.

Dr. Swenson moves really close, right beside me, and somehow smoothly snakes her stethoscope under my double layer of shirts. I jump at the touch.

"Sorry, hon, I know it's cold."

"Yeah," I agree, in a small voice, almost a whisper.

"Wow, Ellie. Your heart is beating pretty fast. It's not like you to get this nervous." Dr. Swenson steps back and looks directly into my eyes. "Are you sure you're okay?"

"I'm fine," I repeat again. I sound impatient and kind of rude, even though I don't mean to.

Dr. Swenson moves behind me and puts the stethoscope against my back. This time I man up and don't jump.

"Take a few deep breaths," she tells me. "Okay, good, good," she adds, after I exhale.

She looks in my ears. "Nice!"

She looks in my mouth. "Still no cavities, Ellie. Impressive!"

She feels my neck. "Good."

She looks in my eyes. "I'm just going to shine this light real quick and—" She pauses as she's looking. "You have some absolutely gorgeous green eyes!"

She hits my knee with that little rubber hammer. "Wow! Excellent reflexes, Ellie!"

Dr. Swenson sits back down on the stool. She wheels it a little bit closer. "Well, you look as beautiful and healthy as usual, Ellie. Nothing to keep you from having fun at soccer." She pauses to sign the form in her folder. "You are officially medically cleared to compete," she says, looking up at me.

I immediately leap down off the table. "Thank you, ma'am."

"Whoa, hold up, not so fast." Dr. Swenson calls me back. "I'd like to spend a little more time with you."

I don't even really bother sitting down on the crinkly paper. I just kind of lean my butt against it and fold my arms tight and wait for whatever we're not done talking about.

"So, Ellie." Dr. Swenson pauses to smile. "I've noticed you've gotten a little bit taller this year. Have you started your period yet?"

Oh. Boy.

Do you know how little kids put their hands over their ears and start singing, "I'm not listening, I can't hear you!" This is kind of what I'm considering trying at this point. I mean, could this get any worse?!!! Yes. Yes, it can.

Dr. Swenson sits in front of me, waiting for me to answer. I realize I'm not getting out of here if I don't say *something*. I have a fifty-fifty chance. "Um, no," I stammer. "I guess not?"

"Okay, so has anyone talked to you about getting your period?"

I can feel the heat charging up into my cheeks. I am literally sweating. I straighten up and look at her like, you know, *please don't do this to me. Please.*

But she just smiles again. "Ellie, listen, you don't need to feel embarrassed. It's a *totally* normal part of being a girl." She pauses, then goes on. "Puberty is starting for you, so you are going to want to be prepared."

"Prepared?" I repeat.

"I'm sure you are wondering when it's going to happen, right? And maybe what it's going to feel like and what you need to do when it arrives . . ." She stops for a second. "Are you okay? You look terrified."

I don't say anything.

Not a word.

"It seems like this might be a little scary for you." She smiles. "Let me see if I can help you feel more comfortable. The first time is usually proceeded by cramps, a little lower back or abdominal discomfort. Then you see some blood. Sometimes it's not bright red initially. It's like a dark brown, and that's all good, but it can be scary to see blood coming out—"

"Okay, that's cool." I cut her off. "I'm good, really. You can stop."

Dr. Swenson grabs on to the edge of the desk, pushes off, and rolls the wheels of her stool closer to me. "Ellie, I know it can be a little bit uncomfortable to talk about, but really it is just a *beautiful* part of your journey to womanhood. It's amazing, when you really think about it! Right?" She gives me a genuinely happy look. "Ellie, every single girl in the entire world has a time where she gets her first period. It's just a way of showing that everything is working right, from your brain to your ovaries to your uterus. It's like a miraculous clock! It's incredible, really, and totally normal."

I take a big breath and just stare back at her.

She's still smiling.

"Are you sure you are okay?" she asks. "Nothing you want to tell me?"

"I'm good," I insist, and hope this is over.

Dr. Swenson finally stands and hands me a bunch of pink pamphlets. "Tuck these away for when you want to read more," she tells me. "We can talk again about this at your next visit, okay?"

I nod. We're standing together now with the door open and my foot half out in the rainbow hallway.

"You can call me if you need anything, okay?"

"Okay, thanks." I smile politely and take one step back.

"Ellie?"

I turn.

"Sometimes life is so tough. Missing a parent is—" Dr. Swenson pauses, reaches out, and rests her hand on my shoulder. "I just want to say I'm really sorry you are going through this. I know it's hard. And if you ever want to talk or anything, just come see me, okay?"

27

ELLIE

"IT'S GO TIME, BIG BOY!"

"Wakey wakey!"

"Rise and shine, it's butt-whoopin' time!"

"Pitter-patter, let's get at 'er!"

Someone is talking very loudly, and for a second I completely forget where I am. Then I open my eyes and stare up at Stryker Malloy, smiling down at me.

"Rise and grind, Jackie Chan!" he says. His shirt is still off.

It hurts to close my eyes, but I do. I feel like I got hit by a bus in the middle of the night.

"Good news is, you have five minutes before The Captain considers you late. Bad news is—" Stryker stops and begins laughing uncontrollably.

I open my eyes again, and somehow one brother has

multiplied. Gunner's looking down at me too, with his super-short marine haircut and big toothy smile. He's laughing too. "I see you're pitchin' a tent, big dog!"

Huh?

I look past them. Clark Kent, with his glasses and his chiseled biceps and his sleepy dark bed-head hair, appears behind them. "'Sup boys!" he says.

"Here's what's up!" Stryker says, laughing his head off as he rips the sheet off me. "Jack's got a woody!"

I am completely slow. Slow to move. Slow to breathe. Slow to understand what they're talking about. I look at Clark Kent for help.

"That-a-boy." He grins. "Don't worry, little man, morning wood happens to all of us."

By this point Stryker has fallen back onto his bed laughing, and I still don't get it until I go to sit up and—

Oh. My. Gosh.

Sorry, Jack. I do. I let out a little bit of a squeal.

Gunner winks. "Best way to start the day, eh, bud?"

Clark Kent extends his hand and I take it, letting him easily pull me to my feet. "Don't think about it, big guy," he tells me. "Just push it down, adjust, and let's get at 'er!"

Gunner digs through the dresser and fishes out a pair of sweats and a black hoodie, tossing them both at me from across the room. "How's your mug, you mutant?"

"Fine," I say. A total lie.

Gunner looks at me funny. "Seriously, you okay? You're

acting like a Froot Loop."

I nod and hug the sweats tight to my chest like a security blanket. "Um, I just need to go to the bathroom," I try and explain.

Stryker's back on his feet. "Go take a dump, bro, but make it fast. You still have to make your bed, you're running out of time." He nods toward the clock on Jack's desk.

"Five a.m.!" I sort of let it slip. It's so early. My stomach starts to have the worst nervous feeling. My heart is pounding. I swear I nearly start crying.

Stryker and the boys just look at me.

"Are you kidding me, bud? We wake up at the same time every day!" Clark Kent grabs me by the shoulder and shakes me. "Little man, it's the butt crack of dawn, we've got to hustle, no time for shenanigans!"

He gives me a little shove and I go flying into Stryker, who promptly puts me in a headlock, and I get a mouthful of underarm hair and deodorant.

"For the boys, with the boys, Butter Baby. Say it!"

"You're strangling me!" I cry out.

He tightens his grip. "Say it, Jacko!"

"Say what?" I plead.

"For the boys, with the boys!" he tells me.

"For the boys, with the boys!" I repeat.

"That's not good enough, Jackie Chan." Stryker tightens his grip. "Look at this Nancy, so soft. Say it louder, hombre!"

"For the boys, with the boys!" I scream it, muffled by his hairy armpit, until his grip loosens. I fall to the floor and feel around my neck, clasping the tiny pendant on the chain.

"C'mon, man!" Gunner says, helping me up. "The kid's face is waxed and he still has a nasty dried-blood muzzy on his upper lip." Gunner reaches out and rubs my new lucky-sandpaper head. "Get a move on, big guy. Never thought I'd say this, but just this once, I'll take one for the team."

"Huh?" I say.

Gunner laughs. "I'll make your bed for inspection, ya plug."

I look at him weird. "Wait. What? Inspection?"

"Go!" they all yell at once.

I take a tender step backward toward the door, watching the three of them, each in a different state of undress, madly making the bed I just got out of. Stryker in his boxers, straightening the pillows, and Gunner in sweats and a T-shirt, smoothing out and tucking in the sheets. Clark Kent with his crazy bed head and his sweats and no shirt, shaking out the blanket and draping it carefully across the mattress. He looks up at me standing frozen in the doorway and catches my eye. "Throw on a smile, big guy. Battle through it. Things are about to get a whole lot better."

* * *

In the bathroom down the hall, I splash my face and wash up as best I can, pee (sitting down on the cold toilet seat before I remember it doesn't work that way), slip into the sweats and the hoodie, and follow the boys' voices downstairs. They are all standing in a row dressed in sweats and hoodies. Only there's a fourth person there, and he is not smiling.

I look up into the eyes of The Captain with my mouth hanging open, like he's some kind of mythical hero. He looks like one too. He's pretty much rugged handsome, exactly like Jack and his brothers—same ice-blue eyes, same superhuman athletic shoulders—except he's the older version. His salt-and-pepper hair is buzzed almost to the scalp, and there is a shadow of white stubble on his big square jaw.

"Your haircut is a significant improvement," says The Captain, greeting me.

My heart is pounding and my hands are trembling. I bite down on my quivering bottom lip. I can hardly look at him. I have no idea what to say.

"Thank you, sir," Gunner whispers, prompting me.

"Thank you, sir," I repeat. I swallow hard when I see The Captain's eyes zero in on my messed-up face.

"What in the Lord's name happened to you?" he asks.

I glance sideways at Gunner. But it's Stryker who saves me.

"That was my fault, sir," he offers. "Sauced him with a

puck right in the melon yesterday in The Cage."

I glance at the brothers. Each of them is standing tall, shoulders back. I suddenly straighten up too. "I'm okay," I blurt out. "I'm okay, sir," I try again.

I'm not stupid.

We all stand there silently for a good minute. Then The Captain smiles quietly, first at me, then down the line at Gunner, Stryker, and Clark Kent—*I still have no idea what his name is.* The Captain checks his watch, fidgets with it, and opens the front door. Not a word is spoken. And so I do the only thing I can think of. I follow them all right out that door. Running.

28
JACK ▶

IT'S DARK. I HAVE NARROWLY escaped having to take a bath. I ate Summer's homemade lasagna for dinner, and I am wearing Freckles's fleecy flower-print pajama bottoms and an oversized Patriots T-shirt I found on her floor. And her floor? Let's talk about that. Nothing is put away. It's like her dresser exploded. It's hard to know where it's safe to even step. The floor is pretty much totally covered. Crumpled clothes, books, candy wrappers. The dresser drawers are all open, and there's no desk. I stand on the edge and take a deep breath.

I don't know how she can take it. I mean, it's like—

"This place is a mess," I say out loud.

I am so absolutely beat, though. I don't think I have ever been this tired in my life.

Trying to be someone else is exhausting.

I turn off the light and trample through the clothes, walking right on top of them, and let my body collapse into Freckles's incredibly messy, unbelievably comfortable bed. And it's huge. It's one of those double beds like my dad has.

I close my eyes and I picture my room and my house and my bed. *I hope Freckles is okay,* I think, and stare up at the glow-in-the-dark stars above her bed. I hope Stryker isn't grinding her gears too bad. I think about what a crazy day it's been. "Monday," I whisper up at the stars. *I just have to make it till Monday,* I think, and I start counting stars. It's what I do when I can't sleep. I count things. And ever since, well . . .

Let's just say I don't really sleep that great a lot of the time.

I am almost to that place where I'm just about asleep when I remember what I forgot. I throw one leg over the bed and onto the floor, kneeling, and push away a space on the carpet. *Two hundred sit-ups and two hundred push-ups,* I tell myself, and get to work.

Ellie's body isn't as strong as mine, but I'm not about to stop. I break them into sets of ten. In between, I lie on the floor and count the stars. It takes me a while, but I make it through. And when I'm done, I stay on my knees and do what I have done every night since my mom taught me how. I do the prayer of Saint Sebastian seven times.

The only thing that's missing is my notebook.

I jump up, turn on the bedside table light, and kick through Ellie's stuff until I find a pen and a piece of paper. And then I sit up in Freckles's bed and I write it out, just like I do every night. Everything about my life is about making my dreams happen. I visualize that dream I'm chasing as I write it all down. Just a reminder of what I'm working toward. No one will do it for you. I'll do whatever it takes.

1. Play for Boston College.
2. Get drafted in the first round of the NHL.
3. Sign an NHL contract.

After, I carefully fold the piece of paper, tuck it under Freckles's book on her night table, and turn off the light. Then—

"Sweetheart?" I hear. I can barely see through the darkness. Summer is standing in the doorway, and for a few seconds I wonder how long she's been there and how much she saw.

"Oh my gosh, Ellie, sweetie, I can hardly walk into your room." She laughs, and I can make out her smile and the outline of her long hair. She gets closer and sits down beside me on the edge of the bed. I curl up in a ball and pull the comforter up to my chin and wedge a pillow under my head.

"Ellie, honey, is everything okay?" Summer sets her hand on top of my forehead and runs her fingers gently over Freckles's long hair. I'm not gonna lie. It feels good.

It's been a long time since . . .

"I'm fine," I finally answer quietly, and turn away.

"Well, you're not fine, sweetheart, and it's very apparent that you're not fine." She pauses and takes a deep breath. "Honey, look, it's kind of ridiculous to say you're fine when something is obviously very not fine."

I don't know what to say. I swallow and flip over, facing the opposite wall.

"Ellie?"

"I'm fine, really," I repeat softly, into the darkness.

The room is so still. I close my eyes. For a few long moments, the two of us stay just exactly like that. It's so quiet. Under the covers, her hand finds my hand and holds it in hers. I don't pull it away. I leave it there. I don't move.

"Oh, honey." She sighs. "I know things have been really hard with your dad leaving and . . ." Her voice trails off, and I feel the weight of her arm wrapping around me.

She's so close.

I bite down on my lip.

"Sweetheart," she says. Her voice is barely a whisper. "I know it's so hard to stay open when you feel like closing." She pauses and nuzzles up so close I feel her heart beating.

For a long time neither of us says a word.

"I know you're hurting, honey," she tells me. "And you don't have to keep it all inside."

I can smell her hair, it smells like . . . I take a deep breath and try to swallow back the feeling in my throat. Try to stop everything from spilling out.

"Oh, Ellie," she whispers into the night. She holds me so tight. It's dark. Thank god. Nobody can tell. Nobody can see the tear streaming down my cheek.

29

ELLIE

WE SPRINT THE ENTIRE MILE-LONG steep climb up the mountain in pitch-black silence, and it's only at the very top, on the muddy clearing, that I drop to my hands and knees, panting, and puke. My heart is absolutely pounding and my legs are burning and I am pretty sure I am not supposed to stop.

The reason I am pretty sure is that while I am now flat on my stomach, dying, Gunner is standing over me shouting.

"Let's go!" he yells. "Balls out, bro! You're a warrior, little man. No pressure, no diamonds, dude, get up!"

I don't move. I can't. I have puke burning down the back of my throat and dripping out of my nose. It's so quiet and dark. Clark Kent, Stryker, and The Captain are already on their way down.

"Keep grindin', bro, get up!" I feel his foot jab me in the side. "Stop playin', Jacko! You know it doesn't count till you touch it."

"Touch what?" I say back, but I'm pretty sure he can't hear me because I am talking facedown with my forehead smushed into the muddy ground and a bunch of leaves under my mouth.

"You've got to be kidding me right now." Gunner sounds shocked. Out of the corner of my eye, I can see his ankles. His socks and sneakers and the bottoms of his sweats are covered with wet grass and mud.

"Whatever it takes, man. Let's go!"

"I can't," I say. It sounds more like a whimper than I mean it to.

"You *did not* just say that, bro." Gunner's voice grows louder. "What's got into you, bud? You don't give up. *Ever.*"

There is silence for a few seconds.

I turn my face. I can taste the mud. The ground feels oddly good against my head.

Gunner is practically yelling now. "C'mon, man! Get up!"

I do not move. I stay absolutely still. I close my eyes tightly and think about Jack and how he's probably in my bed, tucked under my covers. *He has it so easy!* I'm cold. I just sprinted up a mile-high mountain. I don't think I've been up this early in my life.

Gunner crouches down. He gets close. "I know how

bad you want it, bud. Keep breathing. Just keep breathing," I hear him say. "Let's go, bro. Fall seven times, stand up eight."

My hands are freezing and trembling underneath me.

"C'mon, man." He pauses for a moment, then gets louder again. "I'm telling you right now. Get. Up."

I hear Jack's voice in my head—"*If you're going to be me, you can't be such a girl!*"

"Bro," Gunner starts again. "If you don't man up, I'm going to get you up, how 'bout that?"

I feel his hulk hands on each arm. Gunner literally lifts me to my feet until we are standing face-to-face.

"Atta boy! Heck, yeah! Gritty, bro!" he hollers, grinning ear to ear, dusting twigs and muddy wet leaves from my shoulders and chest. "Your body can do anything, bud. It's just your brain you have to convince."

I look back at him through the rising light. His face and hair are drenched with sweat; his ice-blue eyes are open wide. He's almost glowing. I think he actually *likes* this.

"Do it!" he demands.

"Do what?"

"You're a piece of work, kid." He shakes his shaved head, still grinning. "Touch the flippin' rock!"

I follow his eyes to the smooth boulder jetting out from the cliff's edge. The sun is just beginning to rise over the green hills in the distance.

"Go ahead," he says, giving me a nod. "Tag it like you always do or we stand here all day, and I don't think the old man is going to be too happy, bud."

I manage a weak smile and begin to carefully step toward the ledge. My legs feel like spaghetti. I reach out and gently lay my hand on the cool rock. And it's so weird, but when I touch the rock, when I rest my hand against it? I swear, a chill goes through my body, and all at once it feels kind of awesome that I made it. That I'm standing. I take a long, deep breath and look down across the valley. The morning sky is this unreal pinkish-orange streak. I can see all the way into town. The view is wide open. It doesn't stop. Off in the distance I can even see the lake. It looks almost emerald green. I take a few steps closer to the edge and look down the sharp, grassy hill we just climbed up. And I'm thinking it's kind of crazy we are up here. That we are even up! That I am awake and that there are so many things happening when I'm usually sound asleep. Which is right about the same second I realize it's suddenly extremely quiet and—

"Hey!" I cry out, and whirl around. "Gunner!" I yell after him.

"Gunner!" I shout. But it's too late; he's already taken off. I watch him bound down the mountain. He doesn't stop.

"You're a warrior!" His voice booms into the morning air. "You're a beast, bro. Do work!"

And I don't know if it's the fact that the sun is rising or the way it felt to touch the rock. I can't really explain it, but this feeling just comes over me, like, *I can do this*.

"I can do this!" I whisper to nobody but me. Then— "Yeah!" I yell out at the top of my lungs into the wide-open sky, off the mountainside. And run.

I run all the way back to the house. Blazing down the steep, grassy hillside, leaping over rocks and branches and slippery leaves, cutting across three backyards, and sprinting down the middle of Jack's now-sunny street. I run all the way, and I don't stop until I charge up the winding path and have my hand on the front door of Jack's house.

"Yes!" I say to myself, out loud. And sure, whatever, *you* try and not be proud. I let out a little bit of a squeal. I do. Which, of course, is exactly when I see him.

Gunner. He's bent over under the basketball net, his hands on his knees, catching his breath.

"That-a-boy, Jacko!" he tells me through his dimpled smile. "Way to suck it up and push through, big guy!"

"Thanks," I tell him, and collapse next to him right on the pavement.

Gunner stares down at me. "What the heck are you doing, bro?"

"I'm resting!" I answer.

"Seriously, you are getting soft, dude." He laughs, then

looks worried. "Bro, are you crazy? Do you want to get us all in trouble? Get up before The Captain—"

I watch Gunner's smile fade and his eyes wander, and I get a very bad feeling in the pit of my stomach. The bad feeling sounds something like this in my head: *The Captain is standing behind me, isn't he?*

Yep.

I get up slowly, turn around, and wipe the dripping sweat from my eyes and face with the back of my sleeve.

"Nice of you ladies to join us," says The Captain.

Why is he calling me a lady? I wonder, confused. I glance at Gunner. Stryker and Clark Kent have suddenly materialized too. Each is standing up straight. Perfectly still. I copy them, shoulders back, eyes on The Captain.

"*Wanting* is different than *doing*," he says.

"Yes, sir!" they answer together.

I'm slow, a second or two off. "Yes, sir!" I manage. I look sideways over at Jack's brothers. Nobody is laughing or joking right now. The sun is in my eyes. The world is waking up all around us. I can hear it all. Like I am extra awake. A dog barking across the street. Birds singing over our heads—

"Men, if you can't commit yourself one hundred percent, morning after morning, day after day?" He pauses and looks directly at me. "If you aren't willing to make that sacrifice, you do not want it as bad as you think."

"Yes, sir!" I blurt out awkwardly. Only this time I'm the

only one. The boys all purse their lips. I can tell they're trying not to laugh.

I feel my head heating up and my heart racing. The Captain clears his throat. "Those who reach the top didn't fall there. Put in the work, boys. Train hard. Do it right."

This time I'm ready for it.

"Yes, sir!" I say. I focus so hard on answering correctly that, again, my timing is a little bit off. A little too soon. A beat before the others.

The boys can't hold it in this time.

The Captain raises his eyebrows and lets out the faintest smile. "It's a lower-body day. Legs feed the wolf, boys."

Legs feed the wolf? Huh?

"Go muscles, not show muscles," continues The Captain. "Deadlifts, split squats, landmine reverse lunges, quick-feet ladder drills, sled pushes, box jumps—working on explosiveness, men. Heavy reverse sled drags for the finisher." The Captain pauses and walks over to Clark Kent.

There is complete silence, and then The Captain finally speaks. "Jett," he starts. "I trust you will follow the protocol? Do it right the first time."

Jett! Of course he has a cool name. I glance at him. Except for the shiny gold pendant we each have hanging around our necks, he's bare-chested, and he looks like a gladiator the way his black hair is slicked back from sweat.

"Jack!"

Oh, no, they're talking to me.

"All you," Gunner says, directing me to do something—only I have no idea what!

"Uhhh." I stall and look back at him, panicked.

Gunner nods toward the ground. "You know how we always start things out, big boy! Warm-up circuit. Let's get it goin'!"

In case you're wondering, this doesn't help.

They're all waiting for me, staring. Jett. Stryker. Gunner. *The Captain.*

"Um." I look blankly at all of them. Then—

Thank goodness. Stryker drops to the ground. "I'll go first!" he says, coming to my rescue. He starts busting out push-ups—he makes them look easy. Like army men, we all drop to the ground too. My hands press into the driveway's rough pavement. And it's so crazy, but after running up the mountain in the dark? I fall into a rhythm with the push-ups. It feels almost automatic, the way Jack's body easily moves. "One, two, three, four, five, six—" The boys bark out the numbers, so I do too, Jack's quiet, crackly voice mixing into the count. "Twenty, twenty-one, twenty-two, twenty-three—"

Gosh, I never thought when I woke up yesterday that today I'd be pumping out push-ups in The Prince's driveway. Let alone *be* The Prince. We stop at one hundred. Stryker shoots me a smile. Nobody helps me.

I jump up myself.

30
JACK ▶

WHEN I WAKE UP IN Freckles's room, in Freckles's princess-sized bed with my hands clasped tight around Freckles's frayed teddy bear, I am half-asleep and completely confused. A million questions run through my head. I'm sure you know them by now. You know . . . *Where am I? How did this happen? Why am I in a girl's body?* And sure, I'll admit it. The first thing I do with my eyes open is lift Freckles's fluffy comforter and look under the covers to see if—

Yep.

Still a girl.

I shut my eyes again, tight, and try and imagine what my brothers would do if they were me—or, I mean, if they were here right now. Jett would probably say, "C'mon, man!" and tell me to throw on a smile. Tell me to toughen up. Take it. Not be so soft. *Not be soft about being a girl.* Ha! That makes no sense whatsoever!

I laugh and flip over onto my other side. Honestly, I never thought I'd say this, but I actually really miss my brothers. The three of them are all the type of guys you want to be around. They teach me everything they know, they challenge me every day, push me pretty hard. We're all chasing the same dream, and we'll do anything to get there. They know what it takes to get tougher and better.

I can't wait to be reunited with the boys.

"Forty-eight more hours," I say out loud. I stretch my arms up over my head in a yawn. Whatever. I mean, things could be worse. I am lying in a massively comfortable bed with the softest sheets, under cozy warm covers. I let my head sink back into the pillow. The sun is streaming in the window and—

I bolt upright.

If it's late enough that the sun is out . . . I turn, almost in a panic, and look at the alarm clock on the night table beside the bed.

Ten thirty.

"Whoa," I whisper. I don't even remember the last time I was able to sleep this late.

Breathe, Jack. Breathe.

I fall back again, close my eyes, and picture what the boys are up to. Same thing every morning. It plays in my head like a movie: sunrise race up to the rock, knuckle push-ups in the driveway. Leg day in The Cage. I open my eyes and look at the button eyes of Freckles's faded bear.

"I hope Ellie's okay," I whisper. Yes. I am officially nuts! I am talking to stuffed animals now. Ha. And holy smokes, my breath smells like feet. "Sick, buddy." I laugh. "Mix in some toothpaste, ya scrub!"

Apparently I'm chirping myself without my brothers around.

I flop over, push Freckles's tangled hair out of my eyes, and I lie sprawled out, my face smushed into the mattress for a solid ten minutes until it hits me. I know just what to do.

It takes me a good forty-five minutes to thoroughly clean Freckles's room to The Captain's standards. First I sort through all her wrinkled-up clothes. I can't tell what's clean or dirty, nothing really smells, so I just pretty much fold them and put them away in her dresser or hang them up in her giant closet.

Yes. Even underwear. You're welcome.

Underneath the piles of clothes I find four empty science-experiment-looking glass cups.

"Gross!" I whisper, and line them up by the door. Gatorade? Or . . . I hold one up to my nose—maybe Hawaiian Punch? Moldy, dried orange rinds, a half-eaten cookie, a shriveled-up apple core. I lob them like little basketballs across the room—"two points!"—into the trash. Books straightened and stacked, soccer gear piled up, seventeen stuffed animals and three dolls, squeezed together like best friends, side by side, lining the entire far wall. Last, I get to work on the bed. I can't see an unmade bed and not make it. It's automatic. I could probably do it with my eyes closed: take the sheet, lie it flat all the way from side to side, line up the edge of with the bottom of the mattress, pull it tight, tuck in forty-five-degree hospital corners, smooth out the wrinkles with my hand. Shake out the comforter, lay it out across the mattress top, line it up twelve inches from the pillow, plump the pillows and place them at the head of the bed. Teddy bear front and center. Why not?

Afterward I sit on the very foot of the bed, on the edge, and inspect my own work.

"Not bad." I shrug. To be honest, though? Freckles's room would in no way pass The Captain's inspection. The garbage needs to be emptied, the carpet vacuumed, and . . . I look around at the dolls and the stuffed animals, the books jammed into the bookcase, the candy on the bedside table, three soccer balls . . . there's just too much stuff in here for The Captain's liking. The Captain does not like stuff.

"The best things in life aren't things," he always says.

I fall back onto the bed and look for the stars. They just look like dumb yellow stickers in the light.

The second I close my eyes, I hear a knock, followed by "Morning, Ellie-Belle!" Summer sings through the door.

I've only known her a day, but I can totally picture her behind the door, smiling, her crazy-long red hair, her billion freckles.

"Morning," I call back and watch the door open and Summer step through, her smile instantly brightening the room.

"Oh my gosh!" she says. Her jaw drops open, and her eyes are huge. "Whoa! Wow! Ellie, honey, it's—" She stops talking, opens the closet, and runs her hand along the hangers all arranged the same way. "I'm actually totally speechless!" she exclaims. "I mean, like, you have seriously blown me away!"

I shrug. "It's okay," I say, trying to act all cool. But I'd be lying if I didn't say it feels kind of good to make her so happy.

Summer turns around. She's dressed in her pajamas still too—a silky lavender bathrobe and fluffy bunny slippers. When she grins, her green eyes light up.

"Wow! Wow! Wow!" she says, gleaming. "I don't know *what's* gotten into you, but I like it!" Summer plops down next to me on the bed and smothers me with a huge hug and a big, wet kiss on the cheek. I kind of back away at first, but then—

I mean. I don't want to be rude. I just melt while she pulls me in. I don't fight it.

She talks to me about three inches away. "Honey pie," she says. Her voice is gentle again, almost in a hush. She just looks at me for the longest time, smiling and brushing the hair out of my eyes. I try not to look away. I try and let it happen. I try and just stay.

"Love cake," she starts again; our noses almost touch. "I'd say this rare but absolutely wonderful occurrence deserves a little celebration, don't you?"

"What do you mean?" I ask.

"What I mean is, we have to celebrate, this is . . ." She leans in and lets our foreheads brush.

"It's no big deal," I say, and jerk back. "Really, it's no big deal. It's fine."

"Fine? Are you kidding me? This is—" Summer stands. "This is spectacular!"

All right, fine. I don't exactly argue when Summer tells me to "climb back into bed and get all cozy and snug." A lot of times, my brothers and I don't even sleep under our covers. That way we won't have to make our beds at five a.m. The covers don't get all messed up.

But, I mean—Freckles did tell me to stay in her room, after all.

Why not!

I easily climb back under the covers and sink into Freckles's cozy bed. Thirty minutes and forty pages into Harry Potter later, Summer appears with a tray of food.

It's like room service! Like a hotel! I sit up and wedge a pillow behind me like I do this all the time.

Summer carefully sets the tray down in front of me on my lap. "Your majesty, Princess Ellie-Belle." She giggles. "For your royal highness we have—" She pauses to sit down on the edge of the bed beside me. The food looks and smells so good! Yesterday I was struggling to get down a spinach–fish oil smoothie, and today . . . I focus back in on Summer.

"We have banana pancakes with fresh raspberries, whipped cream, warm maple butter. Bacon, two poached eggs, and last but not least—" She hands me a cup of fresh-squeezed orange juice.

"Wow, this is so . . ." I try and search for the right words. "Thank you so much." I stare at the plate. I haven't had this many carbs since—

Since forever.

And you know what? Screw the rules. It looks so good!

I hear Stryker's voice in my head, "Yeeeeah, buddy!" as I lift a forkful of pancake and shovel it in. Sometimes the littlest things can make you the happiest.

Summer looks kind of amazed as she watches me. "Whoa, hey, slow down. You must be growing, huh? You are famished. Maybe I don't feed you enough!"

"No, it's just, like, so good," I say between bites, and try to remember to swallow next time and not to speak with my mouth full.

"Well, take your time. Chew." She's smiling, and she's looking at me like she's never seen anybody eat before. We sit together quietly for a little bit.

"So," starts Summer. "I wanted to ask you, honey, did Dr. Swenson talk to you about—" She stops midsentence, and her smiles grows.

I look at her like, huh?

She reaches over and gently sweeps the hair out of my eyes. This time she tucks it behind my ear. "I just hate it when I can't see your eyes, honey." She pauses. "It's just you've been so tired and a little bit moody, and, gosh, ravenous! I thought maybe it might be a good moment to talk about the changes your body's going through and, you know, about *that time*—"

I look up from my plate and think for a second. "Wait, what time?" I ask, confused.

"Getting your period." Summer's voice is soft and calm. Her eyes are sparkling.

Noooo. Not this again!

I pick up the orange juice and start gulping to hide the look on my face, which pretty much says: *Please don't make me talk about this!* But just in case? I set down the glass and do my best—and only—girl imitation of all time. I pout my lips, tilt my head forward, and flip the hair out of my eyes like I've seen girls do.

"Um," I start. "Can we, like, pleeeease not talk about this?" Yes. I make my voice extra high. "Please!" I add.

Summer smiles softly. "Oh, honey, I know it's a little bit uncomfortable, but we *all* get our period. It's going to happen to you too."

"I'm fine," I say.

"I know you're fine," she answers. "Seriously, sweetie, you're acting very different. Are you sure you're okay?"

"I'm fine," I repeat, and throw in a smile.

"Okay, I get it, I get it." She stops and just looks at me for the longest time. "Look, honey, maybe you don't want to talk about it now, but if you do? If you ever want to talk about it?" She smiles. "Come talk to me, okay?"

"Okay," I agree.

"Really?"

"Yeah," I answer, and stuff my mouth with an entire strip of bacon.

Summer stands and moves to the door. "Hey, remember yesterday how I said I had a big surprise?"

I nod and swallow the half a pancake that I just stuffed in my mouth.

"After you're finished, wash up and get dressed. You and I are going on a big adventure!"

"Adventure?" I repeat.

Summer's eyes light up. "Mommy-Daughter Day!"

And look, I know it wasn't in the agreement, but I'm a thirteen-year-old boy in a twelve-year-old girl's body. I'm not in a power position here. I can't exactly demand to stay home. And the crazy thing is, I don't want to be

alone. I wouldn't go broadcasting this on ESPN or anything, but . . . the truth is, I am kind of a mixture of
relieved and excited. Something about Summer makes
me feel calm.

I think about my mom every day.

I miss her so much.

"Sure," I say, and mix in a smile. "Mommy-Daughter
Day? Why not!"

NONE OF THE BOYS TALK in The Cage. I mean, there is grunting. There is sweating. There is more puking (Stryker) and one bloody nose (Gunner), but it's not until we all climb back up the steep basement stairs and I follow Stryker through the back door out to the yard that the boys slowly come back to life.

"Two hours of lifting," says Stryker, flexing his huge biceps. "Look at these guns. Yoked, bro!"

I nod and smile and crash onto the soft grass.

"Oh, yeah," Striker says. "I like the way you're thinking, bud." He crumples to the ground, a foot away. "Just chillin' with my roomie. It's the little things, right, Jackie Chan?"

I smile sideways. We are both flat on our backs. For the first time all day, I kind of understand him.

"Yeah." I sigh and look up into the cloudless sky. "The little things."

Stryker reaches over and plants his hand right on my chest. I feel the heat and weight of his sweaty palm through my soaked T-shirt. "Dude, you killed it on the squats, bro."

"Thanks," I answer, and wonder if his hand is, like, resting or if he's about to pull some ninja-style wrestling move and mash my face into the ground. I turn and look at Stryker. His eyes are shut and his mouth is open. He doesn't talk and he doesn't move.

I watch the sweat drip down the side of his head and have an up-close view of the dark stubble above his upper lip. He looks kind of adorable and peaceful when he's not strangling me. He's probably, like, fifteen or sixteen. He probably shaves.

Stryker exhales long and loud then speaks. "Bagger at the end killed me, bro."

I don't even have to talk. I just nod.

"Play like you're in first, train like you're in second," he tells me. "Right, bro?"

"Play like you're in first, train like you're in second," I agree.

"That's the legit truth, Jackie Chan!"

Stryker's voice gets suddenly quiet, almost like he's whispering, but he's not. "Nothin' better than seein' your little bro battle through it, eh, buddy? You were an absolute gun today."

I smile up at the sky. "Thanks," I tell him. "I mean, as long as I don't walk for the rest of my life." I stop and laugh. "I think we're good."

"Word," Stryker says. "Pay to play, bro."

"Pay to play," I mutter back.

The two of us stay there. Sprawled out side by side on the grass. The sun feels so warm. My lips taste salty, in a weird good way. And I can honestly say not moving has never felt so good. Which is when I hear Gunner yelling across the grass, "Nice of you boys to help out!"

I look up. He doesn't look happy. He's walking toward us, shirtless, and hoisting two giant plastic garbage tubs over his head.

"Yeah, thanks for your support, fellas!" calls out Jett. He's right behind Gunner, bare chested, too, lifting two more huge plastic tubs over his head.

I jump to my feet.

So does Stryker.

"C'mon, man!" Jett shoots us both a look as he sets the tubs down on the grass. Every single rippled muscle in his body glistens in the sun.

I think I might be staring.

"Get the ice!" he yells.

After we finish hauling eight ten-pound plastic bags of ice from this huge freezer in the garage out around the side of the house and into the backyard, I get the feeling Stryker and I are supposed to stand back. Gunner and Jett seem to have whatever it is they are doing down to a science: Gunner empties the bags of ice into four side-by-side giant plastic garbage pails while Jett walks behind him with the garden hose, carefully filling each tub with water. Stryker and I stand obediently off to the side until—

With absolutely no warning, all three of them start *stripping*! Shoes, then socks, then . . . yeah. Um. *Oh my god.* In case it's not clear, what I am saying is THEY ARE REMOVING THEIR CLOTHES! I cover my eyes with my hands.

"What are you doing!" I squeal, and peek out of a little space through my fingers and watch the three muscular stark-white bare butts disappear into the icy water.

Stryker is practically screaming. "Dude, it's freezing! Holy Hannah. Man, do I hate this! This is actually insane. Do we have to get all the way in?"

Jett slides in like it's nothing, of course. He takes off his glasses and tosses them onto the grass. "Up to your midchest, dog. Nipple deep, don't cheat."

Gunner sinks all the way down, disappearing for a split second under the icy water before he pops back up like a killer whale. "Whoooooooooweeeeee! Bring on the pain!!" he shouts, grimacing. "That's #%*! cold!!!"

I cover my face again, then look—

The three of them all stare back at me from their ice-filled garbage-pail Jacuzzis.

"I'm *not* getting in there!" I state very clearly.

No way am I getting naked. No. Way.

Gunner looks genuinely ticked. "Don't be a wuss, bud. Get in!"

"No," I blurt out. "Noooo way. I'm good. I'm absolutely fine here."

I backpedal a few steps.

"What's with you, bro?" Jett asks. He's leaning back in the tub, his arms resting around the top edge. "Must have been that tilt yesterday, eh, bud? You're seriously blowing my mind right now. Don't be a chick!" He pauses. "Let's go!"

I take another step back and almost trip over the stairs to the back deck.

"It's go time, J-Man," Stryker chimes in. "What's your problem? Get your manhood out of your purse, Jacko. You know we do this every time. You always feel better tomorrow. Recovery, bro! Take it."

I shake my head vigorously as I watch Jett settle deeper into the plastic garbage tub filled with ice, the water spilling out over the sides.

My mouth falls open.

"Quit being such a baby," Jett calls out, his dark hair slicked back. "Seriously, you are either gonna get in or I'll get out and dunk you in, you sexy beast!"

For a flash, the mood kind of lightens and the boys all laugh. But just as fast, Jett sounds more serious. "Ten minutes, bro. Get gritty, let's go!" He crouches back down into the icy water. "Figure it out, Jacko. We aren't starting the clock without you."

Stryker cocks his arm back and fires a chunk of ice at my head. "Do it, Butter Baby!" He shouts so loud I swear the whole neighborhood can hear him. "Dude, grow a pair! When did you get so soft? What are you, a girl or something!"

That's it. I don't hesitate.

I don't think too much.

I lose the sneakers first, then the socks, then I strip down to Jack's boxers—I keep those on, thank you very much. Then I march forward and throw my leg up and over the side and—

"OHHHHHMYGOOOOOOOSH!" I scream at the top of my lungs. Then I don't scream, because the cold literally takes my breath away.

I can hear the boys laughing, and for a few of the longest seconds of my life my mind goes completely blank. I shut my eyes. I can hear the words, but they sound like they're in a fishbowl. Muffled. Everything goes in super slow motion.

Jett: "Control your breathing, big boy. Just make it a minute and a half, and it gets better."

Gunner: "Piece a' cake, big man. Battle through it."

Stryker: "Don't piss in your shorts this time, Jackie Chan!"

Jett: "Breathe, bud. Just breathe."

Jett's right. The pain lasts about a minute, then everything just goes numb. I open my eyes and squint at the three of them. Gunner's in the first tub, then Stryker, then Jett, next to me. I'm on the end.

I copy Jett and rest my arms up around the plastic edge.

"Don't think about it, man," he tells me. "Another day at the office, right?"

"Uhhh . . . I, I—" I try.

"Let's talk, big man," says Jett. He gives me a nod and a smile. "Take your mind off the chill. Bro-to-bro bonding."

I shrug my frozen shoulders. "What do you want to talk about?" I ask him.

"Why don't you tell me why you got in tilt yesterday, bud?"

"Uhhh, ummm," I stutter.

Then I have an idea. *I'll just describe Sassy.*

"Well, the thing is"—I look at Jett when I answer—"somebody was saying something and it was really mean."

"Really *mean?*" Jett lets out a laugh. "You are seriously being a girl right now, bud, I swear."

"Yeah, well, what if I am? What are you gonna do about it?" I answer, joking.

See, I can play too. I smile at Jett.

"Oh man, that hurt, bud. It's gonna be like that, huh?"

he teases. "Even though you literally make no sense."

"What I meant was . . . ," I start again, and try and convert it to Malloy language. "The kid's a dolt," I say. I flash back to Sassy in the cafeteria at school. "She's always laughing at me and rolling her eyes and chirping at me—"

"She?" Jett raises his eyebrows and smiles. "Dude, the cold's getting to you."

"I mean, *he*. Yeah, um, like—" I start, then I stop. I don't know how to explain it. "I just . . . ," I try, but then I give up.

"First, little man." Jett hesitates; his voice gets serious suddenly. "Look, it was ballsy to take a go at him. You're a beast, bud. Nails. I'll always have your back, you know that." Jett stops, looks me in the eye, nods, and holds up his fist.

I'm kind of thrilled when I realize he wants to tap fists.

Our knuckles collide, and icy water spills out of both our tubs.

"Let's be honest, though." Jett picks back up. "Clowns just thrive on getting a reaction out of you."

I shrug. "I guess."

His eyes brighten. "There's your answer, big boy. Basically ignore the guy. You don't need that in your life, bro. Let it slide."

I nod.

Jett flashes me his huge smile. "Keep it real, Jacko. Be you. Don't have time for haters. Stay positive. Work hard.

Be humble. Surround yourself with the right people. Focus on what you can control, bud." He winks. "Keep moving forward."

I listen and nod. Even though I don't really understand exactly what he means, every time Jett talks, it makes me think. He has this aura about him. He's just a real confident person. When he talks, you listen and honestly believe him. My eyes catch a glimpse of the shining gold pendant hanging from the thin chain around Jett's neck. I instinctively feel up around my neck too, tug on Jack's identical pendant, hold it between my fingers like a good-luck charm.

"You know what?" Gunner chimes in. "Jett's right, bud, I couldn't have said it better. Guys say stupid stuff, man. Don't listen to what anyone else says about you. Don't get caught up in all that. You got to know when to fight and know when to walk away, bud."

"Scared dogs bark the loudest, bro!" offers Stryker. "Dude sounds like a plug. Probably jealous."

Sassy . . . jealous? I think about this in a cold-induced haze, and for a few more long minutes, the four of us soak in quiet until—

With absolutely no warning?

Jett stands straight up!

Stands. Up.

Yes. I see it. I see—

E-V-E-R-Y-T-H-I-N-G.

"Good sesh, boys!" Jett announces, ice and water dripping off him and gushing out over the side of the tub as he jumps out. The idea to shut my eyes? It's like on some sort of cold delay.

But I do. I shut them tight. And I'm thinking: *Wow. Just. Like wow.* And I kind of laugh. Never thought I'd see *that* when I woke up yesterday.

When I open my eyes, the three of them are standing on the grass with their crazy toned muscles and their white towels wrapped tight around their waists, grinning back at me like I'm an idiot.

"Never a dull moment with this kid. Apparently you missed the memo, big guy." Gunner looks at me, just shaking his head, laughing. "Get out, man! You'll feel like you have pistons coming out of your hips! You'll feel like a machine! Trust me, bro."

I stand up slowly and manage to climb out without doing a face-plant into the grass. Out of the ice bath, my legs almost burn. The air is so much warmer than the water. I stand next to the deck, clutching my arms, shivering. I'm pretty sure my lips are blue.

"Whooohoooo! How good does that feel!" Stryker screams, and nails me in the head with a towel. I copy the boys and wrap it tight around my waist. The four of us all look almost identical if not for age and my and Gunner's buzzed heads.

Jett throws his arm around me and pulls me in. He

smells like salty sweat. He smells like work. "You know that's the best thing about having bros, bud." He pauses and looks down at me with the kindest eyes. "We tell each other everything. No secrets."

"Thanks, man," I say quietly. "No secrets," I repeat.

Honestly, I actually feel a little bit bad for a second. I feel this pang. Like I'm in on something special. Like I'm not supposed to see this. But just when I'm thinking that? Stryker creeps up behind me and rips my towel off and there go—

My boxers.

Sorry, Jack.

"Stop!" I say. Okay. I scream. I wail. I let out the hugest cry.

The three of them are dying laughing.

Gunner can hardly get the words out. "Sometimes less is more, Jacko, and this is one of those times!"

Jett shakes his head, grinning. "Just remember, little buddy, everything shrinks!"

Stryker finally tosses my towel back. "Don't be alarmed, bud, it won't stay that way for long!"

I whip my boxers back up and wrap the towel tightly around my waist.

I don't even get it, but they're still laughing. They can't stop. It's like, I mean, it almost doesn't matter what they're laughing at. We're all so tired and wet and sore and sweaty, and honestly it sort of makes me laugh too.

"What?" I say, and look back at them, grinning.

Gunner comes right up to me and rubs my head, smiling. "Bro, sometimes you're dumber than a box of rocks, but I love you, man. I just love ya."

32
JACK

SUMMER IS DRIVING. SMILING LIKE Summer does. She glances over. "I think we did really well for a quick shop!"

"Sure, I guess," I say, and try and not sound so completely relieved. Never would I have thought I'd actually survive a mother-daughter shopping spree. Summer reaches across the seat and places her hand on the back of my neck. It's weird, but I won't lie. I like it, I guess.

"Look at my little fashionista over there." Summer winks. "I can't believe how much you're growing up. You're really good company, Ellie, and I love the new clothes you picked out. It did seem a little bit like I was torturing you with the marathon bra try-on session, but you need some nice things, honey." She looks over at me and smiles. "You're growing up!"

I flash a smile back. I don't want to seem ungrateful. "So we're done, right?" I ask. "I mean, we're going home now, right?" I think about Freckles's room and her big bed. I could go for a serious nap.

"Home?" Summer sounds shocked. "You're joking, right? Hello! The big surprise?" Her whole face smiles as she says it.

"Oh, yeah." I grin. With Summer it's almost impossible not to smile back.

"You going to make it? Are you still tired?" Summer asks.

"No, I'm good," I answer. I feel like I have to gut it out, you know, for Freckles. For Summer.

"Okay, so the surprise. I'll give you a hint," she tells me. "And look, you'll probably resist this at first, but just hear me out." She smiles at me sideways. "It involves a little bit of a trim."

"A what?"

"Just a little hair snip," she answers.

"Wait, what?" Oh, man. Freckles and I didn't cover this. "Uhh," I stall.

"We really need to do something about your hair."

Man, if Freckles touched my hair, I'd be so heated. But what am I supposed to do?

"Just a little trim, honey, because nobody can see your eyes!"

"Okay," I answer. "Just a little trim." It's honestly out of my mouth before I realize there's no going back.

Ten minutes later Summer and I step through the door of Butterfly Loft Salon and Spa, and I'm standing in front of a shiny, completely white desk with a waterfall backdrop. Like. A real waterfall. With water.

"See, sweetie," she whispers. "Doesn't this place just ooze Zen? It has a fantastic vibe, right?" The biggest smile settles on her face. "Wait till you meet Devon. She's a true artist, you'll see."

Almost at that second, this college-age girl walks toward us. "Hey, lovely ladies," she says, grinning.

She's wearing a short red dress and scuffed-up cowgirl boots. I try and keep my mouth from falling open. This chick is absolutely smokin' hot.

"Too hot for you, bro," Gunner would say.

Seriously, she looks like a movie star. Glossy black hair, perfect face, million-dollar smile.

She looks right at me, eyes shining. "Hey, pretty lady!" she says. Her face brightens, and I immediately feel incredibly nervous because she is extremely beautiful and I've fallen in love. She throws her arms around Summer, and the two of them hug like they're old friends.

"So good to see you, love," says Summer, kissing her on the cheek.

When they finally let go, Summer smiles at me.

"Devon, this is my daughter, Ellie!"

My heart speeds up. "Nice to meet you," I say, holding out my hand and hoping my palm isn't sweaty.

Devon has a strong grip. Firm. "The pleasure is absolutely mine, Elle!"

Elle. Sigh. I love the way she says it. *Elle.* Ellllllle. Elle. Elle. Elle.

Devon looks at both of us with her eyebrows raised. "Okay, fabulous ladies! Well, let's get going." She winks.

Something about her voice sends shivers down my spine.

"Okay," I say. My voice sounds girlishly high and eager. "I mean, yeah, cool," I try again.

Devon motions for me to follow her.

And I do. Oh, I do.

I try to snap out of it. I try not to watch the way she moves when she walks. I try, I do. When we get to the door that says TREATMENT ROOM and Devon stops and smiles again, I take a deep breath, but that doesn't really help because she smells like—

Man, she smells beautiful.

"So, Elle," she says. Her eyes are, like, gorgeous. "This is the changing room."

"Um, I don't need to change," I tell her, and try not to stare. "I'm good."

"Trust me," she says as she hands me a fluffy white robe. "This will feel really good. Relax. Take all the time you need." She glances down. "Oh, and exchange your shoes for these slippers." She points to a pair of fuzzy white slippers set neatly by the bench. "Slip into those puppies and leave all your worries behind."

I won't lie. When I first put on the robe and the slippers, I feel pretty stupid. But then I walk out and I see Devon and I don't have time to be all weird and shy.

"Comfy, right?" she asks.

I nod.

"You are adorable, Elle." She takes a big deep breath and smiles at me. "Soooo, let me escort you to the treatment room."

I follow her into a big room with wood floors and a wall of windows with light pouring in. It's pretty much empty except for a sink and two big leather chairs that remind me of Geno's, except nothing about this place is like Geno's, only the chairs.

"Welcome to my little paradise!" says Devon.

She moves over to the sink and pats the chair.

"Okay, lady, just sit right here, recline and relax."

I drop into the seat.

"Good. Now, let's scoot you forward." She pauses. "That's it, lean back into this little dip in the sink, just rest your head. Perfect!"

I do exactly as she tells me. The chair is comfortable, and every time I breathe in, I smell Devon.

"So, we're going to start with the scalp treatment, okay?"

I look back up at her. She's even pretty upside down.

I find myself staring.

She smiles down at me. "Wow, you have gorgeous green eyes!"

Wow. You do too, I think but don't say.

I hear the water turn on.

"Your mom totally hooked you up with the chakra deep pressure-point scalp massage ritual treatment. Aaaaamazing. You will love it. Close your eyes, Elle, that's it. Nice. Just relax."

I shut my eyes. The warm water feels good. I feel her fingers massaging the shampoo into my scalp. This is weird. But, like, really, really good weird. I take a deep breath. "That smells *so* good," I let slip.

"Oh my gosh, right?" Devon sighs. "So. Good!"

I squint and catch a glimpse of her. She's still smiling, even though my eyes are closed.

"It's a blend of essential oils. Rosemary, lavender, jasmine. Love, love jasmine. Super nourishing."

The more she massages, the less we talk, until this dreamy hush comes over the room and my eyelids feel heavy. I never would have thought I'd be sitting in a chair with the hottest chick I've ever met massaging my head. I usually don't like anyone even touching me.

But whatever. It's just crazy how nice it feels. It's just like—

My whole body has goose bumps. I feel a ripple of good. My shoulders, my neck. I take a few deep breaths. I kind of, like, just surrender.

"How you doing?" I hear Devon.

"This is *amazing*," I say in a whisper.

"Yeah, this is everybody's favorite part. Totally opens up your chi, harmonizes your chakras. Have you had a rough couple of days?" she asks.

"Yeah." I nod. *You could say that.*

"Well then, this is exactly where you need to be," says Devon.

I don't even have to say anything back. She's cool like that. I feel her slip a towel under my neck and drape it lightly around the back of my head.

"Okay, Elle." Devon speaks really quietly, easing me back to life. "You can just slowly sit up and come on over."

Next thing I know, I'm in this barber-type chair, the sunlight pouring in the window like a spotlight. Freckles's long, wet hair is brushed out and hanging down around my shoulders, and Devon's standing directly behind me.

"So, Elle." She's running her fingers through my hair as she talks, smiling at me in the mirror. "What are we doing today?"

Luckily her eyes get all wide before I have to answer. "Wow," she starts, picking up a strand and examining it up close. "How long has it been?"

"Has what been?"

"Since you had a trim?" she asks.

"Oh, uhhh," I stammer, and wish I knew how to not sound dumb.

I watch her study my hair in the mirror. "Let's get the ends cleaned up first, then we'll bring up the layers." She pauses and looks at me. "Sound good?"

"I guess." I grin.

"Okay, so short layers? Long layers? We can go blunt with some bangs just above the brows?"

"Umm—"

"Okay, let's try this." She winks. "Are you a ponytail 'n' go kind of girl? I don't want to give you a cut for someone you aren't."

"Yeah," I say, laughing softly, "wouldn't want to do that."

"You want to keep it long?"

I nod right away. I mean, I don't want Freckles to kill me! Plus Ellie does have great hair. It's really pretty, like Summer's.

"Okay, see, we're making progress, Elle." She smiles big. "I'll just bring the length up a tiny bit, and that will lift your features, give your hair a lot of movement, and let the natural texture come out. Sound good?"

"Sure." I smile shyly.

I have no idea what the heck she just said.

For the start I kind of watch in the mirror. She moves like a pro, holding up pieces of wet hair and snipping.

Every so often she'll pause and her eyes will get all big and she'll say something really nice.

"Wow, you have fabulous color, Elle. It's like dark, rich, copper-red, super vibrant!"

"Thanks," I say back.

"Seriously, Elle, I know a lot of people who would *kill* for this hair! It's gorgeous."

I watch Devon. . . .

Snip, snip, snip.

After a few more minutes, I kind of shut my eyes. It feels good to do nothing. I'm not at all used to this.

That's the last thing I remember during the haircut. That, and Devon's voice: "Just relax, Elle, don't move a muscle. We're almost done."

I didn't know it was possible to fall asleep with a hair dryer blasting on my head. But it all feels so good. The heat, the flowery potion smell.

I wake up to Devon's voice. "Keep your eyes closed," she reminds me in a whisper. She sounds really excited. "You are such a star, Elle. Wow! I need to run and get your mom. Can you keep them shut?" she asks. "No peeking, promise?"

"Promise," I say. And I do, I keep them shut.

I hear the two of them walk back in.

"Ready for the big reveal?" I recognize Summer's voice right away.

"Sure," I answer back.

"Okay!"

"So I can open my eyes?" I check to make sure.

"Go for it!" says Devon.

I open my eyes.

And wow.

Devon stands behind me still, resting her hands on my shoulders, talking to me in the mirror. "How absurdly fabulous are you!"

"Wow," I say softly.

Freckles looks good.

I kind of turn my head from side to side, looking into the mirror, checking it out. I run my fingers through my hair. "Wow," I repeat for the third time, stunned.

"I can finally see your eyes!" exclaims Summer.

"Your head must feel ten pounds lighter. I took a lot out! And look." Devon stops talking for a sec and runs her fingers through my hair. "Look how the length hits right below your cheekbones. Your bone structure is aaaaamazing, Elle! I love the length and the way the long layers frame your face."

I grin. I think I'm blushing.

"You're *gorgeous*, Elle. Gorgeous fair skin, freckles, green eyes." Devon rakes her fingers through my hair. "You don't need to wear a touch of makeup ever! I think women look much sexier when they're natural, don't you, guys?"

"Absolutely," Summer agrees.

I kind of know what they mean. A lot of the girls at Thatcher wear way too much makeup. Ellie has that classic type of pretty. She doesn't need to do anything. She just is.

"Elle, your hair is fabulous!" Devon is still talking to me in the mirror, her eyes all glowy. She runs her fingers through my hair again. "There's just so much dimension and movement, it's like—" She stops, shakes her head, and smiles. "You are stunning, Elle, really." She winks, "I can't even imagine how jealous your friends must be."

33
ELLIE

SIX HOURS AFTER THE ICE bath, I'm standing outside Owen Cashman's door, trying to get up the nerve to
lift my hand and press the doorbell. I have been dropped
off by The Captain. I didn't even have a say. I was passed
out on Jack's bed until I heard the phone ring and bolted
upright, just as The Captain appeared in the doorway.

I didn't even know he was home.

"That was Owen's mom," he told me. "Let's go."

And look, I know Jack told me to stay in his room, but
if you could see The Captain? If you could see the way he
looks at me? You would do just as I did, which is, with
absolutely no delay, jump to my feet, wash my face, and
obediently get into the truck.

I am dressed in Jack's jeans and the black hoodie from
the morning, even though it kind of stinks.

In the truck, we drive through the setting sun in silence. The Captain speaks exactly three times.

At the stop sign before he turns right: "The difference between being ordinary and being extraordinary is that little extra."

When we pass the football field by the high school: "If you're always comfortable, you're never going to get better. You have to understand you're fighting for a job."

And when he drives up Owen's long, tree-lined driveway: "I expect you to step up and perform as well as I know you can. Consistency is key. Everyone's tough. It's a dogfight. Be ready to focus tomorrow."

"Yes, sir," I respond, proud to answer correctly but wondering what exactly I am supposed to focus on.

He looks at me, and I swear to you I count to fifty in my head before he finally speaks.

"Oh-six hundred. You'll be ready?"

"Yes, sir!" I don't miss a beat even though I have no idea what he's talking about. *What does oh-six hundred even mean?*

When I finally get the nerve to actually put my finger on the doorbell, I am giving myself an all-out pep talk.

I can do this, I tell myself. I mean, what's so hard about a stupid boy sleepover, compared to everything else I did today?

I smile and think of what Gunner would say.

"*Get gritty, bro! You can do this.*" I hear him in my head. I press down on the bell, step back, and almost immediately the door opens.

"Hi, Jack," says a lady who I'm guessing is Owen's mom. "You don't have to knock, silly!"

I just look back at her and stand there on the welcome mat.

"Wow, what a sharp haircut," she says, her eyes wide, smiling. "Come on in, the boys are in the usual spot!"

"The usual spot?" I repeat, fishing for some kind of clue.

Owen's mom looks at me strangely. "You're funny, Jack Malloy." She laughs gently. "They're in the basement. You know, your favorite other home."

"Oh, right, the basement," I say, nodding, but I stay exactly in the same spot and pull Jack's loose jeans up.

She shakes her head, "Jack Malloy! How many times have you been here? I appreciate your standing so politely at the door, but truly, it's okay. You can walk in without an escort." She waves me in, leads me to the door by the kitchen, and opens it. "Go on down," she tells me. "The boys will be thrilled to see you!"

34
JACK

AFTER THE SPA, ON OUR way home, Summer pulls up to a big white house with a swing set in the side yard and a pink playhouse underneath a huge maple tree.

"What are we doing?" I ask.

"What do you mean, what are we doing?" she responds.

"I mean, why are we stopping?"

She glances over like I'm crazy. "Sweetie, really? You still don't want to go?"

"Go where?" are the two words that come out before I kind of wish I could take them back. *I sound so dumb.* But I have no clue what we are doing in front of this house.

I turn and look out the window. I know where we are. It's Owen's street. Three houses down from my elementary school and directly across from the big open field where we play capture the flag in after it gets dark. I've spent a hundred nights running around this neighborhood. It's just . . . *what exactly are we doing here?*

I turn back to Summer. She's gazing at me. Like, literally just smiling, and we're sitting in the parked car. I have no idea what she's waiting for.

She reaches over and runs her fingers over my hair. "It's so great to finally see your eyes, sweetheart." She studies me for a second. "We had fun today, right?"

I nod and manage a quiet smile back.

"Are you feeling okay?" she asks.

"I'm fine," I answer, and turn away.

She takes a deep breath. "What's going on?"

"I'm fine," I repeat.

"Well, okay then," she says, smiling. "Have fun!"

I turn to her in a panic. "What . . . what do you mean, have fun? Aren't we, like—"

Summer cuts me off. "Oh, right, I totally forgot!" Her eyes light up, and I watch her jump out of the car. I hear the trunk open. Then she slips back into her seat, handing me a gift bag with sparkly tissue paper sticking out and a big pink ribbon tying it together. "Almost forgot!"

As soon as I see the bag I remember. Freckles. "No birthday parties!" she told me.

"Oh boy," I mumble, and stay exactly where I am, in the front seat. Frozen. "I, um . . . do I have to go?" I try.

"Honey." Summer sighs; her eyes scan my face. "Why are you so afraid of going to Claire's birthday party?

What's going on? Is this about Sassy?"

Sassy? I look back at her and shrug both my shoulders. *I'm so confused.*

Summer smiles and holds out her open hand. It takes me a few seconds before I realize what she's waiting for, and I follow suit. For a moment we sit in the car, neither of us talking. I wonder if maybe she'll let me just go home. Maybe she can tell how rattled I am. Maybe she'll let me leave.

But instead?

Summer squeezes my hand. "Sweetheart, you don't have to spend your time with Sassy. There are going to be lots of girls that you like there. Just don't focus on her and be with your other friends."

I take a big deep breath and look away. I look outside. I look at the perfectly cut lawn and the house and the flowers on the front steps.

"Just go and have a good time and don't worry so much. It's just one night." She pauses and I look back at her. She's smiling wide. "It's just a sleepover!"

"A sleepover!" I repeat, in disbelief. But my panicked expression does nothing. Summer looks a little puzzled at first, then breaks into a huge Summer smile.

"You've done sleepovers before! You've had a million sleepovers!"

I grip my hand tight around the edge of the seat. *I just won't get out! I will not get out. I just won't leave. Only—*

Summer is not exactly on the same page. She eyes my door, stretches over me, and opens it with her reach. "Get out of the car and go, silly!"

"But . . . ," I stammer, and don't move.

Summer leans in, and before I even realize what's happening, she plants a big wet kiss on my cheek. "Go!" she tells me again, still smiling. "And have fun!"

I get out of the car, holding the frilly gift bag a foot away from me as if it has something smelly in it, and take a few slow steps up the front sidewalk until I'm sure Summer and her white Volvo and her big smile are far enough down the street so she can't see what I'm about to do. And in case you are curious? What I'm about to do is make a run for it! I gave my word to Freckles. I told her I wouldn't go, and I'm not going to go! It's as simple as that. I look all around, up the street down the street. For a flash I picture myself hiding at Owen's. Only how am I going to walk in as . . . yeah, that's not going to work.

I scan the side yard to try and plot my escape route, and I am about to take off back into the woods behind Owen's when the front door opens and a lady in an apron starts talking to me.

"Hey there!" She waves.

I'm standing in the front yard, one hand shoved in my new jeans, one hand clutching the frilly gift bag.

The lady begins walking toward me. "Hey," she says. She's smiling. "Are you here for a birthday party? Because if you're here for Claire's birthday party, you're in the right place!"

I just stare back.

"I know we've met before, I'm really sorry." She looks at me, embarrassed. "To be perfectly honest, I can't remember your name. I'm Ruth, Claire's mom, and you are—"

"I'm, um." I pause awkwardly, then—"Elle," I tell her. I say it the same way Devon did. *"Elle."* I let it roll off my tongue and throw in a polite head tilt and a slight grin. I try and seem girlie and normal and not like—

Me.

The lady smiles back. "Elle, of course! That's right. Elle!" She waves me toward her. "Well, Elle, please, come on in!"

For a split second I consider running again. I look to my left, then my right, and imagine myself bolting into the field across the street and staying there sleeping under the stars all night. Man! I'm so rattled.

A chick party! A sleepover? Really!???

The lady in the apron can sense my hesitation. "Come on in, Elle," she repeats, smiling. "There's just a whole mess of girls having a ball in the basement, nothing you haven't seen before, not a thing to be afraid of!"

"Oh, man," I mutter, and take one reluctant step forward, and then another. I can't even believe it when my feet move toward the house. When I follow her. When I walk up the front brick stairs. When I step inside.

* * *

Claire's house is amazing and huge and smells like popcorn, and I can already hear faint laughter and girl shrieking coming from somewhere. I follow Claire's mom through the living room, past Claire's dad and little brothers, who are parked in front of the huge flat screen. I squint to read the score: Notre Dame twenty-three, Michigan sixteen.

"Yeah buddy, beast mode!" escapes my lips as I watch a Notre Dame fullback blast off running up the right sideline. It's pretty much a fact that my brothers are chilling out, relaxing on the couch right now, watching this. "Dude's a tank!" I say, pumping my fist before I quickly remember that . . .

"Wow! I *love* it! A girl who loves football!" Claire's mom says, surprised and smiling. "How awesome is that!"

I look at her and flash a smile. "I could sit up here and watch a little bit," I offer. *I had to try, right?*

Claire's mom laughs. "Oh, but then you'd miss all the fun! If you want, I can put your gift with the other presents, or you can put it right over on the table." She gestures to the kitchen table stacked with a huge mound of colorfully wrapped presents, glittery eye-catching gift bags, and a tower of boxes tied up in two giant ribbons. I take a tentative step into the kitchen and set down Summer's frilly bag.

I shove my hands deep into my new jeans pockets. Claire's mom is just standing there, smiling at me.

"I'm sorry," she starts. "It's just, your hair—I can't stop staring! It's such a beautiful deep red hue." She pauses, eyes bright. "I bet you get that a lot, huh?"

I shrug both my shoulders. "Sort of," I answer.

Claire's mom leads me down a long bright-yellow hallway with a billon framed family photos. She talks as we turn the corner and head down a set of stairs. "We have a lot of food, Elle, I hope you're hungry! Pizza, dip and chips, and my personal favorite, a yummy salad!" She laughs. "Tons of junk and cake, lots of cake! Do you like at least one of those things?"

"Yes, ma'am," it slips. "I mean, uhh, yeah, thanks," I say, sounding flustered.

When I turn the corner at the bottom of the stairs, I'm not expecting it. The room is lit up by a glittery disco ball hanging from the ceiling and music is blaring from two towering speakers—it's loud. Bodies are sprawled out everywhere, two to a beanbag chair, four draped across couches, two playing Dance Dance Revolution in front of a flat screen on the thick, shaggy carpet. I think I'm the only one not dressed in pajama bottoms and a soccer T-shirt and crazy striped socks.

I take a step backward, not forward, and consider running again.

Get me outta here!

My throat feels hot and tight. I wish I was at Owen's, crushing *Call of Duty*. Instead I'm standing on the edge of slumber-party mania, with a bunch of girls I recognize from school, all of them seventh graders. There's so many of them! I scan the faces— Kaitlin, Blair Thompson, Tori, Sassy Gaines, Aspen, Girl Sammie. Besides soccer yesterday, I have never talked to any of them in my life. I told you. I'm shy. I don't talk to girls. I'm not like Sammy. I'm not the type of guy who knows what to say. For a few seconds, nobody even notices me standing there, then—

"Girls!" Claire's mom raises her voice above the noise. The entire room suddenly goes silent, even the music is turned down, and every single one of them stops what they are doing, turns, and looks at me.

"Elle's here!" she announces.

Honestly, I have never been so completely flustered. I stand there with all eyes on me in my new lavender sweater, my new jeans, and nervously lift my hand to my hair and fiddle with it. I can't seem to actually speak, and I'm in the middle of coaxing out a smile and a nod and wondering who exactly Claire is and how I'm going to know it's her when this small blond girl with short stubby pigtails, wearing a T-shirt with sequined letters that spell out BIRTHDAY GODDESS! across the front and a diamond-looking tiara crown on her head comes running at me. I remember her face from soccer.

"Elle!" she squeals. "Oh em geeee! I love your new name! Elle! How sophisticated!" she shrieks in my ear and literally jumps up onto me with a hug. "Oh my gosh,

I'm so glad you're here!" She talks so fast and loud. "You look so amazing! Your hair, it's like awesomesauce! You're so, so, so pretty! No. You are *gorgeous! Très chic!*" she declares.

I step back and try very hard to not, like, make a face that says, *"Whoa. Dude. You are talking way too loud."* Instead . . . "Thanks," I say quietly, and smile.

For a few seconds I stand at the bottom of the stairs, not really sure what to do, but then I see Mackenzie. Mackenzie from soccer. *That Mackenzie.* Only this time she's not in her Thunderbirds gear. She's wearing silky pajamas like the other girls, and her long blond hair is down around her shoulders.

"Elle!" she shouts from across the room, and comes running at me too. I let her throw her arms around me. "Why did we not think of this fabulous name sooner? Elle! I love it. *Love!*" She hugs me for a solid five seconds. I counted. She smells like cinnamon. I try to play it cool while Mackenzie takes my hand and pulls me over to the love seat and sits one inch away from me, her arm laced through mine. "Come snug!" she says.

My heart is racing. My palms are sweating. I try not to stare at her rocket body or her blue eyes, and focus instead on the pink hearts all over her pajama bottoms.

"Oh my gosh!" she exclaims, noticing my staring. "These are *seriously* the most comfy things I have ever worn!"

I pause for a moment and try to think. "Yeah, uhh, they're cool." I nod.

Smooth! Not.

Mackenzie stands back up, staring at me wide-eyed, smiling. "I am seriously so mesmerized by your hair right now! You look hot, girlie, and I mean that in the non-creepiest way possible!"

I manage a shy smile and look around me at the out-of-control dancing and squealing. It's so loud down here. Also? My heart is beating about two hundred miles a minute, because Mackenzie has sat back down and she's still holding on to my arm while we are squeezed together on the couch. Our shoulders are rubbing.

"Hey, by the way," she says, leaning in and cupping her hand around my ear. "I hear a certain *someone* has been acting super sketch." Mackenzie stops whispering, and I follow her eyes to a crowd of girls watching us from the other couch across the room. As she looks, she wriggles closer and proceeds to lace her fingers around mine. My chest is pounding. I'm sitting on a love seat two inches away from Mackenzie, holding hands with a girl for the first time in my life. Man, do I have butterflies! It feels so weird. Weird good. I can just hear Sammy. "Dude, she's bangin'!" he'd say.

I'd be lying if I didn't say I notice that too, but yeah. I know this sounds so soft, but there's something different about Mackenzie. She's just really friendly and laid-back, and nice.

I take a deep breath and look around the room. Holy buckets, am I sweating. *Breathe, Jack. Just breathe.*

For half a second I close my eyes and wonder if I'm dreaming. Only I know I'm not, because when I open them, Mackenzie squeezes her fingers tighter, pulling me toward her, and whispers into my ear again. "Seriously, who does she think she is, right? It's *so* not okay to be rude! I'm just not into that."

I have no idea what Mackenzie is talking about, and I feel bad that I'm mostly focused on the way our palms feel pressed together and the way she smells and how much I want her to keep whispering.

Please. Keep. Whispering.

"I mean, really." She keeps going. "If you don't like someone, just leave them alone, right? Get over yourself."

"Totally," I answer, nodding, eager to impress. "If someone messed with you, I'd rip their head off!" I tell her before I realize what just came out of my mouth.

"Ha, thanks, Elle!" She laughs and scrunches into me even closer. "But, like, I'm not even joking." She pauses, then goes on, "Honestly, she's a total drama queen!"

"Wait." I manage a shy smile. "*Who* are you talking about?" I finally ask.

She leans in.

More whispering? Yes, please.

"Sassy!" she breathes.

35

ELLIE

WHEN I REACH THE BOTTOM of the stairs, the room is completely dark, and the only light I see is the flashing from a giant TV screen. I try and act all casual as I step over three empty pizza boxes and sink into the very end of the huge leather sofa, my knees pressed together, my arms folded tightly. I try to not pay attention to the fact that I am sitting in a mostly dark, smelly basement with six eighth-grade boys, all shirtless, in jeans with their boxers peeking out.

"Duuuude, welcome to the lair! Nice buzz, broskinator!"

I know that voice. *Sammy*.

"Oh, uh, hey," I say, trying to sound laid back. "'Sup, bro?" I almost grin.

Where'd I get that from?

I can see his face now. It is Sammy. When he smiles

through the dim light, this boyish mischief comes out of his eyes. He's sitting on the couch across from me. "Dog, how's your nose since the scrap? Chicks lovin' on your fat lip?"

"I'm fine," I say. It's weird, but for the first time I actually think I kind of sound like Jack. I sit back. I stay quiet. I watch the gun battle on the huge screen. Listen to the explosions.

Owen is sprawled out on the floor. No pillow. "Dutes is so sick," he says. He sounds a little bit like he's in a video-game trance.

"Dutes?" I repeat. I don't mean to, it just comes out.

"Dude, *Call of Duty?*" Sammy tells me. "What's wrong with you?"

"Ha." I laugh awkwardly. "I'm just playin' with you."

"Dude." A fourth voice speaks. "You're crushing my K.D. right now! This guy is running around with Marathon Pro, knifing me in the back."

Then a fifth: "Oh, yeah! Sit down! Dominated! Did you see that?"

One more: "I could sit here all night, quick scoping fools!"

Huh?

Once my eyes adjust to the darkness, with the help of the flashing light coming from the TVs, I scan the faces in the room. It's all the same eighth-grade guys Jack hangs out with at the pool all summer. I don't really know any of them, but I know who they are: Owen, Sammy, Demaryius, this kid Trey. Plus two other guys—and the only reason I know who they are is because Brayden and Dominic Hersh went to my elementary school. They're twins. It smells like sweaty feet down here. Chips, empty soda cans. I'm not really one to call out a mess, but it's seriously kind of gross. I stay huddled on the couch, my legs folded underneath me, until Owen stands, walks over, and shoves the game controller into my hands. "Yo," he tells me. "I gotta take a leak. Take over, man!"

"What? No!" I say a little too loud, and push the plastic thing away.

Owen looks back at me, shocked. "Dude, I don't even know what you're saying right now. Are you kidding? You don't want in? Come on, dude, my K.D. is gonna go downhill, man."

"No, I'm good, really," I answer. I sit on my hands and sink farther back into the couch. "I'm just gonna chill."

"Are you crazy, dude? I'll take it!" Demaryius grabs the controller out of Owen's hands. "That's the first time in my life I ever saw Jack Malloy turn down COD. First time for everything, I guess!"

I sit there patiently for . . . I don't know? At least an hour while nobody even talks. It's so weird! I just stare at the gun barrels on the enormous flat screen, and watch explosions, and shooting, and listen to random video game commentary that sounds something like this:

"Dude, I just *dominated* you!"

"Dude, I absolutely destroyed you!"

"Dude, watch out, they're camping, man."

Camping?

"Dude! There's two campers in that room. Watch out, bro!"

Hour number two is almost an identical scene, except every now and then Sammy brings up girls. And if you'd like to picture this, keep in mind that boys—these boys? They do not stop what they're doing to talk to each other. They talk while focused entirely on shooting zombies and just blurt out random stuff.

Sammy: Dude, seriously! Do you know who is so hot?

Trey: Aspen?

Sammy: Oh, dude. She's so bangin'!

Brayden: She's a ten, bro.

Dominic: Not gonna lie, she can rock the yoga pants.

Sammy: Boys, she'll be all over me!

Trey: In your dreams, maybe. You're in more friend zones than anyone, dude.

Sammy: Whatever, man! Don't mean to pump my own tires, but you'll see. Let me go to work.

Dominic: Sammy, dude. You seriously need to stop talking!

All the boys have a good laugh, even Sammy.

I shut my eyes. I'm so tired from the day. The mountain, The Cage. The ice bath . . .

I have no idea how long I sleep. It's still dark when I open my eyes. I squint through the pulsing flashing light from gunfire and explosions coming from the screen. The boys are still glued to their game. But I only sit quietly for a few seconds before Owen's mom walks in, carrying pizza boxes with a twelve-pack of soda on top. Might be the best thing I've seen all day.

Nobody looks up at her but me.

"Owen," she says, sounding kind of irritated. "Owen, put that thing down and look at me, please!" She stands at the door, her arms full. "Boys, I brought you down some pizza, some wings—they're extra hot—and soda pop. Please try and not make a complete mess, boys? Boys! Owen!"

Owen looks up quickly. "Sorry, Mom, can't talk, I'm . . . His voice trails off, then he picks back up. "Duuuude! Unbelievable! Did you see that? Obliterated him. Playing with the big boys now, son!"

Owen's mom sets the pizza boxes, the wings, and the soda down on the table. I jump up and help her clear a space. I can't even tell you how excited I am to eat. *Food!* She watches as I open up the boxes and lift steaming-hot slices, setting them down on paper plates and handing them to the boys.

"Jack Malloy," she says, sounding grateful, "I can always count on you to be a total gentleman."

After the pizza, we play some football. Not outside. We're still in the half-dark basement. Everyone's still shirtless but me. It's another video game. Owen is particularly awesome at it.

"*Madden* all day all night, baby!" he says, wide-eyed. "Anyone who thinks they can compete with this machine, let's get it. It's about to go down!"

"Dude, I think you may seriously have a gaming problem!" says Demaryius. He playfully shoves Owen sideways, but Owen just pops back up, bug eyes still glued to the screen, grinning broadly, the game controller still gripped tightly in his hands.

They all laugh. Even I do. Owen's so sweet and kind of adorable and it's impossible not to like him. And what the heck, I even play. I grip the controller and just start pressing buttons, even though I have no idea what they do. I watch, smiling, as my little guy runs down the field, ball tucked under his arm, the crowd cheering him on. I don't even mind when they tease me.

"Brutal, Mallsy." Trey bursts out laughing. "Quit playin' with us, you noob!"

"Oh, man, you have to be joking, dude," says Demaryius. "You're running the wrong way!"

"Nice job, buddy!" says Dominic, clapping his hands,

mocking me. "You are good. *Not!*"

Honestly? It's kind of a relief to sit and play and not have to talk. I'm actually having a pretty good time. I'd even use the word fun. And I'm thinking, *This isn't really so bad*—when, as if on cue, Sammy unveils his plan for the night.

He's fiddling with his phone. "Yo, dudes, I just got a text," he tells us, without looking up. "Do you want to meet the girls at the playground?"

The room falls silent for a few excruciating seconds.

Girls? Oh, god.

Trey burps loudly. I can smell it. Pepperoni pizza. "Who's going?" he asks.

"My future wife's gonna be there," says Sammy. He looks up. "No, for real. Sassy, Aspen, Claire, that whole seventh-grade scene."

Demaryius turns to Sammy. "Dude, Sassy Gaines? She's smoking hot, but she's—"

"She wears too much makeup, bro," finishes Dominic. "Plus, she talks so much she would give a woodpecker a headache."

"Duuude," Sammy argues. "She's a ten! She's totally hot. Her body is out of control!"

"No, man, it's not that she's not hot." Demaryius stops to kickoff, then continues. "She's a stunner, I'll give you that. But seriously, dude, she talks too much. I'm just, like, shut up! She's rude too. Fake. It's not cute to be so desperate for attention. Have you ever listened to her for, like, more than five seconds? All she does is make fun of people. I don't even want to be around her. I'm just, like, grow up!"

Brayden flops back on the couch, kicking his feet up. "That-a-boy, just say what you feel, Demaryius. It's called being real! You're the man, buddy!"

"Ha. Yeah. I'm that guy. You're welcome!" Demaryius laughs. "Seriously, dude, nothing's worse than a hot girl full of negativity, man."

My chest tightens and my ears get hot and I feel like I'm hearing something I'm not supposed to hear. I hand the controller to Owen and fold my arms and try and act like I'm totally not listening even though I totally am.

I kind of don't want them to stop.

"Yo, Mallsy." Brayden raises his palm toward me for a high-five. "That chick's in love with you."

Oh my gosh. This is about to get real awkward.

Trey beams me with a pillow. "Kid's head's in the clouds as usual."

Laughter.

"Seriously, Mallsy," Brayden says, nodding. "You can deny it, but Sassy Gaines is all over your action, bro! Have you seen the way she stared at you all summer at the pool? Stalker, dude."

"Whatever," I mutter, shaking my head and trying not to look as absolutely uncomfortable as I feel.

Dominic laughs. "Let's be honest, dude, we all know the ladies love your mug. Face it. You got swag without even trying, bro. You need to capitalize! Get some!"

Oh my god.

"Ha! Notice how he doesn't deny it, stud!" Trey says, laughing. "This guy is all smiles right now. Yeah, Mallsy, pretty sure most guys would love to be you."

I need to change the subject fast. This isn't going anywhere good.

"Come on, please," I try. It's pathetic when I hear how the words sound. "Like, I mean, come on, *pleeeease?* Will you guys just stop?"

Brayden shoves a handful of popcorn in his mouth. "One of those awkward moments where a guy acts like a girl and you don't know what to say. You're hilarious, Mallsy!"

I pretend to laugh too. I can feel my cheeks heat up.

Sammy stands and brushes the crumbs off his jeans. "Okay, no question about it, we're going, right? We're going to meet them? Who's in?"

Owen glances at me, his eyes flicking between me and the TV. "Can't we just stay here?" he asks, sounding nervous. "We can play *Minecraft, Halo, Madden* . . . You choose, Sammy. We can play anything you want, man."

Owen puts the controller down and stands up, walks over to the couch, and sinks down right next to me. "Truth is"—Owen looks at Sammy as he talks—"if we get caught I'm toast, dude. You won't even get in trouble. Your parents let you do *anything*, Sammy. Seriously, man, you could do almost anything and get away with it. Dude, it's different for you, you don't understand. Jack and I will get grounded for the rest of our lives."

Sammy smirks and throws a smile at Owen. "Pull your skirt down, bro! My dude, you're with the master! There's nothing to worry about, dude. Your mom's not going to find out." He turns to the rest of us.

"What about the rest of you ladies?" Sammy asks, eyes twinkling.

Trey pops to his feet. "I'm in!"

"Let's see," starts Brayden, getting up. "Go meet up with a bunch of hot chicks or stay in the basement with you hooligans? Ha. I'm down, let's do it."

Demaryius shrugs, then stands. "You're crazy, Sammy, but okay, I'm in."

Sammy looks at me last. "Mallsy, deal with it, don't even try and front. You're an absolute stud and the ladies love you." He grins. His dimples are huge. "Come on, bro, we all need to let loose once in a while. Come on, buddy, are you in?"

All the boys are watching me.

Waiting.

As if whatever I say goes.

Even Owen looks suddenly excited for Sammy's big plan, like he wants me to say yes. He flashes me the thumbs-up as he moves to his feet.

"Well?" Sammy asks again. "Let's go, my dude. What's the word from the man, the myth, the legend, Jack Malloy?"

All of them are standing in front of me, bare chested, jeans barely hugging their hips, boxers showing, staring at me with big dumb grins.

"Let's go, dude, live a little," Sammy presses. His eyes are wide. "Come on, Jacko, whaddya say, what's the word!"

For a millisecond I soak in the power. I let them linger. Under Sammy's spell, I do not once think of what Jack would want me to do. I told him to not go to Claire's party. He's not going to even be there, he won't even know. I feel oddly bold and brave. For the first time in a long time, I don't even feel nervous or afraid.

I can't believe I say it. Two words. But I do.

I shrug. "I'm in!" I say.

And I'm grinning.

36
JACK ▶

DO YOU KNOW HOW HARD it is to feel manly when you're painting your fingernails candy-color pink with sparkles?

"So pretty!" Mackenzie says. She's scooched up next to me on the couch. "Here," she says, picking out a bottle that's glittery peach. "You do mine!"

"No, really, I'm not good at this," I answer, shaking my head.

"Are you crazy?" She smiles and grabs my hand. "Look, this is so pretty! Please?"

I take the bottle and unscrew the top. She places her hand in my *lap*. I have to concentrate with all I've got. It's like painting a model car, right? That's what I tell myself. That I'm not doing this. That I am not dying a slow, painful I-couldn't-get-any-more-*soft* death. Unreal. *My man card will be permanently revoked after this*, I think silently to myself, and almost laugh.

Afterward, I'm first to help myself to pizza (extra cheese), salt-and-vinegar chips, and gummy bears. I wash it all down with peach iced tea and three pieces of cake (vanilla with chocolate icing). Then it's "present time!" When Claire picks up my bag, I watch her dig through the tissue paper in suspense—I have no idea what I got her. And whatever, make fun of me all you want. I smile when I see her wide eyes and hear her shriek with joy at the sight—"Oh my gosh, a Pillow Pet! I *love* it, Elle, thank you so much!" Claire jumps up from the couch and hugs me tight. I didn't even know what the heck a Pillow Pet was until tonight. *Butter's my middle name*, I think to myself as I sink deeper into the couch.

Next, Claire insists I put on pajamas too. She drags me upstairs to her room and tosses me her fuzzy purple pajamas out of her drawer. "Feel them!" she exclaims. "They're my favorite cozy pj pants. Super soft!"

Yes. Okay?

I put them on.

Now I am sitting on a huge L-shaped couch bathed in disco-ball light, watching some chick-flick on the flat-screen TV, dressed in a borrowed long-sleeved Thunderbirds T-shirt and purple drawstring pajama bottoms. My nails are painted pink, and I'm nestled in between Girl Sammie (who is hilarious and awesome) and Mackenzie.

Not hating the fact that Mackenzie's legs are draped over mine. Nobody would believe me if I told them where I am right now. Jett always says, "You just gotta enjoy the moment, man!" I guess he's right.

I look around the room, mostly quiet for the first time all night. Everyone's eyes are on the movie unfolding on the screen. I am honestly half listening, almost falling asleep, when I hear Claire say this: "Do you know that kid Sammy Armstrong?"

"Oh my gosh," says Tori. "He is *so hot!*"

Sassy sneers from the couch across from us. "Um, ew, no, he's not! Super unfortunate when people obviously downgrade. He's really not attractive."

Sammy? I have to help a brother out. "I think the kid's really nice!" I say, surprising myself. I nod and smile just to make it clear.

"Seriously, did anyone ask you?" Sassy snaps. "Shut up, no one cares!"

Sassy laughs, and Aspen does too. I feel Mackenzie's arm loop through mine and pull me toward her.

"Just ignore her," she whispers. "I don't know what her problem is."

For a moment, nobody says a word. Then—

"Re-*lax!*" Sassy explodes in laughter, her eyes zeroed in on me. "It's called a *joke*. Get over it. People are so immature. God!"

I watch Sassy through the half darkness, across the

room. *Is this girl for real?* Man, she's lucky I'm not me. If she were a guy chirping me like this, I would literally have already put her in a choke hold and not let go. I take a really deep breath and shake my head. *What a clown!* Sassy Gaines definitely acts like a different person here than when she's around me at the pool, or all last year in the hallways at school. She's always smiling and complimenting me. I've never even said a word to her in my life!

Sassy suddenly leaps up from the couch and strides into the middle of the room, blocking the TV with her hands on her hips. "Turn it down," she orders.

I don't like the way she talks to her friends.

The room falls silent. The only light is beaming from behind her, on the huge flat screen. All eyes are on Sassy and her ironed-straight, glossy, yellow hair and her leopard-print pajama bottoms, and her dumb way-too-small T-shirt that comes up to her belly button. She flips her hair back with her hand.

"Ahem," she says. She seems pleased to be the center of attention.

"Okay." She pauses to smile and giggle and exchange knowing glances with her exclusive little club—Kaitlin, Tori, Aspen, Blair—eye-rolling, real-life Barbies sitting shoulder to shoulder on the far couch. "So this movie is totally boring, and it's time to talk about boys!" (Pause for squeals.)

"Wait, first—" Sassy stops and looks to her posse.

"Someone bring me honey Dijon chips, I want them so bad!"

Tori jumps up obediently, like a dog, and brings Sassy a bag of chips. She even opens it for her.

"You are my guardian angel, boo! Love you!" says Sassy, sitting back down.

"Okay, losers!" Tori moves into Sassy's spot. "Say one guy you like. I'll go first!" She stops and giggles. "I totally and completely heart Demaryius Jones."

"Oh my gosh, yes!" Kaitlin squeals. "He's *so* hot!"

"Total doll," Claire agrees.

"He's really smart too. He's in math with me," adds Blair.

Everyone turns to Mackenzie.

"Kenzi, you go!" demands Sassy, leading from the couch.

My heart starts beating. I can't believe I'm saying this, but I kind of want her to say my name.

"I don't know." Mackenzie shrugs. "Someone else go, this is dumb!"

"Yeah, seriously," I whisper back.

Two days ago I didn't even really know she existed. Now? I take a really deep breath and feel her shoulder rub up against mine.

"Okay, boo." Sassy turns to Girl Sammie. "Your turn, smunchkin!"

"Okay, well, don't laugh?" Sammie's nose scrunches

226

up and she pulls her knees up, hugging them as she talks. "Okay, so! You guys promise you won't laugh?" She giggles.

"Promise! Say it, Sammie!" Aspen eggs her on.

"I am in love with Owen Matthews. He's funny and—"

"Awesome!" I finish. I can't help it. I almost lose it and start laughing.

Sammie buries her face in her hands. "Oh my gosh. Do. Not. Tell!"

That's it—the floodgates are open. They all start talking at once. It seems like every guy I know gets covered.

Tori on Dominic: He's a cutie. Not gonna lie.

Kaitlin on Trey: He's nice. He helped me with my French homework every day last year.

Sassy on Brayden: Um, no! Gross.

Blair on Sammy: I think he's totally cute, but he's a total player. He never dates one girl. He just, like, hops around.

Aspen on Keegan Lowe: He's a little immature.

Sammie on Robby Donovan: He's really good at basketball. He's funny!

Mackenzie on Mason Rice: He's kind of adorable. I can see how a lot of girls fall for him. But he's in sixth grade! So, no!

Claire on Danny King: Really, really smart. I have science with him!

Sammie on Everett MacGregor: He's cute, but he's kind of a jerk.

I feel softer than a pillow sitting here actually listening to this. I am about to get up and hide out in the bathroom when the name Porter Gibson comes up.

Girl Sammie sounds much less jokey when she says, "He can be a serious jerk, but, I mean, I feel so sorry for him. My parents are friends with his parents, and his brother died last year. He had, like, bone cancer. He was only *fifteen*. It was *so* sad. Porter's had a really hard time." Girl Sammie leans into me. "Super sad, right?"

I can't even look at her. My eyes wander straight ahead. Everything gets fuzzy. I just stare into the TV lights. I instantly feel sick. That explains why Porter's always such a jerk, I guess. I legitimately feel bad for the guy. That's the honest truth. God, if something happened to my brothers—

My heart starts racing, and the fight flashes in my head—my blood-spattered shirt, knocking him down with one punch. I went ballistic! I held him down. I went all out. I just unloaded on him, man.

I'm sitting sandwiched on the couch between Sammie and Mackenzie. And it's like, for a few seconds nobody is in the room, everything falls away. I have the worst feeling in my gut. I start thinking about my mom. Everything changed the day my mom died. *Everything*. I remember that day like it was yesterday. I swallow back the feeling. I push it back inside. I tilt my head to keep the tears from leaking out.

"Hey," Mackenzie whispers. "You okay?"

"Yeah." I nod and manage a tiny grin.

Mackenzie sighs and leans her head on my shoulder. "I got your back," she says in a soft voice, so nobody else can hear.

Sassy has the stage now. She's in front of us again, going on and on about some kid they all call The Prince.

"Reasons everyone's obsessed with The Prince, in no particular order," Sassy announces. "Number one!" She pauses dramatically. "He is *so* hot and he has really pretty eyes and long eyelashes that are like . . . oh my gawd!"

"So ridiculously hot!" Blair shouts out. "He's good at everything!"

"He's so polite! It's adorable," says Claire. "He's, like, rugged but gentlemanly. He's, like, a knight!"

"I know, right?" Girl Sammie even speaks up. "He's like confident but not cocky. He's so nice!"

"Have you seen his abs?" asks Kaitlin, giggling. "Like, seriously! Oh. My. God. Just . . . wow, words cannot describe! And his hair?"

"Luscious!" Tori finishes. "So dreamy! So pretty to look at. Gawd. What a cutie!"

"Totally." Aspen sighs. "No guy even comes close to how hot he is!"

"He's delicious," Sassy declares. "I absolutely am in love with him, and I am *not even kidding*!" Then she lowers her voice, almost to a whisper, obviously wanting all of us to pay attention. "I wasn't going to say anything, but . . ." She hesitates, grinning.

"What? Tell us!" Tori squeals, giggling.

"Well," starts Sassy. "He's a *seriously* good kisser!"

"Oh my gosh!" says Claire. "Where'd you hear that?"

Sassy's eyebrows go up. "Trust me," she says, smiling and pausing to glance around the room. "I love it when The Prince grabs my hand and kisses me. 'You're all mine,' he tells me, usually in a whisper, like, *right in my ear.*"

"Oh my gosh, seriously?" asks Claire. Her eyes are big.

"Seriously!" Sassy brags. "He told me that this summer at the pool, behind the locker rooms."

"Oh my gosh, he whispers in your ear? That's literally the sweetest thing in the world! You two look really good together, boo," Blair says. "You guys are both really attractive people. You'd make the cutest kids!"

Sassy sighs, smiling. "I know, right?"

I don't know who this Prince clown is, and honestly I feel sorry for him if he's mixed up with *this* girl. She's an idiot. People like this fire me up every time. I have to chirp her! C'mon, man! Bust her chops, have some fun.

"I'm friends with him," I tell her, working hard to keep my face straight. I don't even know who "him" is. I just want to really grind her gears, get under her skin. "Yeah, uhhh . . ." I pause for a second and try and think of the way the guys talk in the locker room. "We hang out sometimes. It's chill. Casual."

Ha. I bite my lip so I don't laugh in Sassy's face.

"Oh, so you're, like, friends with The Prince? Yeah, right!" Aspen's eyes narrow on me. She looks suddenly angrier than before. "Don't flatter yourself, Ellie. In your dreams you are."

"Don't believe me, whatever," I tell her. I toss in a grin. I can tell I hit a nerve. This girl is too much.

"Excuse me while I laugh out loud." Sassy begins hysterically laughing. "You? Friends with The Prince? Hahahahaaaa! That's the funniest thing I have ever heard. Save yourself the embarrassment, Ellie, and just quit."

Mackenzie tugs at my elbow. "Don't even talk to her, just ignore her," she says.

Girl Sammie whispers too. "Don't pay attention to her, Elle."

Sassy rolls her eyes and sighs loudly. "Seriously, *some* people's lack of maturity is almost impressive. Do you think getting your hair blown out and calling yourself by a new name suddenly makes you sophisticated? *Paaaah-lease!*"

I feel my adrenaline rush. I'm thinking to myself I should probably stop. *Drop it. Man!* This girl rattles me so much. I just look back her, like, are you kidding me right now?

"What a joke," I mutter.

"Come on, you guys!" Claire sounds bummed. "This is supposed to be a party! Can we all agree to be nice now?"

For a minute or two the room grows uncomfortably quiet. Nobody speaks until Sassy reaches for her phone, buzzing, tucked in between her pajamas and her hip. "*Excusez-moi!*" Sassy announces, with a terrible French accent. She drops her eyes to read her texts. After a few seconds she looks up from her phone, grinning.

"Things are about to get real cray-cray," she says. Her eyes are all wild. "Everybody get up," she orders, floating across the room, practically skipping toward Aspen, and pulling her to her feet. "We're going on a little rendezvous!"

"Um, you guys," Claire starts. She looks freaked. "If we go and get caught, seriously, it's so not going to be pretty if my mom finds out."

Sassy rolls her eyes, "Oh, come on, please, don't be such a baby birthday girl. It's a party. You turned thirteen, not seven! We're not in fifth grade anymore, boo. We have to have some big-girl fun!"

Aspen jumps up. "Let's do it!" she squeals.

Tori's next. "Okay, I'm in, even though I don't know where we're going!"

Kaitlin, Blair—they cave too. Even Claire jumps up. "Okay, fine, let's go!"

Sassy laughs, turns to me, Sammie, and Mackenzie—the last ones not standing. She's smiling. "I think you three better come too, because, Ellie, I am happy to tell you and your dreamland imagination that you will now have a chance to prove me wrong."

"Huh?" asks Girl Sammie. We all look back at Sassy, confused.

"You're so pathetic you need to make up stories about someone. We're going to the playground and—" She stops and glances at Aspen, just long enough to make us all wonder what she's up to. "The Prince will be there," she goes on, looking directly at me. "So now, Ellie, you can totally embarrass yourself in front of all of us, because I happen to know him personally, if you know what I mean." She stops again, looking around at all the girls and smiling. "The Prince is all mine, everybody knows it, and you are about to get humiliated. *Badly*."

She waits for a beat, then adds, "Or, if you all want to be little babies, you can stay here."

"Okay, okay, you guys, stop arguing!" Claire tries to pull me up, but I don't budge.

"Come on, let's just go," Girl Sammie gives in. "A little midnight adventure, right? It will be fun."

Even Mackenzie falls under Sassy's reign. "I'll be with you the whole time," she whispers to me as she moves to her feet. Now all the girls but me are ready to leave. I stay right on the couch. Jeez! This Sassy girl is seriously insane. She won't quit. Just for the record, I am biting down hard on my bottom lip so I don't say something I might regret.

Sassy looks at Aspen and Tori. Clearly they are in on some big inside joke.

"Come on, Ellie." Sassy turns her eyes back to me with a big fake grin. "Prove me wrong. If you know The Prince like you say you do, you wouldn't be so afraid. Am I right or am I wrong?" She tosses her hair as she says it, laughing. They are all staring down at me, alone, swallowed up by the gigantic empty couch. And look, I try to keep it in, I try not to speak. Heck, if they want to go and be idiots, I'm okay right here on this seriously comfortable sofa. Simple as that. But I can't take it. This chick is crazier than a sack of rabid weasels. *Fine.* I say it, okay?

"Who is The Prince?" I finally blurt out.

All the girls look back at me like I'm completely nuts.

Sassy smiles at her posse, then whips her head back to me, standing with her hand on her hip. "Seriously, Ellie, I knew you were totally lying. Some people are actually so pathetic it's ridiculous. *You*, friends with The Prince? That will never, ever, *ever* happen!" Sassy begins hysterically laughing. "Oh my gosh," she gasps, bent over. "I can't stop laughing!"

That's it. I stand up. I have to. Without a word I move to my feet and get right in her face.

"Well, who is he?" I repeat, my eyes meeting hers. I can feel myself getting heated. My fists are clenched.

"'Well, who is he?'" Sassy mimics me, making her voice higher and singsongy. Some of the girls are giggling uncomfortably . . . then a stunned silence as Sassy stands in front of me with the biggest smirk on her face. "I'm sorry, excuse me," she continues, "does my always being right offend you? Or do you just like to stare?"

What a piece of work.

I keep my mouth shut. I grit my teeth. I just look back at her like, *Are you for real?*

Sassy hesitates for a second, grinning wide, then begins laughing again. "Who's The Prince?" she repeats, mocking me. "Oh my god. Like you don't know! Please, keep embarrassing yourself, Ellie! Like you don't know who The Prince is!" She looks right at me as she says it. "Duhhhhh! The Prince is Jack Malloy!"

37

ELLIE

SAMMY PRACTICALLY SHOVES ME OUT the back sliding-glass doors.

"Dude," he whispers, "this will be mad fun, I promise!"

When I step out into the night, the warm fall air hits my face. It smells good out here. Better than the basement. The seven of us stand outside in the huge yard. I tilt my head back and look up at the night sky full of stars. *I've never seen so many stars*, I think, smiling softly as I take it all in. I've never been outside in the middle of the night. I've never snuck out before! My heart is kind of racing, but in a weird good way.

Sammy plants his hand on my shoulder. "I can't believe you're finally loosening up, man, I've been begging you to sneak out and meet up with some ladies all summer! I love it, bro! The new you! Breaking some rules!"

I look back at Sammy. "Wait, hold up," I say, stalling.

Maybe this is a bad idea.

I look around at all the boys. Sammy and Owen on either side of me, Brayden, Dominic, Demaryius, Trey. All of them have a crazy-wild look in their eyes, the way you feel, I guess, when you're about to do something that you know you're not supposed to do.

Sammy tightens his hand on my shoulder. "We'll be fine!" he promises. "Loosen up, man. I'm proud of you. Even the great Jack Malloy needs to have a little fun!"

I grin lightly at Sammy, at all of them.

Trey laughs. "Dude, we need you. You're the chick magnet! No Jack, no fun."

Brayden nods, smiling. "He's right, man."

"Okay, fine, let's do this," I finally say, throwing my hand in the middle like the Thunderbirds do at soccer. The boys all follow my lead. One hand on top of the other. I feel the weight. I hold them all up, my hand anchoring the bottom.

Sammy laughs. "Say something inspiring quick, man. This is just a little bit girlie, bro!"

All the boys look at me, waiting.

"Any day now, big guy!" Demaryius says, grinning.

"Yeah." Trey shoots me a quick smile. "We don't want to *be* girls, bro, we want to *see* girls!"

They all laugh.

"Easy, boys, settle," I say, surprising myself at how

confident I sound. Then it comes to me in a flash, thank god—

"For the boys, with the boys!" I whisper into the starry sky. I can tell by the look in their eyes I said the right thing.

"For the boys, with the boys!" they all chant in a hushed, laughing whisper. Our arms shoot up into the night, and we all take a few steps toward the woods separating the elementary school playground and Owen's backyard. Sammy moves beside me, his shoulder brushing up against mine as we make our way across the grass toward the wall of trees.

"Dude, that little huddle action might be the girliest thing I ever did." He laughs. "But I like it, man. A little bro bonding to get 'er going!"

Then?

"Last one there is a girl!" Sammy shouts, and we all take off!

By the time we reach the woods, the race is on. I can barely see in front of me with the trees blocking the night sky. It's dark and silent except for the light, rhythmic sound of my feet barely skimming the ground, and I blow by them all, one by one. Nothing slows me down. Jumping over things, getting snagged by branches. I even crawl under a log on my hands and knees. I fly through those woods. I outsprint them all.

"You're a savage beast, Jacko!" calls out Sammy from behind.

"You're the man, buddy!" Demaryius hollers.

"You're hard core, dude!" says Brayden.

"Wait up, fellas!" shouts Dominic.

My legs fall into an easy stride. I breathe in the warm air, the quiet. I can't believe I'm still up, running through the woods in the middle of the night. It seems like I've been up for days. I think back to the mountain, my hand on the rock, the ice tubs. . . . Jett, Stryker, Gunner—they'd be proud of me right now. It's weird, but the darkness makes me faster. I feel almost invincible tonight. And I emerge first out of the woods, first to run on the wood-chip-covered playground, first to the swings by the kindergarten windows.

"Nails," I whisper to myself when I stop, my hands on my knees. I lift my head and smile at the guys. One by one they arrive, breathless. Now that we're out of the woods, I can see everything again. The stars are like glitter, crazy bright.

"Dang, Mallsy, you've got wheels," Demaryius says, slumping over, panting.

"Thanks, man." I grin.

I've heard it before. But this time, I believe it.

38
JACK ▶

THIS IS SO NOT A good idea, says the voice in my
head. Why? Um. Yeah. Glad you asked. I am clutching on
to Mackenzie's arm like a scared little girl as we tiptoe
up Claire's dark basement steps. Chirp me all you want.
I don't care. This is kind of intense. I've honestly never
snuck out before. Would you, if you had my dad? I can
hear him; he's in my head—"*When you get out of bed every
morning, you have choices to make. One bad decision is all it
takes.*" I push that all away. I block it out—I mean, I am
literally not myself right now.

Mackenzie looks me in the eye. "You ready?" she
asks.

I slowly nod my head. Yes. There's nine of us pressed
together in a clump, huddled by the back door. Whispering. Giggling. It's too late to turn back.

"Here goes nothing," I say softly, mostly to myself. Then—

I step into the night and run.

It's all for one and one for all the way we bust across Claire's huge backyard and hurtle through the thick, scratchy bushes on the side of the house. You'd think we were running for our lives, the way we race right down the middle of the dark street! It's like, one in the morning. There are no cars. The houses are all dark. It's so quiet. It seems like the entire world is asleep. Nothing is moving but the nine of us, giggling down the empty street in our pajamas.

By the time we slow down to a jog at the elementary school entrance, everyone just bursts out laughing. Not going to lie, I do too. In the middle of the night in the dark, things that usually aren't funny are. Do you know what I mean? I look up at the flickering stars. My mind is racing with so many thoughts. Thought number one? This is freakin' nuts! I'm running with a bunch of girls in borrowed drawstring purple pajama bottoms, Thunderbirds T-shirt, and Elle's sneakers. I put my hands on my knees and catch my breath. I'm still trying to wrap my brain around the fact that we're supposedly meeting all *my* friends—Sammy, Owen, Demaryius, Brayden, Dominic, Trey. I can't wait to see Sassy Gaines's dumb face when she realizes I'm not even there. Ellie, I mean.

She won't be there. I'm positive. That's one thing I'm sure of. We shook on it, right? For a second I think about the fact that I promised her too, but—

No. No way. I'd bet on it. She'd be too freaked out to go to Owen's by herself. I picture Freckles safely tucked in my bed. I hope she made it through the workout today. Man! Saturday mornings are rough. Grueling. I picture her sound asleep in my room, with Stryker. I hope that made things a little less scary, to have someone there. To not be alone. Stryker can be a goof, but he's my brother, man, and I love him. I always feel better when my brothers are around. They're my best friends in the world. I lie awake a lot, worrying something bad will happen to my brothers or my dad. Lately I have all these things I do. Like, I have to put my hockey equipment on just a certain way or I have this bad feeling like something is going to go wrong. Something terrible will happen to my family. I don't have anybody else. They're all I've got. They're everything to me. I have to act tough. Man up. Keep it in. I've never even talked about it with anyone before, not my brothers, not my dad. They'd think I'm so soft. . . .

It's been a year and seven months since my mom died. I act like I'm okay all the time. Like I'm so strong. Nobody knows how much it hurts. I haven't told anyone how I feel. I don't want people treating me different—it will just make it worse.

I'm standing in the dark in the middle of the elementary school parking lot, suddenly worried about a million things: *Is Elle okay? How are we even going to switch back? What are we going to do . . . like, lie on the cots in the nurse's office and click our heels?* My head is spinning when I feel a hand slip around my arm—

"Hey, girlie." I hear her voice before I see her eyes. When I turn and look, she's even prettier outside under the stars. Mackenzie.

"You okay?" she asks in a gentle voice, falling in step with me as we walk up the hill.

I let out a breath. "I'm fine," I say, and crack a smile.

"Okay, just promise me you won't get into it with you-know-who." She pulls me along, her arm in mine. "She's so not worth it. Promise, okay?"

"I'll try," I answer with a shrug.

"Try hard." Mackenzie smiles big. "We have too much fun, right? Life's too short for that stuff!"

"For sure." I nod. "Couldn't have said it better," I add, looking at her smiling.

Mackenzie returns my grin and shakes her head. "Seriously, girlie! You have the best smile ever!"

Blair, Tori, Sassy, Aspen, Sammie, and Kaitlin are waiting by the basketball court when Mackenzie and I walk up. I glance up at the net. The hoop is low enough that I can dunk with both hands. I've done it a few times, just messin' around. Sassy, of course, is talking loud, being as obnoxious as ever.

"Ahem," she says, looking straight at me. "Not to be rude? But girls trying to show off and act like they are popular when they are clearly not is literally the most counterproductive thing possible. Seriously? Just stop."

Man. I don't know how much longer I can take this before I snap. I just look at her in her dumb leopard-spotted pajamas and her tight cropped shirt and I shake my head.

Apparently she is not done. She won't quit. Sassy tosses her hair back and glances at me as she says, with a dumb half smile, "Do you think annoying people ever realize how annoying they are to everyone?"

"Come on, you guys." Claire wiggles in between the bunch and throws her arms around both of us, me and Sassy, pulling us in. "Look, let's just have fun. We're meeting the boys, right? Where are they, anyhow?"

Yeah. Where are they? I think, pulling away and looking around. Couldn't be better timing. I need to get away from this girl. *Man, I can't wait to see Sammy's face!* I think to myself, smiling and shaking my head.

Sassy sees me smile. "Oh, you think this is funny?" she asks. "You think I'm joking?" Her voice grows louder and louder, echoing across the empty basketball court. "Does anyone else feel like Ellie is going to *wow* The Prince on our starry night of adventure?"

She waits for a beat, and there's a hushed silence. "No?" She picks right back up. "Yeah, me neither!" She bursts out laughing.

"Sassy, come on," says Mackenzie. "Be nice."

"What?" She laughs. "Everyone was thinking it, I just said it!"

Man, every time Sassy talks, I just shake my head.

"Come on." Mackenzie places her hand on my elbow and pulls me forward. "Seriously, Elle, I can't take her anymore, really. Let's just start walking. They'll catch up."

At first I can't see anyone. I just see the jungle gym, the slide, the baby swings.

Then I see a bunch of—

"Sammy!" I say. I don't even realize it comes out of my mouth.

Mackenzie stops and turns back to the other girls. "Sammie!" she calls out to Girl Sammie. "Come join us!"

Girl Sammie runs to us and grabs my other arm. "Yay! Adventure!" she squeals as we walk toward the boys.

This time I say it my head. *Sammy*, I think, and look at his silhouette across the playground. With each step I take, we get closer and closer and I'm grinning big as if he'd somehow recognize that it's me. I smile. I shake my head, I give him a nod.

Sammy, man! Owen! Demaryius! Trey, Dominic,

Brayden! Little reunion tonight with the boys!

Oh, man. My heart drops.

I stop.

"No worries, Elle," Mackenzie whispers. "We'll have fun, I promise!"

Noooo. Please tell me I'm not seeing what I think I see.

"My hair," I say. I say it out loud, in disbelief.

"What? What about your hair?" asks Mackenzie. "Your hair looks totally gorgeous, Elle, I love it. Don't listen to anything you-know-who says. Really, seriously. Are you okay?"

I'm at a loss for words right now. I honestly don't know what to say.

Elle is standing across from me, six feet away, in my black Bruins hoodie and jeans.

"You shaved my head?" The words slip out.

"Wait, what?" asks Mackenzie, looking confused.

"My hair, it's—" I stop before I say the word "gone."

But trust me.

I'm speechless.

39
ELLIE

I ALMOST DON'T RECOGNIZE MYSELF. I have no idea what Jack has done, but I look like . . . I don't know. Something is going on with my hair. It looks—

"Wow," I say softly into the dark. Our eyes meet. Mine and Jack's.

I guess I look pretty shocked.

Dominic grins. "I know, man," he whispers, staring at the girls too. "Some hotties, right?"

"No, it's, um," I stammer and scan the line of faces standing six feet away—

Kaitlin.

Blair.

Claire.

Aspen.

Tori.

Sassy.

Mackenzie . . .

Jack!

Sammie.

What I'm thinking specifically is: *This can't be good.*

Sammy hits me with his elbow. "Dude," he whispers, staring at Aspen. "I got to wife that!"

"Huh?" I say. What does that even mean?

"Jacko!" Sammy is shaking his head. "You don't understand, man! I'm seriously in love!"

40
JACK

WE ALL STAND ON THE playground, staring at each other. The girls and I in our pajamas, the boys in jeans and sweatshirts, lined up facing each other with nervous starlit smiles on the Riverside Elementary School playground. We're on the little kids' side. Short, fat slides, baby swings, wood chips, jungle gym. Everybody is checking each other out. I have to continually remember that Sammy, Owen, Demaryius, Dom, and the rest of the boys . . . they have no idea it's really *me* over here, staring at them, smiling.

You're Freckles, remember? Thirty-six more hours, at least.

I can't help but look at her—or me, I guess—across the way. My eye and my nose look a little bit better, but man, I'm pretty ugly without hair. No flow. Dang. It's really gone. Like, *no* hair. None. Right down to the wood.

Well, I won't have to comb it, I guess.

I try and picture who convinced her to do that. My money's on Gunner. I bet they went to Geno's. No doubt. Gunner probably ordered up a fade and got one too.

I can't believe how ugly I look.

Mackenzie leans over. "Wow, The Prince got a little haircut, huh?" She giggles.

"Yeah, looks brutal, right?" I laugh nervously.

"No, not at all. I think it looks good, actually. Manly!"

I turn to her. "Yeah?"

"Totally, right?" asks Mackenzie.

I shrug and smile. "If you say so."

Sassy overhears us talking and decides to put on a show. She clears her throat. "Okay, everyone, question!" she says. She's not really talking loud enough for the guys to hear. Just the girls. "What does it take for a hopeless girl to realize someone doesn't like them and it's time to give it up?"

"Sassy, really, stop," Girl Sammie speaks up. "If you don't have anything nice to say, don't say it at all."

"Everyone honestly just needs to relax." Sassy laughs. "It's a joke, obviously. Just proving a point!" Sassy turns to me with a big fake grin and whispers over Mackenzie, "Ellie, seriously, you're probably the biggest scaredy cat alive!" She pauses. "*You*, friends with The Prince?" She rolls her eyes and lets out a loud laugh. "You're a pathetic little liar."

Oh, it's gonna be like that, huh? I think.

I'd be lying if I said this girl doesn't rattle me. I'm fired up. My fists are clenched. I'm not going to stand here and let Elle get ripped like this. I have to do something—

I step forward, pulling away from Mackenzie. It all happens quickly, before I lose my nerve. I catch Freckles's eye and, with a nod, signal her to follow my lead.

She does, thank god. She steps forward too. We meet in the middle, the boys behind her, the girls behind me. I can feel everyone's eyes on us.

Elle is looking at me like I'm nuts. "Are you crazy? What are you doing!" she whispers.

"Just listen," I say, my voice hushed. "Get closer."

She leans in. For this to work, I know I have to make it look like the guy makes the first move.

"Closer," I say.

She takes another step until the toes of our sneakers are almost touching.

"Perfect."

Elle's standing eye to eye with me. You can picture this, right? Me staring into my own eyes, my own busted-up nose, my ugly mug, my bald, shaved head. Oh, man. Elle looks completely freaked.

"Grab my hand," I whisper.

"What? Are you crazy?" she asks again.

"Just do it, please."

Then? She breaks into a quiet kind of smile. I'm

actually surprised. I haven't seen myself smile like that in a really long time. There's a little bit of fire in her eyes.

"Okay." She laughs softly. "Like this?"

I hear all the girls almost gasp. I swear, I do.

I glance around real quick. I sneak a look at the girls, first, then the guys. Sassy's eyes are about to fall out of her head. Everyone looks amazed and enthralled. Even Sammy is standing there with his jaw completely dropped.

"Go ahead," I tell her. I am looking right into my own eyes. "Plant your hands on my hips and pull me in close."

Elle's eyes—my eyes—get big. "Are you serious?"

"Trust me!" I repeat. "Please just—"

I don't even have to finish. Elle reaches out, rests her hands on my hips, and pulls me in. We're chest to chest. I don't exactly know what I'm doing, but by the sound of the absolute silence, whatever we're doing is working pretty well. I'm the perfect height for Elle. I rest my head on my own shoulder, put my mouth up close to my own ear. She . . . I . . . smells like sweat.

Man, this is nuts.

"Elle," I whisper. "What I'm about to tell you to do is going to sound insane. Please, if you ever want this mess to end, just trust me and go with it, okay?"

I feel her chest against mine. She takes the biggest breath.

"Okay," she says. I hear her. It's the slightest whisper.

"Awesome," I breathe. "Okay, on the count of three, I want you to let go of me, look at me for three seconds, then pull me toward you and kiss me right on the lips."

"What?!!" says Freckles. I feel her pull away, but then—

She stays. She holds on. I feel her heart beating through my own Bruins hoodie.

"Just go with it," I whisper. "Trust me," I promise.

I watch my own body, my own face, look at me for a second, then—

She does it. So clutch! She steps right toward me and pulls me in.

"Do it," I mouth.

And BOOM! She kisses me with my mouth half open, right on the lips! It's weirder than weird, kissing yourself. I can't possibly explain it. You can probably figure it out! Kissing yourself does not make any fireworks go off, or funny feelings shoot through your body. No sparks. No butterflies. I don't think either of us should ever officially count that as our first kiss. That's what I'm thinking as her lips are planted on mine. Man, this is more of a take-one-for-the-team kind of kiss. The team being me and Elle. And I sell it! I let her pull me in. I close my eyes like I see couples do in the movies. I make it count. It lasts a solid five seconds long. Then? I step back, I make a face like, "WOW!" I mix in a smile. Then I get right close to her ear.

"Perfection," I tell her. "Now put your hand up against my cheek."

"Are you crazy?" she whispers, sounding shocked. "Jack, what are you—"

"Just follow my lead. I'll explain everything."

She does it. She lifts her hand slowly and cups it against my face.

"Nice." I grin. "You're good at this." I wink. "Okay, one last step." I pause and take a deep breath. "Take my hand," I whisper, grinning, "and walk away fast."

"Wait, what?" Elle looks back at me, absolutely flustered. And for those next few seconds, it's like time just suspends. I can hear every whisper, I can hear the night, the stars. Then—

She does it! She smiles ear to ear and takes my hand!

"That-a-girl," I say. I actually say this, it slips out. I'm legit proud of her, as strange as that sounds. It's a ballsy move, everything she does. She plays me really pretty decent! I'm not embarrassed at all. She looks smooth. She lets out the tiniest grin and takes my hand, weaves her fingers through mine, and the two of us walk away in the stunned silence toward the far-off older kids' playground on the other side of the school. I scan the darkness as we walk. Look up at the sparkling stars.

"Just keep breathing," I whisper. "Keep moving forward."

Elle looks at me and laughs. "You sound just like Jett."

"Ha, yeah." I grin. "I guess I do."

It's so weird, it's like she knows me now. I guess I kind of know her too.

I turn to her and smile and hold on to her hand tighter as we walk. When we are a good ten yards away from them all, I look back over my shoulder at Sassy.

Oh, yeah. You think I can resist? No. She's the biggest clown of all time. I make sure to toss in a wave and a really big smile.

41
ELLIE

OH MY GOSH. MY HEART is racing! My cheeks are sweaty hot. Jack is holding my hand, and the two of us are walking away from everyone fast!

"Are you crazy?" I ask.

"Just let's go, I'll explain," Jack says, gripping my hand tighter. "Keep walking for the swings." He nods toward the older kids' playground on the other side of the school. "Nice hair, by the way." Jack shakes his head and smiles. "You could have made me look somewhat decent." He stops, drops my hand, and runs his fingers over the prickly buzz.

"Dude," he says. "That feels so weird!"

I start to explain. "Sorry! I, um—"

"Let me guess." Jack begins to walk, weaving his fingers through mine again, leading me along. I'm surprised how relieved I feel at the touch.

"Gunner took you to Geno's?"

I nod.

"He ordered up a fade?" Jack smiles and shakes his head.

"Pretty much, and he got one too," I tell him, remembering it all. The chair. The clippers. The clumps of thick, dark hair falling to the floor.

Jack's eyes bug out. "Gunner buzzed his hair, for real?"

"Down to the scalp," I tell him, relieved that this fact seems to make Jack happy. We keep walking. Still holding hands. It's weird, but it doesn't feel strange anymore. It feels like I'm with a really good friend.

At the swings, I let go and look around. There's nobody in sight. All the other kids are back on the other side of the school, where we left them, at the kindergarten playground. It's quiet, and dark, except for the stars and a chorus of chirping crickets and the occasional frog.

I drop into one of the two side-by-side swings and push off, swaying lightly in the dark. For a minute neither of us talks. Then—

"Elle," begins Jack, sitting back in the swing beside me. "Hey, like, what did you tell The Captain about hockey tomorrow?"

I look back at him, confused. "You have hockey tomorrow?"

Oh, god.

He just stares straight ahead with this sad, blank look. "Man, I've never missed a practice in my life," he speaks into the dark. "We have a game Monday night." Jack turns back to me. He looks bummed. "I don't know what else we can do. I guess you'll just have to act like you're sick."

"Sick?" I picture myself with a washcloth draped across my forehead, pretending to shiver under Jack's thin blanket in his bed.

Jack pushes off, swinging back. "Look, the thing is, The Captain will tell you to play even if you're sick."

"Play if I'm sick?" I repeat. *My mom would never do that.*

Jack takes a deep breath, stopping the swing. "'Be a man. No excuses. Skate through it.' That's what he'll say."

I nod. I feel bad for him.

"Are you a good actress?" he asks, sounding suddenly hopeful.

I look back at him with my most reassuring smile. "Well, I'm you, aren't I?"

"True," says Jack, finally cracking a smile. "Just . . . I'm warning you, all right? It'll get heated. The Captain, I mean. You know, be prepared."

"I can handle it," I tell him. Even though I'm not exactly sure I can.

For a long time we don't swing. We just sit and hang, our hands both up, gripped around the chains, staring into the quiet, shady darkness.

"Well, what about you?" I ask, looking his way. It's so

strange to look at myself sitting there. I flash a smile. I try and lighten the mood. "You weren't even supposed to be here!" I let out a tiny laugh so he knows I'm joking. "I told you to stay in my room. Thanks a lot!"

"Yeah, ha. Sorry about that." Jack stands, takes a few steps and jumps up, grabbing the monkey bars. I watch him—with *my* body—use his arms to pull himself up and right over the top bars. He makes it look easy. I look pretty strong. Once he's sitting, he reaches down to help me.

"I got it," I tell him, hoisting myself up. We sit together, high off the ground, our butts balancing on the hard metal bar, our shoulders brushing, legs hanging down.

Jack looks at me and just shakes his head. "Weird, huh?"

"Totally," I agree. We exchange knowing smiles.

"Ahh, yeah . . . while we're sort of sharing information . . ." Jack looks embarrassed. "I went to soccer after school Friday."

"Wait, you went to soccer?" I overreact. Then stop myself. I haven't exactly followed his instructions either. I mean, I shaved the kid's head! I almost cried in front of his brothers. I came to Owen's. I snuck out. I did almost everything he asked me not to do.

Jack nods and grins. "Coach Carolyn loves you, by the way. She's cool, she's chill. She's actually really fun. And also?" He turns and looks at me as he says it. "You're really fast, Elle. You're really, really good."

"Thanks," I answer, and let out a smile.

"Um, also, after soccer . . . uh, well—you kind of had a checkup."

"Wait, what! You went to Dr. Swenson?"

"Yeah." Jack laughs. "You seriously don't want to know. Let's not even discuss that."

"Oh my gosh." I giggle. "I can't believe this."

Jack lies back, resting his shoulders on the parallel bar behind us. I copy him. Not exactly comfortable, but it will do. We are close. The entire side of my body is lightly touching his. I breathe in the warm quiet, stare into the stars. Normally, being out here at night in the dark would make me scared. But I'm not.

Jack whispers, "Better than your stickers, right?"

"Yeah." I sigh. "You got that right."

More quiet.

"Hey, what about The Captain?"

"What about him?"

"Like, um, he can be kind of, uh, intense. He wasn't always like that . . ." He trails off.

"The Captain's fine." I smile to try to help him not worry. "We've barely talked."

"He's not exactly the talking type. Well, what about my brothers?" he asks.

"I actually love your brothers!" I answer quickly. It's true.

Jack exhales loudly. "I didn't expect it, but I miss them, they're—"

"Kind of awesome," I finish for him. "My turn," I say. It's like a game. Twenty questions. "What about my mom?"

Jack's eyes light up. "Dude, your mom is *awesome*, man." He goes silent for a few seconds, turning back to the stars.

I suddenly feel awful.

Jack. His mom.

For a good minute it's totally quiet. I think he even closes his eyes.

"Jack?" I finally say his name.

"Elle?" he whispers back. His words sound dreamy under the night sky.

"So now what do we do?" I ask.

He turns and looks into my eyes—which is weird for obvious reasons! I'm looking into my own eyes, and he's looking into his. We both start to laugh.

Jack takes a deep breath. "This is so nuts!"

"So nuts," I repeat his words, shaking my head slowly. "I don't know what we can do besides find that nurse on Monday."

"Wait, like . . ." Jack turns to me again. "What did she say? Can you remember?"

"Something like . . ." I think for a moment. "'See the world through eyes anew, until you learn what's deep and true—'" I start, but then I forget the rest.

"'Heart and courage to speak and feel, will . . .'" He stops. "Dude, that's all I can remember. What do you think it even means?"

"I don't know," I answer softly.

Jack moves over just a little bit closer.

We turn back to the stars and the darkness. It feels good up here, lying next to him on the monkey bars. For a long time I just stare up and trace the sparkly lights, draw lines with my eyes . . . connect the dots. Only after a long, extended quiet, my mind begins to race—

"What was that kiss all about?" I blurt it out. "That was, like, um—"

"Messed up!" Jack shakes his head, and we both begin to laugh again.

"Kissing yourself." I stop. "That's the weirdest thing I've ever done!"

He grins. "Kissing and hugging and looking into your own eyes?!! Oh my god!"

We almost fall off the monkey bars laughing, like really laughing hard. It takes a few minutes before we settle down. When I finally get quiet again, and feel the growing hush, I sit up and stare straight ahead into the dark.

Jack sits up too.

"Hey," Jack says. He lifts his arm and rests it around my shoulders, pulling me in like Gunner and Jett. "The reason I did that? The kiss, I mean? I had to do it because your friend Sassy, she's, like—" He stops. "She's unreal."

My stomach drops. *Jack likes Sassy?* I don't have feelings like that for Jack, but after everything we've been through, I just didn't expect—

"Wait," I start. I look right at him. "You mean you think she's nice? You *like* her?"

Jack's eyes get crazy big and wide. "Nice? Like her?!! Are you kidding me? She's the lousiest person I've ever met in my life!"

"Jack! Please don't say that. She hated me before, now she's going to, like, never talk to me again!" For the first time I recognize a desperation in my voice that I haven't heard since—

Since I've not been me.

Jack just shakes his head and inches over. We couldn't be sitting any closer.

"Elle," he says.

"Elle?" It took me till now to realize he has changed my name.

"Elle." He smiles with his eyes. "Sounds good, right?"

I nod. I like the way that sounds.

"Look, seriously, Elle, listen," Jack continues. "Sassy is brutal, man! She's, like . . . she's really not a nice person, trust me. She said some—"

"Really mean things?" I interrupt.

"Exactly!" His eyes get big, he's not kidding around. "You get it, right? I had to do that. I had to. I can explain it

263

all later, but . . . I couldn't allow someone to walk all over you like that."

Honestly, part of me is so touched that Jack stood up for me. Relieved that someone else saw what I have been pretending not to see. I think this whole time I just thought I was doing something wrong. That there was something wrong with *me*. But this other side? God. I hate to even admit this part—I know Sassy can be mean, but I've never had another best friend. We've been friends since kindergarten. For the first time, what I am actually thinking, what I really feel falls out of my mouth.

"Without Sassy"—I look down—"I don't even have any friends."

"You're kidding me, right?"

"I'm serious," I say. I'm so embarrassed, I just look at the ground as I talk. "Sassy's been my best friend since—"

"Elle, the girl is a clown! Nobody needs a friend like that, she's—"

"I know she can be bad sometimes," I cut him off. "But, I mean . . . when she's nice, she's really nice." When I hear myself say the words, something just clicks in me.

Sassy hasn't been nice in a really long time.

Jack is looking at me like I'm crazy. "Are you kidding me, Elle? Seriously?"

"You don't understand! She can be—" I stop. I stop because for the first time I realize how pathetic I sound. *I can't believe I'm defending her.*

"Elle, look." Jack takes a deep breath.

I lie back again. My eyes scan the sky.

Jack lies back too, and we talk into the darkness. "Trust me," he says. "Stay away from her, Elle. Really, I swear to you, dude, friends don't treat each other like that." Jack turns to me again. Our faces are so close. "And you're kidding me about friends, right? Mackenzie and Sammie, they're both awesome. Don't you get it?"

"Get what?" I ask.

"You're amazing, Elle," he tells me. "Everybody loves you."

I don't know what to say back. It's just about the nicest thing anyone has ever said. I feel tears gathering in my eyes. It's almost like Jack has a sensor—even though it's dark, he can tell.

"Oh, hey, whoa, whoa, whoa! No tears, Freckles!" He bursts out laughing. We both do. Then we both just look up into the night for a long time until Jack finally says what we've both been avoiding.

"How are we ever going to switch back? What are we going to do?"

"I have no idea," I answer. "I guess we'll just have to figure it out."

"I guess," he breathes.

I give Jack a little nudge with my elbow. "Never thought I'd be out in the middle of the night looking at the twinkling sky with *The Prince* of Thatcher!"

"The Prince, please!" He grins, laughing lightly and shaking his head. "Promise me you'll never say that again."

I flash him a smile. "Face it, they're all in love with you! Don't get a big head."

"Whatever," he says, and grins.

For a minute again we don't talk. Then it just comes out.

"Jack, I'm so sorry about . . ." I pause.

"About what?"

"About your mom," I whisper.

I can hear him breathing. I feel his arm up against mine.

"Yeah," he finally says. His voice is so quiet. "Thanks."

42
JACK

WE'RE ABOUT TO JUMP DOWN off the monkey bars. We're about to jump down onto the ground and just make it through the last twenty-four hours. We have a plan. We're going to meet at the nurse's office door before the bell rings Monday. We're going to figure this out together. I have no idea how. But for the first time since this happened, I feel more sure than ever it's going to work out.

"After tonight, we just have one more day," I say.

"One more day," she says, echoing me, her eyes lighting up.

We hear them coming at the same time and both kind of take a deep breath.

"Here we go," Elle whispers.

"We can do this," I tell her, under my breath.

The entire group—six guys, eight girls—are walking toward us through the dark. I can hear Sassy, of course. She's so loud. I can hear her irritating snorts of laughter.

I look at Elle. "We got this," I tell her.

We both leap off, landing with a thump on the wood chips.

Sammy walks right past me, straight for Elle. He has on that goofy smile of his. He doesn't even try to keep his voice down. I can hear everything he says.

"Bro," he tells her, "you are an absolute stud!"

For a second I'm worried Elle might laugh, but she really is a good actress. So clutch.

"Whatever." She nods at Sammy. "I don't kiss and tell." She looks at me as she says it with a smile.

"She's a stunner," Sammy says, his voice cracking. "I've always loved redheads."

Demaryius just shakes his head. "Gorgeous *and* athletic. Dude, you have good taste."

"'Sup stud," Trey says, slapping Elle on the back. "A girl who can rock red hair? So hot."

You should see the look on her face when I catch her eye. They're all talking about her to, well . . . *her.* I can't see because it's dark, but I guarantee she's blushing.

The girls. They are just as bad—

Claire runs at me with open arms. "Oh my gosh! Oh my gosh! Oh my gosh!" she whispers, kind of loud. "I had absolutely *no* idea! Wow! Just, wow! Oh my gosh, seriously, Elle, this is, like, this is *epic*!"

"This is a major development!" Tori squeals, walking up behind me. "He's such perfection. He's *so* freakin' hot! Oh my gosh, you're literally the chosen one, Elle!"

I look at her and almost shake my head and laugh. That's the first time Tori has even talked to me tonight. She's suddenly a whole different person. Wow. True colors are coming out.

Kaitlin giggles. She's grinning too. "Looks like you won the lottery, Elle!"

I take a deep breath and catch Mackenzie's eye. Dang! I didn't think about that. Now how will I ever have a chance with her if she thinks . . . whatever. I can't worry about girls. I have to stay focused on making it through the next twenty-four hours. Then, you know, maybe I can fix this. Make it all right. I look at her through the dark and smile lightly.

Mackenzie sneaks up beside me. "Hey," she says softly. "That was kind of—"

"Surprising?" I finish for her. We both sort of laugh nervously.

"Yeah!" She grins.

"I know, random, right? Whatever." I try awkwardly to brush it all off. "I think Jack and I are just really good friends," I say. I have no idea where I am getting this stuff from. I sound like a friggin' girl. It's embarrassing! Man.

269

"Well, you're lucky, Elle." Mackenzie smiles and raises her eyebrows. "I'll tell you a secret," she says, leaning in and whispering again. "I used to have the *biggest* crush on Jack Malloy."

"You did?" I say. I let out a shy smile into the night. This feeling goes through my heart. I can't explain it. Mackenzie is just so, like, full of life. Her eyes are so bright, even in the dark. There's something special about her, it's hard to describe.

"Well, yeah," she goes on. "Major crush on him since, like, sixth grade. But don't worry, I'm over it." She grins at me. "He's all yours now!"

"You're over it?" I repeat. My heart sinks. "But wait, it's not like that, we're not, I'm not—"

Oh, man, this is so messed up.

"Well," she says, her eyes twinkling through the dark. "Whatever, it's all good! I'll always have your back, no matter what. Elle, seriously, I'm so pumped for you, girlie! Also, I'm really glad that he just walked up to you like that. You should have seen Sassy's face!" Her eyes jump to Sassy and Aspen, glaring back at us from the two side-by-side swings. "Oh, man." Mackenzie sighs. "I don't have a good feeling about this. This is going to get bad. Stay close to me, Elle, okay? I should have done more back at Claire's. I should have said something. I should have spoken up. Sassy's seriously scary intimidating. She makes everyone kind of terrified, right? She's a total

bully! Someone needs to stop her. She's out of control."
Mackenzie threads her arm through mine. "I don't know how to stop her, but, like, don't worry, okay?"

"Oh, I'm not," I say, looking right back at Sassy. "Trust me."

For a good twenty minutes we all sort of laugh and talk and joke around. Sassy and Aspen are off on the swings, doing their roll-their-eyes-and-glare-side-by-side thing. The rest of us are standing around the monkey bars. Trey is making us all laugh, showing off, doing pull-ups.

I see the headlights in the parking lot. Then I hear her. Owen's mom.

"Oh, man!" Owen cries out. "I knew it, Sammy! I knew this would happen."

"Owen! Boys! Get over here this instant!" Owen's mom gets closer. She's wearing her bathrobe, and she looks angry.

"Oh, snap," I hear Sammy whisper into the dark.

"We're dead." Owen sighs.

Then—

I watch Owen elbow Elle. "Dude," he whispers to her. "I think she called your—"

"Jack!" I hear. I feel instantly sick. I turn to Elle. Both of us stand there totally frozen. The panic in our eyes is equal. I can tell in one look that Elle knows how quickly this is going to go from bad to so much worse.

Suddenly, nothing about Sassy Gaines matters any-more.

Everyone else standing here? They all fade away. My eyes move between The Captain, getting closer, and the stunned look on Elle's face. And the voice in my head is shouting now: *Why am I even out here? I'm so stupid! I should know better! Why'd I even come? I should have just stayed at Elle's with Summer, then I wouldn't be in this mess now!*

Only then do I remember—as I watch The Captain get closer and closer with each step, in his jeans, his gray army sweatshirt, his Red Sox cap. He's not coming for me.

I turn to Elle again. She has her hands hidden in the front pouch of my black hoodie. She glances at me ner-vously. My heart is absolutely pounding. Everything in front of me appears to slow down. Everything is going horribly wrong. I watch The Captain stop and turn to Elle.

"Jack," he repeats. I can tell by his voice how livid he is.

"Yes, sir," Elle stutters under her breath. For a sec-ond I'm relieved she knew how to answer back. But then he reaches out and grabs on to what he thinks is *my* shoulder—hard.

"Get your tail in the truck," is all he says.

The Captain takes Elle by the arm, my arm, grabbing her. The look in his eyes is so intense. Elle glances at me as she walks past. She looks petrified.

"I'm sorry," I mouth as I watch her being dragged off.

"Monday!" I call after her. I say it loud enough for everyone to hear.

I can see her look back over her shoulder at me.

The look in her eyes is total fear.

THE CAPTAIN DOES NOT SAY one word as I walk behind him across the front of the school, down the hill to the truck. He doesn't yell. He doesn't even turn and look. He just walks out in front of me, at least ten steps ahead. And when we get to the truck, he gets in, reaches over, and unlocks the door on my side. I take a big breath before I vault myself up into the front seat and shut the door.

I can do this, I can do this, I tell myself.

I swallow back all the fear that is charging up my throat. Try and block out my own voice yelling in my head: *I caused this whole mess. I should never have snuck out! I should have thought about Jack. I just got carried away and—*

I glance sideways at The Captain. He looks so angry, like he's not even breathing. He's just—

Fuming. Eyes straight ahead.

Oh my god. I ruined everything. I can't even imagine how much trouble Jack's going to be in.

The rumbling engine is the only sound, and I look out of the corner of my eye at The Captain again. But it's like I'm not even here. He just drives. He does not even say a word. He backs up the truck, pulls forward, and turns out of the school.

And I get it. I get this thing. It's like . . . not talking? The complete and utter silence . . .

The darkness.

I think it's honestly worse than if he was saying something. Anything! Worse than yelling. Oh, man. I bite on my lip. I breathe in.

Hold it together, Elle, I tell myself. *You can do this. You can do this.* I say it over and over and over again in my head.

God, do I feel bad for Jack. My mom would never . . .

I lean my head against the window and stare into the dark, watch the streetlights on the side of the road flash against my eyes. I don't say a word. Are you crazy? I've only been a Malloy for a day and half, but I get it, okay? I know the drill.

Do not speak unless spoken to.

When The Captain pulls into the driveway and gets out, he doesn't slam the door. He shuts it and goes into the house and just leaves me there. Sitting alone. For a moment I'm relieved. But then it occurs to me that I'm sitting by myself in a truck in the middle of the night. I open the door and ease myself out.

Standing in the driveway, I flip up the hood on the hoodie and slip it around my head. It feels like a helmet, I guess. I keep my hands in the front pocket, walk up to the house, and open the door, preparing myself for the big conversation that's obviously about to unfold. The yelling and the grounding, the-stay-in-your-room-for-the-rest-of-your-life-ing. At least I won't have to make up some big excuse tomorrow for hockey. But when I step inside, it's dark. The house is completely silent. Pitch black. I feel around for the banister. Then I slowly and quietly make my way up the stairs. I slip into Jack's room. My eyes adjust a little. I can barely make out the lump that is Stryker, sleeping. I take a huge breath and pull back the covers on Jack's bed and, without a sound, slip under them. I don't even care that all my clothes are still on, the hoodie still pulled up around my face. I lie on my side, facing Stryker.

"One more day," I whisper out loud. It just comes out of my lips. *I can do this. I can do this.* I keep saying it like it's some kind of nursery rhyme in my head. I close my eyes. I feel so tired.

44
JACK

AS I THROW MYSELF DOWN the elementary school's sloping front hill, I can hear them shouting after me.

"Elle!" they yell. "Come back! Hey! *Ellllllllle!*" I'm pretty sure it's Mackenzie and Sammie and maybe Claire. Nothing matters. I don't even really care. It's like everything I was worried about before is gone. I don't stop at the bottom when I'm safely out of sight. I don't kneel down and tighten my sneakers before I take off. It's exactly one point seven miles from the school to my house. We've raced our bikes a thousand times, we've measured it out. I know it by heart. I know exactly what I have to do. And I don't care that I'm running down the dark, empty street in purple pajamas, or that Elle's long hair is spilling out behind me. My head is spinning, my heart is pounding.

One foot in front of the other. I run as fast as I can. It's so quiet. So dark. I feel like I'm moving through space. The air feels soft. The only sound I hear besides my breath is my feet striking the pavement. My head is filled with so many thoughts. I hear Jett's voice, calming me down. *"The only thing you can control is how hard you go."*

I kick into some higher gear.

I have to get home.

The closer I get, I'm an absolute mess. I'm sweating. I'm panicking worse than I even ever have. Everything in my head is spinning. My chest feels tight. I'm telling myself to calm down. *Calm down, Jack! Get a grip!* Honestly, I don't know if I'm more worried for Elle or more worried for me. I've worked so hard, and now it's all down the drain. He'll probably not even let me play. Make me call the coach and apologize for—

For what?! I don't even know. That's The Captain. Do the right things the *right* way. Use your head. I can picture him sitting at the kitchen table, staring silently at Elle. This is *my* mess, and he's going to take it out on her. Oh, man, if she cries? It's over! And The Captain doesn't even know about the fight at school! This is all just him heated over the playground thing. I've let everybody down. I want so bad to make my dad proud—show him that I can do what I'm supposed to do.

When I finally hit my street, I slow down to a jog, then

walk. There's an eerie stillness in the air. I look up for the stars, but suddenly the sky is darker now. *Hopeless*, I think, and drop my eyes.

"Pull yourself together," I tell myself out loud. I whisper it into the darkness as I approach my own house. Only when I finally get there? Suddenly my big idea seems really, really dumb. What am I going to do!!? Ring the doorbell!? Throw a pebble at my window!? I'd probably break the glass. I'm such an idiot! What was I even thinking, coming here? I stand there in the driveway I've stood in a million times. The same driveway where I've shot a million pucks. The same exact spot we train, the same place I push Gunner on a sled with weights. I stand there, then I crumple to the ground. I sit with my head in my hands.

The house is totally dark.

There's not even one light on.

I walk alone in the dark all the way back to Claire's. I'm getting closer. I'm almost there. My hands are cold and clammy and my legs are trembling. I'm just so tired.

As soon as I see her, my eyes flood with tears. I can't hold it back anymore. The car stops. Summer jumps out. And I lose it. I burst into tears. It just comes pouring out. I begin to sob. I fall into her arms. I just kind of melt. Summer wraps her arms around me and holds me so tight.

"Oh, sweetie," she whispers. "Oh, honey, Claire's mom

called. You had me *so* worried, why did you—oh, shhhh . . . sweetheart." Summer kisses me above my ear, on the side of my head. "Oh, honey. I'm here. Just let it go. It's okay. I'm here. I love you. We'll figure things out."

It's dark and quiet except for my sobs. Summer doesn't let go. She just holds me. She's strong. "It's going to be okay," she tells me in the softest whisper. I'm crying so hard snot is pouring out of my nose—her shirt is soaked. "It's okay," she whispers again and again. "It's okay, sweetheart—I know you're hurting. You don't have to be afraid anymore. We'll get through this. It's going to get better."

"JACK!"

I open my eyes and squint. The light is on. The Captain is standing in the doorway dressed in jeans, same gray army sweatshirt, same red baseball cap from last night.

"You have exactly five minutes to get up, get your bag, and get in the truck."

That's all he says. Then? He's gone.

"Um, I'm, uhhh . . . sick!" I call out, pathetically weak. "I don't feel well," I add.

The Captain appears in the doorway again. He stands there looking at me, his arms folded across his chest.

"Can you breathe?" he asks.

I nod yes. "But, um, my eye. It hurts."

"Can you see?" he asks.

"Yes, sir," I answer softly.

"Well then, you can skate."

"But, I, I—" I start, but then I stop. The look on his face makes me shut up.

He checks his watch. "You are wasting time, Jack. Four minutes. You better have your butt in the truck."

I wait for The Captain to leave and glance at the clock. It's 5:55 a.m.! What do I even do? *I promised Jack.*

Stryker flips over and looks at me like I'm nuts. "Dude, are you crazy? You're never late to hockey. C'mon, man! Get up!"

"I can't, I just, um—"

"Get up, man! What's wrong with you, dude?" Stryker sits up, groggy, rubbing his eyes and yawning. "I'm going to take a leak." He stands and looks back at me from the door. "Bro, Captain's gonna lose it. You better move."

Oh my gosh! What do I do? What do I do?

I sit up. I listen to the seconds ticking away on the clock. My heart is racing. *Think, Elle, think! I made it through this far, right? The mountain, the lifting. I can do this,* I tell myself. I know what Jack said. But if you could see the look The Captain gave me—

You'd do just what I'm doing, which is getting up immediately out of this bed. When The Captain tells you to go, you go. I hightail it to the bathroom and nearly collide with Stryker in his boxers, no shirt.

"Uhhhh," I stammer, sounding like a total nervous wreck.

Stryker yawns, stretching his arms up above his head. "Bro, what's wrong with you?"

"It's just, oh my gosh," I say. I feel like crying, but I don't. Instead, I look at him and take a deep breath. "Stryker?" I say. Then just blurt it out. "Where's my bag?"

"Settle, man." He looks at me, confused. "Dude, you're acting nuts, but whatever. You piss. I'll make your bed and get your bag from The Cage. Chill, little man, clear your mind. Figure it out, bud. *Do not freak out.*"

Do not freak out. Do not freak out. I repeat it in my mind. I slip into the bathroom, splash my face with cold water, look in the mirror. Jack's eye and nose are better. Still a little bit sore and purplish yellow.

"Hockey, okay, you can do this." I exhale and force a smile. Then I turn toward the window, pull the curtain away, and peek out. It's still dark. The Captain is already in the truck in the driveway. The headlights are on. "If you can see, you can skate." I mutter The Captain's words, like that's going to somehow help.

One minute later, I'm busting down the stairs, dressed in the same clothes I was wearing last night. Jeans. Black hoodie. Slipping on Jack's sneakers. I've honestly never been so grateful to anyone in my life than when Stryker—still dressed only in his boxers—suddenly appears out of the basement carrying Jack's enormous bag of equipment.

"Stryker, oh my gosh, I love you!" I say. It just tumbles out.

He looks at me with a puzzled expression. "I love you too, man. I don't know what's gotten into you, big guy, but you're gonna do big things today." He pauses and flashes me a smile. "Breathe, man. You got this. You're a stud."

I take the bag, throw it over my shoulder and turn to go—

"Whoa, bro, you're unreal this morning." He laughs, pulls me back with his palm planted on my shoulder, and hands me two hockey sticks. "You're gonna need your twigs, bud."

"Thanks," I manage. Stryker has a calmness that kind of rubs off on me. I look at him and feel like, you know, maybe this might work out somehow.

"And hey, bro?" he adds.

I pause in the open front doorway and look back at Stryker.

"Whatever it takes, man," he tells me. "Don't give up. Ever."

I heave Jack's hockey bag into the back of the truck and jump up into the seat that I was sitting in, like, four hours ago. Now I'm wide-awake.

I'm wide-awake and going to play hockey!

The last time I went public skating, I was ten years old. I glance at The Captain. I don't look too long. He's intimidating, with his silence. Before we back out of the driveway, before the truck moves? The Captain, without looking at me, hands me a mug of something that smells disgusting. I take it from him and slowly put it up to my nose. *Oh my gosh. So. Gross.* But I don't cringe. You think I'm nuts? I'm not about to tick this guy off. I have to suck it up. I have to do this for Jack.

"Thank you, sir," I say, bringing the plastic cup to my mouth. I take a big swig and try not to grimace. Then I just count to five, close my eyes, and drink the rest of it.

The Captain does not speak the entire way to the rink. Not a word. I keep my head turned away. I try not to throw up the fishy banana smoothie. I watch the light rise out the window on the highway. A violet blue haze. There's way more people up at 6:17 a.m. than I thought. Cars whizzing by us, traffic. By the time the truck pulls into the rink, I feel the worst pit in my stomach. I have no idea how I'm going to pull this off. But I have to try. It's too late now. I put my hand on the door handle and take a deep breath.

"Jack," says The Captain, finally breaking his silence.

I turn and look back. He's not smiling. *What did I expect?*

"Yes, sir?" I say. I keep my hand on the handle. I do not move.

"This can all be gone in an instant."

"Yes, sir!" my voice trembles, and I go to move, but I feel his hand grab me by the shoulder and pull me back.

"Did I say you're dismissed?"

I feel this awful pang in my heart. "No, sir!" I answer nervously.

"About last night," he says. "Look at me."

I turn. I do. I turn back toward him. "Sorry, sir," I say softly. I won't lie. I'm working with everything I have to hold back tears.

He doesn't bat an eye. "No excuses."

"Yes, sir," I answer quietly.

"There's no gray area. It's black and white. Men do what they have to do. Boys do what they want to do."

I have no idea what that means or what I'm supposed to say. We sit in the truck in total silence for at least a minute. Even the engine is off. I watch other boys get dropped off, laughing, smiling, bags over their shoulders. They all look bigger and older than Jack.

What have I gotten myself into? I think, and watch them disappear behind the double metal doors of the rink.

Finally The Captain takes a deep breath. "Go," is all he says.

"Mallsy, got the flow chopped!" I hear it as I approach the doors, Jack's huge hockey bag strapped over my shoulder. I'm clutching his two sticks.

I glance back. The voice is coming from a tall, bright-eyed kid with stringy, long blond hair sticking out of his baseball hat. The closer he gets, the bigger his smile grows. "'Sup, dangler! Nice buzz cut, looks good, bud. Getting ready for game day! Sick style, Mallsy. I love it, man." He grabs the door of the rink and holds it open for me.

I guess I'm lucky everybody loves Jack. I grin awkwardly

at Happy Blond Kid and focus on fitting through the door with this huge bag. Inside, the air hits my face. It's cold in here!

Happy Blond Kid walks a few steps behind me. "Time to do work," he says.

I glance back over my shoulder and give him one of those guy nods and keep my eyes focused straight ahead, walking down the hallway.

"Mallsy!" Happy Blond Kid calls out to me. "Where you goin', bro?" He laughs. He's stopped in front of a door a few yards back. "Unreal." He smiles and shakes his head as I stop and walk back toward him. "Ha! Classic!"

When I walk into the crowded locker room, nobody even looks up. It's like an entire world in here of wide-awake, laughing, chattering, bare-chested, smiling guys. There's music blaring from speakers attached to the wall. Every guy is sitting, half-dressed, side by side on wooden benches. Hockey bags cover the floor. And *man*. It stinks in here. I have to concentrate hard to keep my nose from scrunching up.

I sit down in the first empty seat I see and throw the bag down on the floor.

The kid next to me looks up under his baseball cap.

"That's Bugsy's spot, bro."

"Oh! Sorry." I jump up and move to the only other empty seat across the room. I have to sidestep a zillion hockey bags, Jack's huge bag of gear slung across my back. *Okay*, I think, throwing it down again. Settling back into the seat, I glance nervously around.

This is going to be . . . interesting, I think, and almost laugh out loud. I have absolutely no idea how to put this stuff on.

With the music blaring and guys talking and laughing and tossing things at each other, I come up with a pretty decent plan: my own solo game of Simon Says. Only nobody is calling out moves. It's just me watching Happy Blond Kid across the room. I copy every move he makes.

He strips down to his boxers. I do too.

He reaches into his bag and fishes out—

A jockstrap.

You can't not laugh. I try not to stare as I watch him slip it over his boxers. Then? I copy exactly what he does. And voilà! I am now standing with a hard shield protecting Jack's, um . . .

Stuff.

Next is this strap thingie that looks complicated. What the heck is this? I put it on—it's like a belt with these hanging buttons and hooks. Whatever. I have no idea. I just play the game and copy the next move. Happy Blond Kid sits back down on the bench, pulls big gold socks over his shin pads, first the left, then the right. He stands and—oh, that's what it's for. I almost nod. The hooks on the belt hold up the socks. This isn't as hard as it looks. Happy Blond Kid steps into a pair of giant pants that look like padded shorts. I find Jack's and step into mine too.

Okay. Next. Skates. First the right, then the left. I start at the bottom and pull the laces one at a time, work my way up to the top, pull real hard, and tie them at the top like a sneaker. Okay. That's it, right? I look around. No. Not yet. Shoulder pads. Elbow pads. Jersey. I slip the jersey over my head, one arm at a time, only it gets hung up on the shoulder pad. Oh, great. I kind of laugh. I'm sitting in a room with twenty guys, with a jersey stuck up around my eyes.

"I got you, Mallsy!" says the kid next to me, yanking the caught-up jersey down.

"Thanks, man," I say. I grab Jack's helmet. Throw it on my head. Slip on his gloves and stand in my skates.

I feel like I'm going into a battle. I follow the guys. And it's Happy Blond Kid who looks at me funny right before we file out.

"Mallsy, better bring your stick." He laughs. "What's up with you, dude?"

"Oh, thanks," I say through the face mask, embarrassed. I grab one of Jack's sticks, clutching it like a sword in my leather-palmed glove. And that's it. I fall back in line. Somebody's dad smacks us on the back as we file by. "Keep it rollin', boys!" he barks, half smiling. "Show 'em what you're made of!" We march out like an army.

I'm the last guy out of the room.

46
JACK

WHEN I WAKE UP IN Elle's big bed, sun streaming in the window, the comforter pulled up to my chin, I honestly feel better than I have in a long time. I curl up and dig the sleep out of the corners of my eyes. I feel like I haven't slept that well in forever. I didn't toss or turn, or wake up sweaty and worried like I usually do. I just slept. Long and deep. And opened my eyes, and it feels good—

It feels good for about three seconds. Then?

I remember.

I remember everything.

The look in my dad's eyes. The fact that I'm missing hockey for the first time in my entire life. What a complete wreck I was last night. I was crying so hard. The messy kind. Big, gasping breaths. I couldn't even speak. I remember Summer tucking me in. Sitting with me. I didn't say a word. All I did was cry. I remember sobbing my eyes out before I finally fell asleep.

Oh, man. I flip over and smash my face into the sheets. Breathe in the clean.

Less than a day to go.

I'm going to miss this bed. My mind begins to fill with the obvious thoughts: *safe to say, I'm probably grounded. I'll probably have to transfer to Saint Joe's.* I picture myself in the tie and that dumb navy-blue blazer, tan pants. Elle's brave! Man. She got into the truck. She went home. I can't believe she did it. Ballsy move. Took some jam! This makes me laugh. Well, obviously Elle doesn't really have—

Ha. Yeah. Don't want to think about that. I close my eyes again. I'm so exhausted. I don't think I ever want to get out of this bed.

"Ellie, hon?"

I hear a light tapping on the door and look up.

"Sweetheart." Summer pokes her head in, then enters, sitting down quietly on the bed. She reaches out and places her hand against my face. "Hey, honey," she says softly. "How are you feeling? A little bit better?"

"A little," I answer slowly. My voice sounds scratchy.

Summer looks at me gently and takes a deep breath. "At some point, sweetheart, we're going to have to talk about what exactly happened, but for now?" She pauses for a long time, smiling at me with her eyes. She leans in and kisses me on the forehead, keeping her lips there for a long moment. "Oh, honey pie," she whispers. "Sometimes you just need your mom."

Downstairs. I walk into the kitchen wearing Elle's big fuzzy slippers and slip into a seat at the table by the window. It felt good to wash my face and pull my hair back. I'm wearing baggy sweats and a perfectly broken-in Boston College soccer T-shirt—I vaguely remember shedding the clothes from the party and putting these on last night. I watch Summer by the stove, flipping pancakes until she looks over and sees me sitting at the table.

"Oh, hey, hon," she says, turning to me, smiling. She's dressed in the same yoga outfit from the day I met her. "Did you take a nice bath?" she asks.

"No." I shake my head and manage a slight smile.

"No? Well, did you at least splash your face? That's always a good step."

"Yeah." I nod.

"Well." Summer grins. "I hope you're hungry, I made enough for an army!"

The word "army" makes me think of my dad. And I'm pretty sure a worried look fills my eyes.

I wish I was at hockey right now.

I glance up at the clock. The boys are probably just leaving the rink, bags on their shoulders, walking across the parking lot, laughing, joking. No better way to start the day than skating. I love the feeling after a good skate. Going back to the house, working out with my brothers. Every Sunday.

Summer hands me a glass of orange juice. "Sweetie? Hey, you okay?"

"I'm fine," I lie. "Thanks," I say, and lift the glass to my mouth. I'm suddenly so thirsty I guzzle it all in one long gulp.

"So listen, are you up for soccer? Because if you are, we have to leave in—" Summer pauses and glances at the clock. "About an hour. Look, honey," she goes on. "Last night was a lot. I don't know what's going on. But I'm going to leave it up to you. I trust your judgment. And like I said, we really do need to talk about what happened. But we can do it after soccer."

I look up at her. She's just, like, so nice. Her eyes are so bright. I love Summer. I know that sounds weird because, like, I hardly know her. It's just—

It feels like I do.

"Honey?" she says, still standing, smiling down softly. Waiting for me to speak.

"I'll go," I answer quietly. I try and smile too. At least Elle told me it's okay with her. It'll be good to sweat. Good to move. I don't even care if I see any of the girls from last night. I don't care what anyone says. I'm just going to keep my mouth shut and try to have fun.

"I'm really glad to hear you're up for soccer." Summer breaks into a huge smile. "And if you're going to play," she goes on, walking back to the stove, "you're going to have to eat."

She returns to the table with a plate full of stacked, steaming pancakes. They look so good. They may or may not be in the shape of a heart! Summer's so awesome. I unfold the napkin on my lap and take a good look around. Elle's kitchen is pretty much the opposite of ours. It smells like butter and sugar, or like—vanilla. Vanilla cake. And everything is bright and warm. There's flowers on the table. Summer brings herself a plate too and sits down across from me.

I wait for her before I eat. That's what we used to do with my—

She looks at me. "Dig in!" Her eyes are really, really pretty. They look exactly like Elle's. Same freckles, same long, deep-red hair hanging down past her shoulders, parted in the middle. And I know this sounds weird, but I just look at her and I practically feel like crying all over again.

"Thank you," I say, taking my first bite, then quickly shoveling in another.

"I'm glad to see that smile," Summer says. She winks through the yellow-and-pink flowers. And the two of us eat in silence. But it's not the empty kind of quiet. If that makes any sense at all.

47
ELLE

I FOLLOW THE REST OF the boys down the long hall, marching single file in our skates and equipment/armor, across a rolled-out black rubber mat, sticks in hand. Everyone's hyped, shouting out random let's-get-fired-up-type cheers in deep he-man sounding voices.

"Make a little noise, boys!"

"Time to get after it! Let's go, boys!"

"Battle it, boys! Can't wait for tomorrow!"

I stop at the gate right before I step onto the ice. It's a tiny step down, and I freeze and brace myself. I feel like a scared baby deer, if you've ever seen one. I have the serious jitters; my legs are shaking, I'm trembling—I'm pretty sure my feet are going to come out from under me as soon as I step onto the ice.

What am I doing? This is insane! is what's going through my head. And right when I am actually considering turning around and making something up, this big man dressed in an all-black Boston Junior Bruins warm-up suit and a shiny black helmet walks up behind me and scares me half to death!

"Let's go, Mallsy! Be ready!" he barks. He's chomping on gum. He has a whistle around his neck. "Get out there and show 'em what ya got. Dominate, Malloy! Let's see what you're made of!"

Um. Yeah. Look, I don't know what the deal is with guys hitting each other. But what comes next is another smack on the back. *Whack!* I almost choke. I'm not expecting it! This springs into motion the next range of events. Let me spell it out so you can (please) *not* laugh.

The slap on the back, the push, the forward lean, the step down onto the clean white ice—

It's so crazy! I don't even have to think! I dig in with my right foot and push off. Only instead of falling on my face like I thought? Jack's body goes into some kind of effortless autopilot! Everything just, like, clicks! I don't have to even think. I can hear the ice crunch under my strides, first my left foot, then my right. I feel the cold air in my throat—I can see my breath—oh, wow! The nervousness just vanishes. If you could see my eyes through the cage on my face mask, you'd see I'm smiling so hard! Jack's good! He's fast!

I can't believe it took us this long to figure it out. Jack has my body, and I have his: *I can do anything he can do!*

Everything on the ice is easy. It flows. I dig into the ice, push off the edge, and just glide. Push and glide. I start to go faster and faster. It feels so smooth. I follow the rest of the boys. I take big, powerful strides around the surface. Guys are stretching, playing with the pucks, getting warmed up—I can't stress how easy it is! And not just skating: stick-handling the puck! It's like I have a string attached to the puck. It never falls off. I pull it side to side, from the left to the right. One side to the other. It's one fluid movement. I flow through the first part of practice.

And when the big guy in the black helmet blows the whistle and calls us to the center, I'm the first one in. I take a knee just like the other guys do.

The coach chomps on his gum and spits on the ice before he talks. He waits until the boys settle down. While he's waiting, I look up in the stands. I see The Captain looking back, watching me. My heart begins to pound, and I'm not gonna lie. I'm more nervous right now than I've ever been. It's like I'm suddenly not worried about anything but right here, right now. I don't want to mess up. And kneeling here, with all the guys, I feel confident, almost proud. I can see why Jack loves this. He's really good. He's playing with the best.

The coach looks right at me as he talks. "Boys, we've got our first game tomorrow, and we have to practice today like we're going to play tomorrow. I want to see intensity. Win our battles. Execute. If we do that today, we'll win our game tomorrow." He pauses and looks for a moment around the team. Again his eyes stop and zero in on me. "All right, men! Let's go!"

For the next fifty minutes I am focusing with everything I've got. Warm-up drills, skating drills, passing, warming up the goalies with shots.

I line up the puck and I shoot, following through. Somehow my body knows what to do.

"Mallsy, nice rocket!" I hear.

With ten minutes to go, I'm basically in love with hockey. I've never had so much fun. Jack's so good and so strong and quick. It's almost like he can dance on his skates, the way his body moves with so much grace. The last drill is a shootout with a chaser. The coach dumps the puck in the corner. Two guys chase after it; the guy who gets to the puck first tries to score. I wait my turn. I can hardly hold it in. I'm so happy, I glance up at The Captain. I swear I almost want to wave!

I step up to the line. It's me against a guy who's a lot bigger than Jack.

"You boys ready?" asks the coach. But before I nod yes, he fires the puck deep in the corner. "Get after it, Mallsy!"

The other kid has a jump on me, but I chase it. We both head into the corner at full speed, and I beat him to the puck. I get there first. The battle is on. I'm not even thinking; my body just moves. I'm reaching for the puck when the kid cross-checks me hard across the chest. It's not just a shove. It's a blast. It sets me back. The kid starts chirping me right there in the corner as we fight for the puck. "You want to go, rookie?" He gives me another shot, slashing me on the arm, checking me into the boards, cracking my shoulder. My first instinct is to just shove him back. But I know that would be dumb, to let this kid draw me in to that. Instead I battle for the puck, dig it out, and head straight for the net. Fake the goalie by shifting the puck to the wide left, and when he bites—cut back and slide the puck past him into the open net.

"Yes!" I whisper to myself. I try not to celebrate. *"Be humble,"* Jett said. I try and act like I score all the time. But man, did that feel good, to take control.

The kid skates up behind me as we fall back into the line.

"What are you doing, rookie?" He gets right up in my face, stares at me and shakes his head. "Why'd you come at me like that? We have a game tomorrow, man! You want to go, man, you want to throw bones?" He gives me a little shove again.

What? He came at me! Kid's got a chip on his shoulder, is what first runs through my mind. But something happens in this moment, and I take a step back. I give him a nod—I shrug it off. It's like Jett and Gunner and Stryker are all here with me now—*Scared dogs bark the loudest.*

Don't have time for haters. Stay focused. Keep your head up. Keep going.

And for the rest of the practice, I feel a jump in my step. I feel stronger, faster. I play with an edge. And when the coach blows the whistle at the end, I'm actually wishing it wasn't over. I'm so pumped! I feel like I can do anything. I feel so strong. Time flew by! It was like—

I fell into a trance.

It was like magic.

We take a knee at center ice. I'm breathing pretty hard. I feel the sweat dripping down the side of my face. The coach chomps on his gum and just looks at us for the longest time. All you hear is quiet, and the buzz of the lights overhead.

"Boys," he finally says, pausing to spit. "I normally don't like to single one guy out, but today I saw something and—" The coach stops again, his eyes narrow. It gets real quiet. My heart starts pounding.

Maybe I did something wrong?

When he starts back up he's looking at me. "If we can play with the heart and intensity Mallsy showed today, we'll be all right. Tough, tough kid. There's no quit in him." The coach stops and gives me a nod and a smile, and I feel all the guys look at me. They begin clapping their sticks against the ice.

"Mallsy!" "Stud!" "Atta boy!" "Rookie's a dangler, man!"

Coach waits for the guys to settle down. "Malloy." He

looks directly at me again. "You went into the corner real aggressive, but you didn't bite when Boomer cross-checked you like I've seen you do before. Good discipline. Boomer's a pretty imposing guy. Being able to have guys on your back and take those hits in traffic and still take the puck and put it in the net—well done." He looks around at all the guys. He speaks slowly, carefully choosing each word. "I want that intensity tomorrow, boys. The retaliator always gets the penalty. Play with passion, but use your head. Tomorrow's going to be a battle. We are going to outwork and outplay. We are going to bring tenacious effort." He stops again, a smile finally taking over his face. "We're going to take a note from Mallsy and fore-check like crazy."

"Mallsy!" The guys all clap their sticks again.

"First on puck and drive to the net. Get some rest tonight, boys. Eat well. Recover, stretch. Come ready to work hard and execute for sixty minutes tomorrow night!"

I'm skating off, soaked in sweat. I'm smiling so big right now! I worked harder than I have in my entire life. I played tough. No matter how hard it got, I never quit. I glance up at The Captain, watching from the highest seats in the arena. Man, he's going to be proud! The guys are all whacking me on the butt with their sticks. In a good way.

"Great practice, kid! Wouldn't expect anything less from you, Mallsy."

"Let's get it, boys!"

"Let's get this thing started tomorrow, boys! Crushin' it, Malls!"

The kid who cross-checked me, the one who took the cheap shot? He comes up behind me as we file off the ice. "Sorry, Mallsy," he says, cracking a smile. "I lost my head, man. No hard feelings?"

"Sure, man. Forget about it," I tell him. It's so easy. It just falls out of my mouth. "No worries, bro," I say, and mix in a smile. And I mean it.

48 JACK

SUMMER TURNS INTO THE SPORTSPLEX, but instead of going into the drop-off circle, she takes a right and pulls into an open space in the parking lot.

"I thought for a change I'd come with you!" she tells me.

We walk in together, side by side. It's different than getting dropped off by my dad. He usually parks the truck, gets a cup of coffee, and appears at the start of practice. He stands in the same spot. Every time. He doesn't talk to anyone. He just keeps his eyes glued on me from the highest seats in the arena. He watches everything. Then we go over it on the way home. Usually how I screwed up. What I did wrong. How to get better. Make adjustments. "It's the little things, Jack," he tells me. "You have to do it right."

Whatever.

I glance over at Summer. She throws her arm around me as we walk, flashing me a big smile. "Am I going to ruin your reputation if I give you a hug?"

"No." I grin. I lean in. It feels good. "Not at all," I say.

"And look, don't worry, I'm not going to cheer or anything." She laughs, "One, I don't know a thing about soccer, and two, I think you're pretty much perfect, so I'm a little bit biased." Summer's eyes light up. "I brought a really good book." She smiles as we walk up the steps. "I won't make a peep. Just know I'm here, okay? I'm not going anyplace."

Inside, the Sportsplex is packed. Humming with kids with sweaty red cheeks, colorful jerseys, packs slung around their shoulders. A traffic jam at the snack bar, kids slurping back slushies, little brothers and sisters swarming around the video games, the trophy case. Summer and I walk through all of that and go separate ways when we reach the turf. She gives me a quick smile and walks off with her book toward the rest of the parents and the stacked metal bleachers.

I scan the fields for the Thunderbirds and their pink-striped socks. I'm hoping I'm a little late and I don't have to talk. Hoping everyone's already kind of warmed up and I can just, like, slip in, unnoticed.

Yeah. Not so much.

When I jog out onto the turf, the last field on the end? They all look up.

Sassy.

Aspen.

Claire.

Mackenzie.

Girl Sammie.

Before anyone even has a chance to say anything about what happened, I'm saved by a whistle. Coach Carolyn.

"Let's go, girls, bring it in!" she hollers out, standing in the middle. Same black warm-up, same visor, same ponytail. Big smile. We gather in the center. One tight pack. I feel Mackenzie's hand grab on to mine.

"So glad you made it," she whispers, and smiles.

"Lots to cover, ladies. Last day of tryouts." Coach Carolyn's tone is all business. "Today is going to be similar to Friday. But last time I looked at your passing and receiving skills and how you can combine with your teammates around, and today I'm going to look more at your dribbling skills and your one-versus-one attacking goal."

I keep my eyes on Coach, but I still feel it.

Sassy.

She's glaring at me. I see her out of the corner of my eye. It's, like, the meanest look I've ever seen. I glance toward the sidelines and look for Summer in the crowd of parents on the metal bleachers. She's there just like she promised, reading her book. I take a deep breath and turn back toward Coach Carolyn.

"So just like Friday, everybody is going to make mistakes. I just want to see how you react to mistakes. Put your best effort in, okay, ladies?"

Everyone's nodding. You hear some feet shuffling.

"Okay, so this is how practice is going to look—we're going to warm up, we're going to break into stations, we're going to rotate through the stations, then end with some one-v-ones going to end line and wrap up with one-v-ones to the big goal. Sound good?" She looks at me and smiles.

"Yes, ma'am!" I say. It slips out. Automatic.

I hear Sassy say under her breath, "What a kiss-up."

After the first hour, I'm pretty sweaty. I've been playing hard and manage to keep myself out of any major Sassy conflict. I stay far away from her, and if she comes near me, I keep quiet. No talking. No eye contact. When I feel like I want to punch her in the face? I just look toward the bleachers at Summer. With her shiny, long red hair, it's easy to spot her. She's the only mom not watching, just reading.

"Okay, girls, bring it in!" Coach Carolyn calls us in for the last drill. I'm breathing hard. The tryouts are pretty intense. I slip in between Girl Sammie and Mackenzie. I feel a little bit like they're my bodyguards, the way they leave a little space for me in the huddle and make sure nobody else is between us. Coach Carolyn's instructions are kind of complicated. In hockey I just know where to go, I don't even have to think. But out here on the turf, I have to really concentrate and listen.

"We're going to finish with one-v-one to goal. Everyone who is in a red pinnie, I want you starting next to the goalpost, balls next to the goalpost, keeper in net. Everyone in a yellow pinnie, at the top of the penalty arc. I'm going to play the ball into the attacking player. Defender, you can start to defend as soon as you hear my foot hit the ball."

Oh, man. I hope I got all of that. I'm in yellow, I get to attack. I fall into line at the top of the penalty arc, behind Sammie and a bunch of girls I don't really know. Sassy, Aspen, Claire, and Mackenzie are all in red. They line up with the balls next to the goalpost. I count it out in my head: *nine players on attack, nine players on defense.* The first few times through, I take a couple of runs against different defenders. First Aspen, then Mackenzie, then this girl Addi. Each time I put the ball in the net, I hear Sassy in line, chirping.

"Oh, that was totally lucky."

"Wait till you have a real defender against you."

"You started before she was even looking!"

I'll admit I'm pretty heated. The girl's such a joke. *She's getting to me*, I think, and glance over at Summer. Still nose in the book. Still peaceful. I fall back into the line with the forwards at the top of the penalty arc. I can't help it. I look. I warned you what I'm like—I count in line. Two in front of me and two in front of her. "Yes,"

I say under my breath.

I'm going head-to-head against Sassy.

Coach Carolyn plays the ball into my feet. I see Sassy running straight at me, full tilt, no brakes on. I don't know how else to describe it, but something inside me just clicks. It's so easy. My feet—they just move without me even thinking. I take the perfect outside touch around Sassy, and yeah, I'm thinking, *awesome. I beat her completely.* And all of a sudden I hear footsteps. I can see Sassy out of the corner of my eye, sliding to take me down.

I quickly touch the ball to the outside again and, in one leaping move, hurdle Sassy's sliding leg, setting myself up, cracking a perfect low strike to the near post, beating the goalkeeper's outstretched arms. It all goes in slow motion—it all slows way down. I look back at Sassy, still on the ground. I don't have to say a word. The sound of the ball hitting the net was pretty loud. That sound alone stopped everyone in their tracks. All the girls are staring, mouths open. Coach Carolyn is going nuts. "Woo-hoo, Ellie! Now that's what I'm talking about! That's how you attack the goal!"

I move back into the line. Yeah, I'm grinning ear to ear. Girl Sammie is just looking at me, speechless.

"Wow! Where'd *that* come from?" she asks, surprised.

I know exactly where that came from. Or, I should say, *who.*

I've been thinking about that since the second the ball hit the back of the net. I definitely don't have moves like that! In hockey, sure. But not in soccer. That was all Elle! One hundred percent! The way my feet knew just what to do.

I am her and she's me!

I shake my head. I have the biggest smile plastered on my face. "That was all Elle," I say out loud, almost laughing. Unreal. "Those moves were so sick!"

As the boys would say, "The kid's a dangler!"

And then I laugh because, yeah. If anyone is listening, I'm not sounding too humble. This is so flippin' crazy. This is nuts. And I'm proud of Elle, more than I could possibly explain. I'm so pumped! I glance over at Summer, and at that exact second, that very moment, she looks up from her book and flashes me a huge smile. I turn back to the net, watch Sassy slowly moving back to the end of the defenders line. And I'm feeling kind of suddenly grateful. Relieved. I didn't snap. I didn't hit her or chirp her, I just—*we* just—fair and square beat her.

49
ELLE

WALKING OFF THE ICE INTO the locker room, I can't even think straight, I'm so amped! Inside, the room is crazy loud, country music blaring, guys joking, laughing, goofing off, unwinding. I sit back on the bench and take it all in. Number one, I can't leave this out: it really *stinks* in here, but I guess—yeah. Ahh, wow. I'm pretty ripe too. The guys are mostly half-dressed. Sitting back, pads off on the top, bare chested, big smiles. A whole lot of chirping back and forth. Nobody's talking about practice. It's like as soon as we stepped off the ice, they left it out there. They've all moved on.

"Pumped! I'm going to the Pats game today!"

"Fitzy, dude, you're so lucky!"

"Ha, Brownie, nice lip lettuce, bro!"

"Hot shower. Refill the tank. Not leaving my couch

today. Giants, Eagles, Bills, Pats. If any of you hooligans want to come over."

"Riles, I hear you hooked up with Shaylee!"

"Holy smokes, Riiiiles! Did you get any, you huge beauty?"

"Shaylee Landon is perfect. I honestly don't think she can get any hotter."

"That new twig is sick. Where'd you get that? That curve is sick, buddy. You're gonna be sniping with this. I want it!"

I kind of like the background noise. The way they're all laughing and joking around. I could get used to this. I take my time. I don't rush. I sit back and soak it in. I feel totally spent—in the best way. I put the equipment back in the bag, zip it up, slip back into my jeans and hoodie. I stand and throw my bag up on my shoulder. The guys are cool when I get up to go.

"See ya, big dog!"

"Unreal, Mallsy, good skate!"

"Get it tomorrow, man!"

It's funny because, just like I did on the way in, I follow Happy Blond Kid out of the dressing room, through the long hall. I try and be cool, keep my smile inside. But it's hard to not, like, grin at all. I feel so hyped! Proud, I guess. Jack's gonna kill it tomorrow—I have absolutely no doubt!

I bust outside the wide double doors into the fresh air

and the morning sun with pretty much a swag in my step. The bag doesn't even seem heavy anymore, strapped over my shoulder, sticks in hand. I look straight ahead and see the truck waiting by the curb. I turn to Happy Blond Kid.

"See ya tomorrow, man."

Happy Blond Kid calls after me, "Expecting big things from you, Malls!"

I throw the bag in the back and jump up into the front, excited. I look right at The Captain, flashing him my best, biggest smile. I'm sure he's going to be proud. I'm sure he's going to be impressed! But as soon as I see his face, my stomach just drops. The Captain doesn't even turn toward me, he doesn't even look! He just puts the truck into drive and pulls out of the parking lot. And in a matter of seconds, I go from feeling like I'm on the top of the world to feeling like . . .

Crap.

I passed out in the truck. I know this because when I wake up, we're pulling into the driveway and I have dried-up drool on my bottom lip. I kind of jerk up. I glance quickly at The Captain. To my surprise, he looks back.

"Are you happy with the way you played?" he asks, very matter-of-factly.

"Yes, sir, I think I played pretty well," I answer quickly, confidently.

The Captain turns away, looks out the window. Then,

after a long silence, he finally speaks as he opens the truck door. "*Good* is not enough. If you play like that, you're not going anywhere."

"But . . . ," I start. "I mean, the coach said—"

He stands outside the truck, the door open, his jaw clenched. A minute passes. Nothing. He shakes his head. "Frankly, if you can't handle the corners and finish your checks, if you can't be a man and figure it out—" His tired-looking eyes are fixed on me. "You can't be complacent. If you can't fight tooth and nail, if you can't be mentally tough, if you can't start doing what you need to do, there are a hundred kids ready to step in and take your spot." He lingers with a shrug. "Maybe you're not like your brothers. Maybe you don't want this."

I watch the truck door shut.

I watch him leave.

I sit in the seat, and I feel this anger just well up in me. It starts in my gut and charges up my throat. It's like an alien force. It suddenly hits me that I have a choice. Without thinking, I jump out of the truck and swing the heavy door closed. I grab my bag, my sticks. I stride with purpose to the house. I drop my bag and set down the sticks inside the entryway, and I turn toward the kitchen, my heart pounding. The Captain is standing by the sink, pouring himself a coffee. His back is to me when I walk in.

The boys are all there, the three of them around the

table, sitting, eating breakfast. They all look up. It's absolutely uncomfortably quiet. Gunner and Stryker's eyes are bugged out, as if they can immediately tell what's going on. Jett looks worried. "*Settle down*," he mouths.

The Captain turns back around. His big square jaw, his ice-blue eyes. He looks right at me. And that's it, I don't even think, the words tumble out—

"Why are you always on everyone's case!" I say, my voice growing louder. "Can't you say one positive thing, ever?!! No matter what Jack does, it's never enough!" I stop and swallow hard, realizing my slip. "I mean, no matter what I do," I correct myself, quick. "Nothing is good enough for you!"

The quiet is unsettling. The boys all just stare at me, stunned. The Captain stays exactly where he is. Stone-faced. Stewing. A long time passes. Nobody speaks. Stryker's fork is halted halfway to his mouth. Nobody dares to even move. The Captain finally takes a deep breath, the kind we can all hear and can see, the way his big barrel chest rises, the way his eyes narrow on me.

"Jack, I'm only going to say this once." He looks like he might explode. I watch the words leave his mouth. Each one comes out as its own complete sentence—

"Go. To. Your. Room."

"Fine!" I answer, dangerously loud. No "yes, sir." No "I'm sorry." I am not polite. I do not feel like being nice! I don't even regret anything. I can't stop. I feel this power rising up. My face begins to feel extremely hot. "Do you have any idea how mean you are?" I look him in his eyes. I begin to shake. "You're so, you're so—" I pause, I glance at Stryker, Gunner, and Jett; all of them are watching this in total shock. I get the feeling maybe nobody has ever done this before. I don't even care!

"You're so hung up on how perfect everyone should be!" Yes, I'm shouting now. I take a step backward. "I don't even know if you even love your kids!" I whirl around. I storm off. I stomp up the stairs, one at a time. And this is the craziest part. For the first time, I'm not really scared at all—I am not even crying. I'm just—

God. I'm MAD!!!! And when I get upstairs, I go straight to my room, and I do something I've never done before.

I slam the door.

Hard.

50
JACK ▶

THE FIRST THING SUMMER SAYS when we get into the car is, "Want to get you-know-what and go you-know-where?"

Whatever that means, her eyes light up.

"Sure," I say, smiling back. It can only be something good, right? I'm still so pumped. I'm pretty sure Elle made the team, for one. And two, I'm not gonna front, that was straight-up fun!

Pulling out of the Sportsplex, I feel like I'm leaving everything behind. My worries about my dad, about hockey. I don't know why, but I feel a hundred pounds lighter. The day is warm for September. The sun is bright. Summer has these glamorous big, black oversized sunglasses on, and all the windows are down. Red hair is blowing all over the place. Hers and mine. Leaping up and dancing as the wind blows past us. Summer reaches out, pushing a button on the dashboard.

"Let's open the sunroof and get this party started!"

Her hand moves to the stereo. She turns the volume up until I can actually feel the vibrations moving through my body.

"Who is this?" I ask through the wind, over the music.

"What?" Summer shouts back, and we both start hysterically laughing, because our hair is going crazy and all the windows are down and I can't hear a word she's saying over the sounds.

"Who is this?" I repeat, louder, through my laughter. Summer's red hair is swept up and flying behind her like a cape. I catch a glimpse of myself in the mirror on the side of the car. My hair—Elle's—is flying too. I smile really big. The air feels so good.

"Who is this?" Summer laughs. This time I can hear her. "You know, silly!"

"I do?" I'm practically shouting.

Summer shoots me a grin. "The Beatles!"

We turn into a gravel parking lot full of cars. The sign says LUNA's in three-foot-high red scripty letters. The building is kind of a shack, with one of those window counters. But if it's a shack, it's a popular one. We walk across the pebbly lot toward the line of people stretching down around the corner of the building: moms, dads, babies in strollers, sleepy college kids, old people. We fall in line too.

"This place must be good," I say, excited.

Summer props up her sunglasses, pulls me in, and kisses me on the head. "Must be? You headed too many balls out there today, silly! We've only come here a hundred times."

"Oh, yeah, right," I say.

"So are you getting the usual?" she asks.

"Yeah." I nod. "The usual."

I hope the usual is something good, I think to myself, as we get closer to the front of the line. I know it's crazy, but I'm already hungry again. Starving. And my stomach kind of hurts.

"What about you?" I ask Summer.

She winks. "Oh, you know my thing."

I nod and laugh again, stepping forward to the walk-up window.

"Hey, Summer!" says the girl. Her face lights up when her eyes land on Summer. The girl is kind of short and pudgy, with a sparkly diamond in her nose. "Hi, Ellie!"

"Hi." I grin back. I love how everyone loves Summer. She has this way of making everyone around her feel special. Something about her energy, it's almost impossible to describe. She just has so much life in her. I watch her step up to the window, and I feel kind of proud. For this second, it's like—she's with *me*. She's my mom.

"Ellie, you remember Janie Tate, right? She babysat you."

Janie Tate blushes. "Well, that was a long time ago," she tells me, with a big smile. "But you sure were one cute baby! You used to have the most precious little baby-doll ears!" She pauses. "What can I get you two *mamacitas?*"

Summer puts her arm around my shoulders. "I'm going to have a coffee, dark roast, thanks, and yes, I will definitely get a vanilla ice cream cone. And you?" Summer looks at me. Janie Tate's waiting with her pen and pad.

"Um, I'll have, uh—" I stall. I scan the menu up above the window.

"French fries, please, and, uhhh, a vanilla milkshake?"

Summer pulls me in tight, her voice tickles in my ear. "Same order every single time. We're two totally predictable peas in a pod."

Ha. I guess Elle and I think alike.

It only takes, like, a minute. "Here you go," says Janie Tate, handing Summer her coffee and her cone. "And for Ellie." She hands me my shake with a straw and a ridiculously huge paper basket of crispy, hot, golden fries.

Summer lingers at the window. "You want some vinegar, too, right, hon?"

"Sure, yes, please!" I grin. That's totally a Canadian hockey-trip thing. *How does she even know that!* I think, and shake my head. Vinegar and fries. Best combination ever. I'm not even shocked anymore. Really. This day is getting better by the second.

It's hard not to eat in the car. I'm staring at the fries and I want to inhale them. But we have come to an agreement. We are going to wait and get to the "spot." Wherever that is.

Summer's kind of a rebel. She ignores all the rules. She shines me a smile, turns the music up loud, and we barrel down the smooth roads through the sun before finally turning down a long, bumpy dirt lane. Gigantic fields of yellow sunflowers are on either side. I'm kind of in suspense, looking all around. Until—

"Wow," I say when I realize where we're going. Down the hillside, through the tall trees, I can see it right in front of me, stretched out for miles.

"The lake," I say aloud in the car, gazing straight ahead.

I love the lake! It's cold and deep. My mom used to bring us. Not to here, since I don't know where "here" even is. Same lake. Just, like—a different spot. My brothers and I would all race to swim out to the raft and play King of the Mountain, shoving each other off a hundred times. Jett and Gunner would pick me up by my feet and my hands and literally have a contest to see how far they could hurl me. Ha! We'd stay out there all day until we were totally sunburned and exhausted. Then my mom would stop for ice cream or pick up Lombardi's pizza. I don't mind thinking about those memories. It actually feels good. Lately I've been worried that I was starting to forget. Forget, like, the little things.

We stop at the lake's shore, because if we drove any farther we'd drive right into the water. I follow Summer down a well-worn dirt path, and in twenty or so steps we are standing together, looking out at an endless stretch of shimmering blue-green water.

"I like being here," I say, mesmerized.

I feel Summer's hand smooth over my hair. "I love it too, hon. Especially with you."

I look around—the water, the faint green hills across the lake in the distance. This is totally the coolest little hidden spot, tucked away. I'd never find it in a million years. I'd never even know it was even here.

We sit shoulder to shoulder on the warm, smooth rocks, a few feet from the water. Summer's holding her "mmmmmmmm . . . truly amazing cup of coffee." I'm working on my extra-thick vanilla milkshake.

The sun is blazing.

There's not a cloud in the sky.

This spot is completely quiet. No sailboats. No Jet Skis. The water is so clear it's see-through. A giant pool as far as you can see. I dig into the fries and polish off the milkshake. Neither of us says a word. The view is doing the talking.

I ditch my turf shoes, my shin guards, and peel off my

striped pink socks. Summer kicks off her flip-flops, and the two of us lie straight back on the hot stones, our feet dipping into the cool lake water.

"Feels good." I sigh.

"Mmmmm," agrees Summer. She takes off her shades and shuts her eyes.

I watch her for a moment, smiling. Then I copy the same pose. The warmth of the sun feels good on my face.

We lie like that, side by side, solar panels soaking up the heat and the quiet for a long time. And when Summer finally talks, she talks up into the sky. I feel her hand rest on mine. "You know, at some point we're going to have to talk about last night, right?"

"Yeah." I whisper, and open my eyes.

I watch a hawk, way, way up, soar and swoop over the water.

"Soooo?" Summer asks again. Her voice is warm. There's a lightness.

"Um . . . ," I start. But . . . what do I even say? This wasn't about anything she thinks.

I exhale loudly.

I feel Summer squeeze my hand. "I see you're having a hard time starting, so I'm going to give this a shot," she says, pausing. "I think this was a little bit about you and Sassy, and *a lot* about your dad."

At first I'm like, wait, how did you know? But then I quickly remember she's talking about Elle's dad, as much as I wish she could somehow make me understand mine.

I keep my face to the sun. I bite down on my lip to stop myself from saying anything dumb.

"So, yeah, this Sassy thing, I just—" Summer hesitates. I glance at her just as she looks at me. "Honestly, honey— I don't need to know the details of what happened. All I really care about is that you feel safe. That you know you can talk about anything with me, even when it's hard." She smiles softly.

I look back up into the sky. I shut my eyes.

"It's not just middle school," Summer goes on. "Trying to change other people is a waste of time. It took me a long time to learn that. Figuring out what matters and what doesn't." She exhales. "It's not easy—"

"Yeah." I sigh. I think I get it—*I didn't have to beat the snot out of Porter Gibson. I don't always have to fight.*

"And it's hard, right, I understand. Believe me. Every bone inside of you wants to take the bait, but when you don't—it feels so good."

"Yeah," I say. "I guess that's what I did today in soccer?"

"Exactly! I saw it."

I peek at Summer as she's talking. Her eyes are closed, but she's smiling. She pauses for a long moment and squeezes my hand. "I want you to know how much I believe in you."

I breathe. I don't even care that's she's talking about Elle. I feel this overwhelming attachment to both of them.

There's a hushed quiet, then Summer laughs lightly and says, "Not done yet." Big breath. This time she turns and waits for me to look. "Running away like that. You scared me. That's not okay. That's not safe. And—"

"I'm sorry," I tell her. My voice kind of cracks from the lump in my throat.

"I just—" I start. I don't even know what to say. I don't have words.

"Ellie, honey, it's okay. I don't expect you to be perfect. You're going to make mistakes. My god, you're twelve years old. I want you to make thousands of them! That's how you learn, right? That's how you grow." Summer smiles softly. Her eyes are so green. She's like this mixture of wildly rugged and graceful at the same time. The way she talks, the way she listens.

"You're such a great kid, honey. I love you so much. I just want you to live your life, and go after your dreams and—" Summer gets really quiet again.

"For a long time, with your dad—when he left, it happened pretty fast. It was hard. I kind of checked out for a while."

Summer stops, and during this pause, suddenly all I can think about is my dad and how much he must miss my mom—I guess I haven't thought of that.

Neither of us says anything for a long time.

"Honey," says Summer. "I feel tremendous sadness when I think about how much you must miss your dad.

When he first left, it didn't sink in. And . . ." She trails off. She exhales. "I had a hard time accepting it." Summer tightens her hand around mine. "Sometimes we miss people, and it's beyond words."

All I can think about is my mom. I squeeze my eyes to try to hold back the tears. I turn away, I try to hide it.

"Oh, honey, pushing away those feelings doesn't work. Let it out. It's okay. It's part of being human."

I slowly turn back to Summer. I can't keep the tears in, and I finally just let them fall. Summer cups her hand against my face. Her smile grows even wider as she looks at me. I watch one lone tear trickle down her freckled cheek. She looks beautiful.

"Honey, what I want to say too—" She stops, breathes in deep, and sits up.

I sit up too.

We both look out at the water.

"I know it hurts and things change and it's overwhelming sometimes, but at some point—I simply refused to let what happened between me and your dad stop me from living. I promised myself to live my life as I want to, to say whatever is on my mind, to not let what anyone else thinks stop me. To have fun." She pauses and wipes the tears running down her cheeks. "Life is precious," she says, giving me that kick-ass Summer smile through the tears and wrapping both her arms around me in a big huge hug. I adore her. The way she makes me feel. Like everything is going to be okay. Like I can do anything.

Then, in true Summer style, she suddenly jumps to her feet and exclaims, "What are we doing sitting here! Let's go swimming!"

That's Summer. She can talk you into anything. I don't even think about it, really. We both strip down to our bras and underwear and run barefoot and squealing into the icy cold water. I think this will be one of my favorite moments ever. Does that sound crazy? With someone I've only known for three days? But it feels like forever. We run through the water whooping with joy, crying, and laughing. We dive in and swim out into the deepness.

51

ELLE

WHEN I WAKE UP ON *top* of Jack's bed—not under the covers—I don't know how long I've been sleeping. And yeah, I'm nervous. I get up and tiptoe along the white strip of tape balance beam and quietly open the door one tiny inch, peering out. I don't really hear anybody until—

"Bud," calls out Jett. "That you, man?"

What is he, telepathic? I thought I was quiet. My heart kind of leaps. Also? I don't want The Captain to come up here and yell at me. I quickly shut the door, return to the bed, and do a belly flop, burying my face in the pillow.

"Bud," Jett repeats. I glance back at the door. I see him in his glasses, peeking in. "You okay?"

He walks into the room in his USA Hockey T-shirt and sweats, his eyes all bright, carrying a plate of food and a glass of milk.

"Dude, *do not* spill this. You know this is major house rules violation, like—I'm seriously risking my life here." He stops next to the bed, looking down at me with a huge toothy grin. "Buddy! Good to see that smile. I made you an omelet." He sets the plate and the glass carefully on Jack's desk.

"Thanks," I answer. "But I'm not really hungry."

"Not hungry?" Jett flops right on top of me, pinning me into submission. "You have a game tomorrow, man," he whispers. "You need fuel for the rocket!"

He's playing with me. I get it. I don't fight it. Jett's body draped over mine feels like a giant human blanket. Also, I love him. He's like a big teddy bear with a lot of muscles, and I can't see his face, but I can tell by his voice he's trying to cheer me up. Jett always smells good, he smells like . . . the way the shampoo smells when you're standing in the shower and you pour it out into your hand.

He digs his elbow into my neck. "C'mon, little man, what's up, bro? No fight left?" He sits up, laughs softly, and rubs my buzzed head. I watch him stand, walk a few steps, and fall backward like a tree onto Stryker's bed. I roll over onto my back. We both stare at the ceiling in silence.

Jett sighs loudly. "How are you feelin', buddy?"

I shrug. "Been better."

"Listen, bud," he says. "I don't know what The Captain said for you to snap like that, but I know what it feels like when you think you've let him down."

I can see out of the corner of my eyes that he's watching me from across the room. I don't look. I keep my eyes on the ceiling.

"You're brave, bud. You showed some stones. There's no shame in that." Jett pauses for a moment. "You said some stuff that, to be honest, I've wanted to say. Not gonna lie. We all have, bro. I usually just keep my mouth shut."

I turn and finally look at him. He grins with his eyes. "Look, bud, I'm old enough now to realize this—you just have to accept him for who he is. He's not gonna change. Not that it makes his crap okay, but—" He pauses for a moment. "He's hurting too, man. I know we don't talk about it, but ever since . . . ever since Mom . . ." Jett's voice wavers.

There's a minute of silence.

He gets real quiet.

"I know he can be tough, bud. But everything he does is for us. We're all he has."

I don't even know what to say back. I never even thought of it like that. I take a really deep breath. We look at each other across the room.

"Dude." Jett's face brightens. "What'd he say to you anyway that got you so heated?"

"Pretty much he thinks I suck," I answer.

Jett laughs. "Well, *that* sounds real familiar." He cracks

a smile. "He's told me that before, once or twice. Bud, you should know by now, he's never satisfied. He's a maniac. But he's our dad. He loves you, man."

"Well, he has a funny way of showing it." I mumble that.

"Dude, it's like the four of us, man. One minute we're fighting, the next minute we're best friends. Shake it off. People are going to say what they're going to say. Me? I don't really care what anyone else thinks. I told you, bud, you have to learn to let it roll off you. Be yourself and have fun."

"Easy for you to say," I sigh. "You're so—"

"First of all, you're nuts!" he cuts me off. We exchange a smile. "Second of all." Jett's eyes light up. "Dude, when I watch you on the ice . . . I don't think I have ever seen someone with the kind of talent you have. You can't teach that. The truth is, you're better than any of us. That feeling of proving yourself all the time? Use it. Let it drive you. Accept everything outside your control and go harder. Don't think about tomorrow, just think about right now."

My insides kind of leap, and all I can think of is how much I wish Jack was here too. That he could hear this somehow. That he could know.

Jett gets up, stands, and looks down at me. "Look, man, it happened. It's over with and—"

"And what?"

Jett shrugs it off. "And don't be a knucklehead. Eat some grub," he tells me, eyeing the plate of food he brought me. "And let's go shoot some pucks, little man."

"But The Captain, he'll . . . I mean, aren't I in trouble?"

Jett shakes his head, letting out a smile. "Captain's not here, bud. He left for work."

"Are you sure?" I ask.

"Dude, you're my little brother," Jett says, his eyes fixed on me. Reaching out his hand, he pulls me to my feet. "I'll always look out for you. I love you, man."

52
JACK

AT HOME, I SMELL LIKE lake.

"Honey," Summer calls up to me from the bottom of the stairs.

I look down, waiting by the banister until I see her face.

"You should really wash off." She laughs and wrinkles up her nose. "I need to too. We both smell like—"

"Slimy lake weeds," I finish, and laugh, picking a stringy green vine off my leg.

"Make sure to really wash your hair well," she tells me. "Oh, I bought you some conditioner at Devon's. It's in my bathroom. Go ahead and use my tub, hon. Take a nice bath."

A bath.

"Okay," I say with a shrug and a grin. *Twist my arm!*

When I step into Summer's bright, sunny bathroom, my eyes kind of pop. It's, like, entirely white and really, really clean. Calming. And the tub? The tub is massive! I could fit three of me in here and there'd still be room.

It takes me a little bit to get it all dialed in: figure out the fancy faucet, holding my hand under the water till it's hot, stripping down to Elle's sun-crusted, lake-smelling underwear and bra. Waiting, watching the water slowly rise. Last, before I climb in, I pick up one of Summer's seven bottles nestled in the corner on the white tiles: "'Love Bomb Bubble Bath, pure spruce essential oil,'" I read aloud, shrug, and quietly laugh. What the heck! I dump it right in. And *bam*! Bubbles! Instantly the air is filled with the most soothing scent, clearing my nose as I breathe it in. It smells like orange peels, plus Christmas.

I finally shut off the water and test the temperature with my toe, easing my body in nice and slow until I'm sitting like a king, surrounded by Christmas tree–scented bubbles! The water feels so good, so warm. I would never have imagined three days ago that I'd be here, soaking in a hot bath underneath a skylight. I look up through the window at the dusty blue sky, the afternoon sun. Only Summer would think of putting a window above the bathtub, right? I laugh. Awesome.

I lather up with the bar of soap and breathe it in too. It's like some sort of flowery goodness. Potent.

Okay, I'll just say it. It smells like—

Girl.

I smile, lean back, and rest my head against the edge of the tub. The water is up to my chin. I'm, like, smiling ear to ear. I mean, c'mon, man! Can you see me! In my bra, my girlie flowered undies. I've become totally soft. As Stryker would say, "Butter." And you know what? I shake my head and laugh. It's weird, but whatever, man, I'm honestly okay with that. I learned a lot from Elle.

I play over the last three days in my mind—starting with the fight, Porter, the nurse, seeing Elle crying that first time. I think it's safe to say I've changed. We both have. It's crazy. Nothing has turned out the way I thought. I literally did not know how hard it was to be a girl. Seriously. It's not easy, it's harder than it looks!

I relax and close my eyes, and I feel this deep peace wash over me, like—somehow, everything that has happened was meant to be, and for the first time in a long time, I'm not scared, I'm not afraid. I dunk under, feel the water glide over my skin, the tingle of the heat. And as I hold my breath, smiling, under a thousand white magical bubbles—out of nowhere I feel this energy rumble through my body from my toes right through my chest. This big surge. It feels totally weird, but it feels totally good! And look, the lights don't flicker. There is no sonic BOOM! But the next thing I know, I'm—

Shooting up out of the water and it's—

Freezing frickin' cold!

It's like something out of a movie, the way I come up for air, my mouth open, water splashing, spitting out water. This rush of adrenaline shoots through my heart and I look wide-eyed all around.

"It's so friggin' COLD!" tumbles out of my mouth. It only takes a second for my eyes to focus, my head to adjust—I'm standing in a garbage pail full of ice! I look right down the line, Jett, Gunner, Stryker, standing in ice baths, chest deep—

"It will get better, balls out, big guy!" says Jett, overcome with laughter.

"Settle down, Nancy," Gunner says, shaking his head, grinning.

"Easy, Butter," chirps Stryker from the very end.

I can't get over the sight of my brothers—each of them bare chested, ice up to their nipples! *I'm back! I'm back!* I can't stop smiling. I don't even care how cold it is! I don't even care how the heck it happened.

"WOOOOOOOOOHOOOOOOOOOOO!!!" I throw my head back and let out the biggest yell. "I'm back, man! I'm back!" I say, splashing the icy water with my hands.

"Holy smokes, dude, settle down!" Jett looks at me, smiling, "You okay over there, big guy?"

My heart is racing and I have to dunk under the water again to calm myself down. I plunge under. I count to three. Then I whip back up, opening my eyes, and yes! I'm still here. I'm back in my body, smiling this big goofy smile. I feel up around my neck and grip my mom's pendant—the one we all wear. I hold it up to my cold, quivering lips and kiss it. And I know, I'm back. It's real! The looks on my brother's faces, their reactions looking at me are pretty funny too. You can probably guess. Jett catches my eye, smiling, shaking his head. "You're crazy, kid," he says with a laugh.

Yeah, I think, smiling and sinking down into the water. *You have no idea.*

After a few minutes, the ice works to calm me down. My heart returns to a normal thump. I just relax. I don't fight the cold. I picture Elle, laughing, back in my hot bath. For a few minutes it's real quiet; the four of us just sit. It doesn't really get better than this. Four brothers. Like I said, we all have the same dream.

Gunner breaks the silence. He's looking square at me. "Took a lot of courage to do what you did."

My stomach kind of flutters. Do I want to even ask? I brace myself and look back. "Uhhh, yeah, what do you mean?"

Gunner's eyebrows raise. "After hockey, dude?"

Elle went to hockey! My heart starts to race. I bite my lip.

Gunner shrugs both his shoulders, gives me a nod. "Maybe you don't want to rehash it. That's cool. Couldn't have been easy though, bro. I'd be lying if I said I haven't wanted to say pretty much exactly what you said."

It's kind of quiet for a minute, then—

I can't take it. "Uh, what'd I say?"

Jett laughs, "Bro, stop playin'. You okay?"

I mix in a grin, I keep my mouth shut. I swallow hard and brace myself.

"Dude," Gunner goes on, "I wish I had said what you said. I watched you in the kitchen, man. You told him how you felt."

Gulp. I'm pretty sure I know the *him* they're talking about.

Gunner winks. "You're the youngest and the strongest, man. I'm proud of you, bud."

Whatever Elle said, the boys seem impressed.

Stryker nods, then kind of laughs. "Just let The Captain cool off more before you have to face him. Go to bed early, before he gets back."

"Okay," I say, and nod.

Jett locks eyes on me. "I'm sure it was hard to hear, man, but I don't know. I think he respected it."

I can't even imagine what Elle said. I'm kind of proud of her, and also a little bit nervous. Talking back to The Captain? *Nobody does that. Man.* I can pretty much kiss hockey good-bye. I forgot to write my goals down last night. I didn't do my push-ups or my sit-ups. I didn't say the prayer.

I take a deep breath and look at my brothers. I love them so much. And I'm here, I'm back. I feel like I got a second chance. I sink down into the icy water as far as I can, all the way up to my neck. I let Summer's voice run through my head—"*It'll be okay, things are going to get better.*" I think that should be my new mantra.

Jett's voice snaps me back. "Just be prepared, bud. Captain's probably going to come down hard on you tomorrow when he picks you up at school."

I just nod. I bite on my lip.

Jett's eyes brighten. "It is what it is, and you gotta deal with it when it comes, bro. He's gonna be heated."

"Yeah." I exhale.

Jett reaches out and rubs my prickly, wet head. "The only way to go through anything is to go right through it, little man." He winks and gives me the softest smile. "It'll be okay, bro. I'll be right there with you."

YES. YOU COULD SAY I am in a state of shock! One second I'm soaking chest deep in our ice-recovery garbage pail, and the next? I'm all of the sudden up to my chin in hot water, immersed in a gazillion sudsy white Christmas tree–smelling bubbles!

"Oh my gosh!" I say it aloud. I'm pretty sure I look like a cartoon, the way my eyes pop out of my head, the way I frisk my own body with my hands, checking to make sure I'm me again! "Oh my gosh!" I practically yell. I'm laughing, like, loudly, when I figure it out. The fact is, I'm wearing underwear and my little white bra in the tub! So just like Jack. *Always the gentleman*, I think, shaking my head, smiling. Yep. I'm squealing, I'm splashing!

"Honey? Ellie, honey?" I hear my mom outside the door. "What's going on? Is everything okay in there?"

"Everything is SO great! Mom, I love you!" I exclaim, much too loudly. I feel this rush of relief when I hear her voice. When I picture her smiling behind the door.

"Well, good," my mom calls back. "I love you, too, and I'm glad you're enjoying yourself in there!"

"I am!" I sing, smiling ear to ear. Still in the tub, I wiggle out of my bra and I'm-not-even-gonna-ask mud-streaked underwear, and I toss them out of the tub onto the tile floor. I lean back and, with my toes, turn on the water—hot—and let it run until I feel the heat tingle all the way through my body, up to my chest. Then I soak, exactly like that.

I think about Jack. I think about the boys. I can just picture how happy he is to be back with them. Joking and laughing in the backyard in the sun.

I'm glad I left his boxers on! Ha!

"Unreal," I whisper into the bubbles, and go all the way under. When I pop back up, my heart kind of pangs. Like, am I really back? I feel up around my head, my long wet hair. Still me. Still here. I smile and breathe it all in. So much has happened. So much has changed. I feel like I have a new start. A new chance. It's like, I'm me, but I kind of feel, I guess—

Stronger.

I rest my head on the edge of the tub and close my eyes, and I just soak and think about how happy I am. How excited I am for school, for *everything*! I open my eyes.

"Mom!" I yell.

There's quiet for a while.

"Mom!!!" I repeat.

"Honey?" I finally hear.

"Come on in!" I tell her. My entire body is submerged under the bubbles. Just my face is popping out.

The door opens, and god, I'm so happy when I see my mom's eyes, her face, her awesome smile.

She puts the toilet seat cover down and sits on the edge. "What's gotten into you, hon? You're full of energy, huh? Feeling better?"

I look back at her with the biggest, brightest smile. Half of me wants to jump out of the tub soaking wet and hug her so tight. But I stay right where I am. I take a deep breath. "Mom, I just wanted to tell you . . ."

She sits, just smiling, waiting, her eyebrows arched. "Yes?"

"You're seriously the best mom in the world. Don't ever leave me, okay?"

"Oh, honey pie," she tells me, looking down. "I'm your mom. You're stuck with me." She laughs. "I'm all yours. I'm not going anyplace."

After my mom goes back downstairs, I stay in the bath until every inch of me is wrinkled and clean and soft. I wrap the big, cushy white towel around my naked body. When I enter my room? My jaw actually drops.

"Whoa!" I say, walking in. Then—"Jack." I laugh.

The entire room is absolutely picture-perfect. My bed is made, my teddy bear perched happily on the pillows. I scan the walls. Everything's put away. I open my closet and stare at the shirts—coordinated by color and all pointing just so, in the same direction. I find my pajamas, neatly folded, and head back to the bathroom. For the first time in my life, I actually carefully hang up the towel. Then I stare at myself—my real self—in the mirror. I've never been so happy to see my own reflection. I lift my hand up to my face and run my fingers over my cheeks. My freckles! I smile at myself. It's weird, but I think you can understand my excitement. I brush my hair, and I leave it down. I quietly look in the mirror for the longest time. I don't mean this in a way that's like, stuck-up or conceited, but I actually feel really kind of pretty. I take a deep breath and slip into my clean undies—and . . .

"Mom!" I shout. I shout at the top of my lungs. "Mom!!!" I am half laughing, half crying.

My mom bolts upstairs. "Honey, what in the world is going on—"

I don't have to say a word. My mom is so awesome. She's not embarrassing or dramatic. It's crazy, but it's not at all awkward. She just takes one look at my face and glances down.

"Oh, honey," she says, smiling. She's almost laughing too. "This has been a weekend to remember." She walks over to her cabinet and takes out some, um, products. She hands me a cottony pad. "Just take off the sticker off and—"

"I know," I cut her off. "I mean, thanks." I smile. Okay, I'm a little bit embarrassed, but also feeling so lucky. Not because I got. You know. *That.* More because my mom, she's—

I throw my arms around her waist. I do. Standing there in my underwear, in front of the sink, in her big, white bathroom.

"I love you so much," I say into her chest. I hug her so hard. I let the tears kind of flow. I don't hold them back.

My mom just holds me. She doesn't even have to talk. But after ten seconds or so, I feel her familiar kiss on the side of my head.

"I love you too, honey. So, so much."

54
JACK ▶

MONDAY MORNING I'M THE FIRST one up, bed made, ready. Racing to the mountain, I'm up front, right behind Jett. Gunner's behind me, then Stryker. We run in a pretty tight pack.

"That's it, bud!" Jett says as we sprint up, up, up, in the early morning shadows. I feel this superhuman energy. I'm even stronger than I was before. It's like, I'm back and I'm better, lighter. I've accepted the fact that The Captain is probably going to punish me from now until forever. I've already pretty much given up on being allowed to play in my first game tonight. I won't see The Captain until he picks me up after school. I'm not expecting a miracle. I've prepared myself. From the sound of it, it's probably good I don't see him yet. Let him cool off.

I beat the boys, all of them. It's a full-on jockeying for position, elbows and all. I go all out the last ten seconds, blow past them.

"Got it!" I shout, my hand lunging to be the first to touch the rock, broad smile.

"Not so fast, little man," Jett says, laughing, grabbing me by my hoodie and yanking me back. Dude's a tank, he's strong. He easily pulls me back from the rock, throws me down on the ground. I look up at all three of them laughing, the morning sun behind us turning the sky a pinkish orange. And I'm thinking, I can't complain. I'm lucky. They're tough—they bring out my greatness. I don't let it faze me. I just jump back up. I stand with them, right there in front of Jett and Gunner. Stryker's on the end. Jett plants both his hands on my shoulders, and the four of us catch our breath for a few long seconds, looking out at the view as the morning light rises. I still feel it. The peace I came back with. The gratefulness. The calm I felt with Summer—I took it back with me.

"Dude! Look at that hawk!" Gunner exclaims, breaking the silence.

I look up at the orange sky. "Where?" I breathe.

Only the next thing I know, my sweats and my boxers are ripped down, bunched around my ankles.

"Got 'em!" Gunner hollers. The three of them take off laughing, leaving me standing alone, shaking my head, bare butt, straight up smiling.

I can hear their voices echoing through the morning air, taunting me.

"Figure it out, bud, get gritty!" shouts Jett.

"C'mon, big guy!" Gunner yells. "Let's see how it goes!"

"Let's go, Jackie Chan!" Stryker calls out. "Run somebody, bro!"

I take my time, I don't freak out. I pull up my boxers, my sweats. This time I tie a tight double knot. And when I take off down the mountain, I push the pace, sweating, smiling. It only takes me a few minutes. I catch up.

After, we hit The Cage and lift. I shower and dress in my favorite broken-in jeans—Jett's hand-me-downs—and my black Bruins hoodie. It smells like hockey.

Breakfast is a feast. Stryker's this morning's chef. He cooks us each a made-to-order omelet, and Jett is a ninja with the blender, mixing up a batch of The Captain's famous protein shake: seven raw eggs, extra spinach, and bananas. The boys all watch me as I dig in, shovel it into my mouth.

"Dude, slow down." Jett grins.

"Little man's got a growth spurt." Gunner laughs.

Stryker pours half his green protein smoothie into my empty glass, burps loudly, blows it in my face, and stands. "Jackie Chan's probably growing hair *down there*, if you know what I mean, boys."

Jett shakes his head. "Dude, c'mon, man, I'm eating. I don't want to talk about hairy nuts."

I keep my mouth shut, but I just watch them. Secretly? I'm loving every second.

When I get on the bus, Owen and Sammy practically make me deaf, talking in both ears. They have entirely different concerns. Sammy is obsessed with the fact that I "got some lip action" on the playground.

"Dude, I thought about it all weekend. I could not think of someone more perfect than Ellie O'Brien, red-haired rocket. I hear she's sick at soccer."

I just grin and shake my head. "Dude, she is awesome. And you better never lay a hand on her," I say, sounding overly protective. "Also, we're just friends."

"Just friends?" Sammy repeats. Eyes are wide, sly smile. "Yeah, sure, man, whatever."

Owen is much more worried about what happened with The Captain.

"Bro, sorry my mom called your dad. I feel so bad," he tells me.

"I'll be okay," I tell him. "Things have a way of working out, man."

Owen smiles. "Dude, I like the positive attitude." He laughs.

I shrug. "My brothers always tell me to focus on what I can control."

"You're lucky you have brothers," Owen says.

"Yeah." I nod.

When the bus stops, I descend the steps into the madness that is Thatcher. The swarming, crowded, loud hallways full of squeals and laughter. I'm only standing at my locker for about one second when I feel a tap on my shoulder and turn around.

"Mr. Malloy," Ms. Dean says, looking extremely serious, as always. She's dressed in a gray fancy suit, skirt, jacket, white blouse.

"Yes, ma'am," I say, immediately straightening my shoulders, looking her in the eye, forcing a polite smile. I try to swallow, even though my heart starts pounding. Porter is standing next to her.

We walk into Ms. Dean's office before the bell even rings. There are two empty chairs set in front of her desk.

"Gentlemen, please have a seat," she tells us, waiting for both of us to sit. I glance at Porter. I give him a nod. He's dressed like he's ready for golf: yellow polo shirt, popped collar, pressed tan khaki pants.

I slip into the chair in my Bruins hoodie and my dirty jeans. Good thing The Captain didn't see me leave. Wearing dirty jeans to school is strictly against the code—same with socks not pulled up, ratty T-shirts, or saggy pants around your butt. Today . . . I don't mind. I'm just so happy to be *me* again.

I dig my hands into my front hoodie pocket.

I keep my eyes on Ms. Dean.

I sit up straight.

I try to remember to breathe.

The bell rings, and the announcements are broadcast over the loudspeaker. Still Ms. Dean just sits quietly behind her desk. I have no idea what she's going to say.

We sit for what seems like five minutes in silence. Porter's breathing heavy, shifting around nervously in his chair. Fidgeting.

I glance sideways. Dude's a mess. His cheeks are all splotchy pink. He's sweating. I'm just glad he doesn't have a black eye. One punch and he was done, man. I don't think I've ever hit anyone that hard.

I don't expect it, what I do next.

I turn to him. I look him in the eye, just like my dad always says.

"Porter, man, I'm sorry. I just want to say, I was out of line. I shouldn't have hit you. I snapped. No excuses."

Porter's eyes go wide. He looks genuinely shocked. He stares back at me. He looks terrified. I see his lips kind of quiver.

"No, man," he says, his voice shaky. "It was my fault. I shouldn't have started it, that stuff I said—"

We both turn back to Ms. Dean. Like, now what?

She's smiling gently. Then the smile grows. "Gentlemen, I'm pleased you both initiated a conscious approach to a civilized conversation. My utmost concern is a sense of safety. This is your only warning. Physical confrontations will not be tolerated."

"Yes, ma'am." I speak softly.

Porter just nods.

More quiet. I can hear two teachers talking outside the door. I hear the clock. I swallow back the lump in my throat. I look at Porter in his chair, his slumped shoulders, his head hanging. It just happens. It feels right. It's not easy. I stumble with the words.

"Hey, man, also," I add, looking right at him, "sorry to hear about your brother."

Porter's eyes well up. I can tell he's fighting back tears. I give him a second.

I breathe in deep. I make sure to face him, squaring my shoulders as I say it. "Thing is," I tell him, "you and me both lost somebody. You lost your brother and my mom, she—" I stop and swallow hard. I have never said the words out loud. "She—" My voice cracks. I take another deep breath, and I look at him again. "She died. It's been—" I stop. I breathe. "It's been a little over a year."

The office is incredibly quiet. I hear the voices outside, the secretary laughing. A phone ringing. I swear to you, I can hear my own heart. Ms. Dean reaches across her desk and hands Porter a box of tissues. He blows his nose, hard. I'm surprised I'm not a mess right now. Ever since Summer and Elle—I feel like, I don't know—

I let the pressure out.

After a few more silent minutes, Porter lifts his head

and looks at me. Not right in the eye. It's more a quick glance. Then he drops his eyes and stares into the floor.

"Thanks, man," he says. He can barely speak. "That means a lot." He slowly turns to me, extending his hand. And yeah, I shake it. His palm is moist with sweat. I grasp it for longer than I need to—a strong, firm grip, the way my dad taught me.

Ms. Dean stands up. "Okay, gentlemen."

I move to my feet.

Porter rises too.

Ms. Dean's eyes shift from Porter to me, back and forth. "I expect there won't be any more physical confrontations."

"No, ma'am," I say.

Porter shakes his head, wiping his eyes with the back of his hand.

"Good," Ms. Dean replies, handing us each a slip of paper. "Here's a note for both of you to return to class."

Porter takes the note. I hear it sort of crumple in his hand. He walks past me to the door. I can tell by his eyes, he's going through a lot.

"Stay strong, man," I tell him. It just comes out. He gives me a nod. He pauses at the door and looks back over his shoulder, as if he wants to say something too.

His eyes are red.

I shoot him a shy smile. "If you ever want to talk, dude, I'm down," I tell him. It feels good to do something different. To not brush it off.

I grab my bag, lift it to my shoulder, and hesitate before I turn to the door. I look back at Ms. Dean, standing behind her desk, wearing her gray suit. She looks like a judge, minus the robe.

"Ma'am, does this mean you won't—" I start, then stop. Maybe I shouldn't even bring it up.

"Mr. Malloy, I am impressed with your humility and thoughtfulness today. You accepted responsibility and showed contrition." She pauses for a moment and just looks at me, her eyes brightening. "I would suspect your father would be quite pleased with how you handled yourself this morning. I know he requires a lot from you." She stops, and a hint of a smile appears. "As long as you continue to use good judgment, as far as I'm concerned, last Friday never happened. You have a clean slate, Jack. Use it."

MONDAY MORNING I WAKE UP smiling, stretching my arms up over my head. Being back in my own bed feels so good. I pull my teddy bear in and give him a squeeze.

There's no place like home, I think, and grin. I flop over onto my stomach and pull open the silky window curtain by my bed. The view isn't as great as the top of the mountain, but I stay perfectly still. I don't move. I didn't miss it—I'm three for three on watching the sun turn on. Through the trees across the street, I can see the morning light fill the sky, finger-painted streaks of orange and pink. Unreal. For a few quiet minutes, I just watch. It's mesmerizing. Magic. I stay there until the sky is blue, a pillow propped up under my chest and my chin perched on my folded arms. And I keep thinking, you know, there's a lot I want to do. I think waking up to watch the sunrise is going to be my thing. It's peaceful. It just starts the day right. It's how I think it's meant to be.

I shower.

I take care of "business." (Yeah. *That*.)

I brush my hair.

I stand, wrapped in a big white towel, in front of my thanks-to-Jack perfectly organized, color-coordinated closet and pull out the first thing I notice—jeans and a new shirt. The shirt is purple. It still has the tags on. I cut them off and hold it up. It's kind of fitted. It's not what I would have picked out, but what the heck, I'll go with it! Pulling it on, I remember yesterday—Jack's hockey jersey getting caught and how the kid next to me yanked it down. Those guys were nice. I stand in my bare feet, jeans, and new shirt, and look in the mirror attached to the back of my door, shaking my head, doing that weird smile you do when you smile at yourself. I almost laugh. It's like, I don't know if you know what I mean, but it's like I'm friends with this girl looking back at me. And it's not so much what I'm wearing. I guess it's more the way my shoulders are back. The way my feet feel planted on the ground. The way I feel strong.

Maybe it's this getting up with the sun, but I'm energized as I bounce down the stairs and walk into the kitchen. I'm the first one up! I hit the lights. I get to work. Tea and two bowls of oatmeal with raisins and honey. I'm pretty proud of myself when I set the bowls down on the table. You should see my mom's face when she walks into the kitchen! She's dressed in her yoga teacher clothes; her hair is down and still wet from the shower.

"Well, good morning," she says, sounding amazed, smiling. "And excuse me, but did someone steal my daughter and bring me back a Martian?"

"Morning," I say, handing her a hot mug. "Peppermint tea with milk, just the way you like it."

She looks at me, mouth kind of open, eyebrows scrunched up. "What's going on? It's not my birthday, it's not Mother's Day. Hmmmm . . ." She brings the tea to her mouth. "Ohhhh, this is perfect, just what I needed."

"No big deal," I say with a smile. "I just, you know, I got up early, and—"

"You got up early?" My mom looks surprised. "How are you feeling? Like, with the—"

"I'm fine," I say quickly, a little bit glad she brought it up and a little bit embarrassed.

"No cramps?" she asks, sitting down at the table.

"Sort of, but—" I sit down too. "I'm tough. I've felt worse."

My mom just gazes at me across the table. Her eyes are all sparkly.

"Did you do something different with your hair or, like—" She pauses and studies my face for what seems like a long time. "Something's different. I can't put my finger on it."

I laugh. "I mean, I got my hair cut."

"No, it's not that. You look gorgeous, but I think you always do. No . . . it's something *inside*," she says, beaming. "It's coming from your eyes."

"Whatever," I say. I'm kind of blushing.

"What. Ever," says my mom, playfully mimicking me.

"I guess I'm just getting older," I say with a shrug.

"I guess you are," my mom tells me, sipping her tea. She sits back, tilts her head, and just looks at me again, smiling her crazy-big smile. I kind of laugh, because it used to really bug me when she did this. I'd get so mad. But this morning I smile softly back at her. I can't get enough.

Look, the last three days have blown my mind. But I'm going to be completely honest: when I step off the bus onto the sidewalk, I get this nervous, fluttery, funny feeling deep in my stomach. And it's not the "girl thing," if you know what I mean. It's the fact that as I make my way through the hundreds of kids flooding out of the yellow school buses onto the sidewalk, I see straight ahead—past the colorful backpacks, the swarms, the fist bumping, the shouting, the high-pitched excitement. I see, in the distance, standing in front of the bike rack, Sassy Gaines and her pack of identical glossy-haired ladies-in-waiting. I take a deep breath. *I can do this.*

I keep my head up. I keep walking. With my backpack slung around my shoulders and the little voice in my head cheering me on, I mix into the sea of eager faces. *I can do this.* I say it to myself as I walk through the open Thatcher doors.

"Good morning," calls out Mr. Santos, the vice principal, dressed in his suit and tie. He's standing where he usually stands, greeting us as we arrive. "Make today count!" he says in his booming voice. "Be the change you want to see!"

He always says that. But for once, I think I know what he means.

Before the bell even rings, I see him from a distance.

Buzzed hair.

Black Bruins hoodie.

He's standing at his locker, way down by the front office. I literally stop walking. I just stop. People are shoving me in the crammed-crowded hall, telling me to get out of the way. The pushing doesn't faze me. I hold my ground. I don't shy away from it. The pulsing noise from the hallway just drops away and everything gets fuzzy. Everyone but Jack. My eyes focus like a close-up camera lens zeroing in on the scene.

Ms. Dean.

Porter.

The anxious look on Jack's face.

The three of them walking across the hallway through the door to the main office. I know something's wrong.

And here's the thing. In this moment, when I see him? I am actually way more nervous for Jack than I am for me. And it hits me right there, in this very second, standing in the middle of the buzzing hallway, kids pressing into me, pushing past me—

I know what a real friend is like.

I know how it feels.

Cue the music! Start the applause! Right there, when the bell is about to ring, this light just goes off in my head. Or maybe I should say a light goes *on*. Four words come to mind: *I do not care.* Or is it seven? *I do not care what Sassy thinks!* She doesn't scare me anymore. I don't want her to like me. I don't *need her* to like me. And when I walk through the door into first period and our eyes connect? When she predictably whispers to Aspen, scrunches up her nose, and laughs? I just, like, smile a totally friendly smile back. I sit down. I take out my books. I look up at Ms. González standing by her desk. I don't even really think about it! It's hard to explain, but I'm not even mad at her—

I just don't care.

There is no superpower involved. No magic, no secret. It's really simple. I don't know how to say it except: if you're lucky enough to get a second chance at something? Don't waste it.

On my way to lunch, by my locker, Sammie from soccer runs up and hugs me! I've never hung out with her that much, but I don't know why. She's, like, super nice and really funny.

She stands by my locker and waits for me to fit my bag in.

"Oh my gosh," she tells me, moving in closer. "Can I tell you something that's a little bit of a TMI?"

I nod.

Sammie takes a big breath. Her eyes are really twinkly, like she has a huge secret. She lowers her voice to an almost whisper. "I just got my period! And I think I might be leaking!"

My mouth falls open. And I hesitate for a moment. I almost don't say it. I almost hold it back, but then, what the heck! It's all about making new friends, right?

"I got it too!" I tell her.

"Shut. *Up!*" says Sammie, grinning. "Oh my gosh, like, my sister told me that when a bunch of girls hang out together, sometimes they all get their period at the same time! Maybe it was, like . . . maybe it was all of us hanging out at Claire's!"

"Maybe." I laugh.

"OMG! We're synchronized, Elle. We're like sisters!"

Sammie says, working to keep her voice down. You can't not smile when you're with Sammie. She's so funny.

"Well?" Sammie scrunches up her nose, sounding a little embarrassed. She leans in and whispers right into my ear. "Will you, like, tell me if I'm leaking?"

"Sure," I say nervously, giggling.

She spins around, looking back over her shoulder at me as she walks like a supermodel striding down the mostly empty hall.

I watch her.

We both start cracking up.

I run up to her and catch up. We're both laughing hard now.

"You're all good!" I announce.

"Phew! Oh my gosh, I know that's so weird, but, it just feels like—"

"It feels really kind of weird, right?" I finish, giggling.

"So. Weird!" says Sammie, threading her arm through mine as we walk together toward the cafeteria, down the long Thatcher hall, past the orange lockers, past two teachers talking.

Sammie looks at me. "The funniest thing is, I was, like, literally so excited to, you know, get it!" She pauses thoughtfully. "But seriously, now that I got it? It seems kind of like a major pain in the butt, right?"

"I guess," I reply with a shy smile. "I mean, it's only been like twelve hours for me."

"Well, gosh, me too, but in my totally inexperienced opinion? Boys literally have it so good! They're so lucky! I mean, could you, like, imagine, if they actually had to have blood come out of their body!" Sammie laughs and shakes her head. "It's just so much easier being a boy. You just don't have to worry about a lot of stuff."

"Yeah," I say as we continue walking. I almost don't say it, but then I do.

"But, like, guys have other stuff that's kind of hard too."

"Oh, really?" jokes Sammie, our arms still looped as we move down the hall. "That's what I love about you, Elle! You're always so, like, considerate and thoughtful. You are the best! We definitely need to hang out a lot more!"

"Yeah," I agree, and grin. "I'd like that."

"You need to come have a sleepover after soccer! Mackenzie too! We can make brownies and just eat the batter!"

"I'm down," I say, grinning when I hear myself, because I sound like the boys.

"And," she goes on, pressing into me as we walk, "we literally need to convince Mackenzie to switch back to Thatcher!"

"Totally!" I agree, remembering what Jack told me: "*Mackenzie and Sammie, they're both awesome.*"

Sammie talks loud as we enter the super-noisy

cafeteria. "Hey, you played like a *boss* yesterday at try-outs! Go get it, girl! You totally rocked it!"

"I did?" I ask before I quickly correct myself. "I mean, um, thanks!"

The cafeteria is packed as usual with Thatcher's entire seventh and eighth grades. It's so loud! In the line for food, Sammie and I pick up more friends—Claire (who gives me a gigantic hug), Addi, Annie Hutchinson, and two girls who are in chorus with me, Emma and Hannah. By the time we emerge from the food line and stand looking out at the swarms, trying to find an empty table, we're like a full-fledged parade. We have picked up three more members—Tatum, Hope, and Catherine.

We stand there, holding our plastic trays and looking out at the maze of crowded tables.

"Where should we sit?" asks Claire. Her eyes, like mine, scanning for space.

At this exact second, Aspen appears out of nowhere. My stomach kind of pangs. To be perfectly and completely honest, some familiar not-so-great-feelings flood back. Aspen glares at me, annoyed, then grabs Claire's upper arm. "Claire, oh my gosh, *what* are you doing!" she demands. "We're over *here*." She gestures across the room. "Come on!"

All of us can't help but look. Our heads all turn like a synchronized dance team.

Diagonally across the cafeteria in the corner, Sassy sits, residing at the head of her "popular" girls table. The queen and her court all have the same blank expression, perfect shiny hair, makeup. Nobody looks very happy.

They are all staring back at us. Watching.

You can feel the tension.

"Um"—Claire stammers at first, then—"I'm fine, thanks," she tells Aspen, looking at me and smiling as she says it.

"Yeah, we're good," adds Sammie, with a gutsy, knowing grin.

Then—

"Elle!" I hear my name.

I know the voice. I know it well.

He has to yell over the cafeteria chaos. When he does, it seems like practically the whole entire busy place gets almost quiet. I lift my eyes and follow his voice, all the way across the room by the guidance doors. "Elle!" Jack has his hands cupped up around his mouth. "Elle!" he shouts. He smiles this big smile and madly waves his arm above his head. Owen, Sammy, Demaryius, Trey, Dominic, Brayden. I watch them all stand up, smiling and waving and shouting to me.

"Elle O'Brien!" they all yell at once. "Elle!!!"

I can't hear what they're saying besides my name, but I can tell by the way they're waving what they want me to do. My eyes light up. I catch myself smiling. I give

Sammie a nod and a big confident grin and mouth, "Let's go!" and I start walking. I navigate around the web of tables, stepping over backpacks and squeezing between chairs. For a second, the noise dampens. I feel everyone's eyes on me. I look over my shoulder. All the girls are behind me, a train of new friends. When I turn back to where I'm headed, I watch Sammy and Demaryius carrying an empty table, setting it down, pushing it together with theirs. Dominic, Brayden, and Owen lift the extra stack of cafeteria chairs over their heads and set them down, arranging them, connecting the two tables into one.

And then there's Jack. He's looking right at me, watching me as I get closer and closer with this big smile on his face. He's standing behind an empty chair, right next to his.

56
JACK ▶

AFTER LUNCH, I AM ALREADY in my seat in sixth-period social studies when I hear a woman's voice over the loudspeaker make an announcement: "Jack Malloy, please report to the main office." Then they say it again, with more urgency. "Jack Malloy, please report to the main office immediately."

My stomach just drops. Getting called out of class in the middle of the day—there's nothing about that scenario that can mean anything good. I stand up and grab my bag, my books. Right away, my heart starts pounding.

Demaryius gives me a nod. "That's you, bro. What's that all about?"

I shrug and say, "I don't know, man." I try to act like I'm not thinking the things I'm thinking, which is that I'm starting to worry about everybody and everyone.

Maybe something happened to my brothers. Maybe my dad's flipped out. Maybe something happened with that crazy nurse and Elle!

My head starts throbbing. I'm sweating, and my thoughts begin to race. By the time I leave social studies and hurry out of the room down the empty hall to the office, I'm feeling lightheaded, dizzy. Hot. I stop right before I reach the guidance counselor's wing, connected to the main office. I pause outside the door, leaning my back up against the lockers. I tell myself to calm down. Everything doesn't have to be bad news, right? I mean, like, maybe it's something good. For a moment I wish Summer was here. I wish she could be the one waiting in the main office. But she's not here, and I am. I take a really deep breath and put my hand on the door knob.

I see Jett standing in his dress shirt, necktie, and a navy-blue Saint Joe's blazer before he sees me. That awful feeling in my stomach explodes into my heart. This has to be something even worse than I even thought. He's talking to Mr. Santos by the front entrance, next to the attendance lady's desk. I walk kind of fast. I try to think brave thoughts, even though I feel more and more nauseous the closer I get.

Jett, in his thick black-framed glasses and his loosened necktie, looks up, sees me, and smiles. And, god, I swear right that second, I can tell. I can tell, like, nobody died. I know what *that* face looks like. I take the biggest, most relieved breath of my life, exhaling the air out of my lungs. But I hurry. I'm still kind of worried. Jett has never come into school to pick me up. I've never in my entire life gotten called out of class.

Jett gives me a nod and a wink as I approach. "'Sup, big guy."

"Is everything okay?" I just blurt it out.

Jett doesn't answer, though. Instead he turns to Mr. Santos, reaching out to shake hands.

"Sir, thank you," Jett tells him, looking him square in the eye.

As soon as we walk out the Thatcher doors, as soon as we are outside on the sidewalk, Jett tells me.

"Dad wants to have a meeting," he says. He doesn't stop or look at me. He tells me as we walk to the truck that he has parked on the curb in the visitors' circle.

"A meeting? Why?" I ask, confused.

"I don't know, man." He raises his eyebrows, looking anxious.

"Oh, man," I mutter. "This can't be good."

In the truck, Jett doesn't drive with the music blasting like we normally do. It's just completely silent except for the thump of the pavement moving underneath us. When we pull into the driveway, I feel like I might puke.

Jett turns and looks at me before we get out. "Bro,

settle down. Just don't think negatively, man. You never know." He pauses and shrugs as he opens the truck door. "It might be something good for once."

"I doubt it," I counter, under my breath.

Jett stands outside the truck and waits for me to get out. We don't say a word as we walk up the path to the door. Then, right before we step inside, he gives me a look. "If it's bad," he tells me, putting his hand on my shoulder, "we're all going to be together, and we'll take it."

The meeting is in the living room, which makes me worry even more. We never sit in there, you know . . . ever since my mom. The double doors with the glass and the curtains, they've been shut. Closed.

Everything about the room reminds me of my mom. The smell. The big sofa, the fireplace, the books lining the bookcase, the framed family photos of my mom and dad at their wedding, my brothers holding me up for the first time on skates—picture proof that there was once a time that my dad was actually happy.

When I walk in, Gunner and Stryker are already waiting on the big couch, still dressed in their matching navy-blue blazers with the Saint Joe's school crest.

"'Sup, man." Stryker nods. He looks just as nervous as I feel. His tie is loosened like Jett's, the top button of his shirt undone.

I sink down into the sofa in the gap of space between

Stryker and Jett. Gunner's huddled on the very end, looking rattled.

Nobody talks.

Nobody moves.

So I sit and stare at the floor.

My dad walks into the room dressed in the clothes he wears to work—tie loosened, crisp blue shirt with the sleeves rolled, dark suit pants. He looks different, clean-shaven; the shadow beard of rough white stubble is gone. He pauses in front of the photos lining the mantel, then clears his throat, and, using one hand, picks up the heavy wood-framed chair from the corner of the room and sets it directly in front of us.

My heart is racing. I'm shaking my leg. Stryker covers his hand over my knee and gives me a look that says, "Stop."

My dad sits down. I make myself look at him. I lift my eyes. And I didn't expect it, but my dad's actually smiling. Like, a gentle, warm smile. I haven't seen him smile like that in so long. I glance sideways at my brothers. They look just as surprised.

"Boys, I'm going to get right to it," he says. My dad's eyes are so blue and clear. He takes a deep breath and looks right at me. "Jack, first, thank you."

I look back confused. Then I realize. *Elle.*

"Yesterday wasn't easy. What you said, it . . ." He trails off. He breathes. "What you said really hit home. I'm not going to mince words. Losing your mom—" My dad just stops. He stops and closes his eyes. He raises his hands to his face and bows his head.

It is absolutely quiet.

Complete silence.

I do not even move. I don't move my eyes. I don't shift. I have never ever seen my dad like this. My dad, he's, like, the toughest, strongest man I know.

"Your mom," he begins again, his voice cracking. "The thing that was most important to her—" He stops.

We all see it.

"It's been tough. I know I haven't been . . ." He pauses again, choked up. His eyes begin to fill with tears. "My job as your dad is to completely love you."

There's a long time again where no words are said. And we sit and watch the welling in his eyes until there's nowhere left for the tears to go, and the grief spills out, streaking down his cheeks.

It's so quiet as it happens. Nobody speaks. I try, through the silence—I try holding my breath, try to keep it inside. Until I can't. I steal a glance at my brothers. Jett, Gunner, Stryker, each wiping away tears.

I feel this gushing relief.

The tears just keep coming.

"You boys are my pride and joy," my dad goes on. "You are the biggest blessing of my life. You do everything right. And I'm not talking about hockey. Hockey is a game, it is not what defines you. You are beautiful young men. You are kind, you care about others—" I look up at his eyes brightening through the tears. I haven't seen them shine like that in over a year. "For the last year, you boys have been raising yourselves. What I had to tell you now, it could not wait. I'm just sorry it took so long," he tells us, breaking down.

"I'm back," says my dad. "I'm here, and I want to tell you how much I love you."

IT IS FEBRUARY FOURTH, WHICH means two things: it is my birthday, and I am turning thirteen.

The first thing I do when I wake up is take out the folded-up piece of notebook paper I found tucked under a book. Yes, it's Jack's. I've thought about it ever since I found it. Sometimes I take it out, carefully unfold it, and look at it before I go to bed. I've been waiting until I turned thirteen to start a new tradition.

I do it right when I wake up, after I watch the sunrise, still in bed and propped up with a pillow.

"Here goes nothing," I say aloud, smiling at my own white, blank sheet of lined paper and putting the blue pen to the page. I'm starting with one year at a time. Things I want to do or try.

"Elle O'Brien, thirteen!!!" I write in shaded 3-D letters.

☐ Try out for spring track!

☐ Get good at hockey!

☐ Try out for *The Music Man* at Thatcher and make it!

Instead of numbers, like Jack, I make empty boxes that I plan to check off when I complete my missions. Laugh all you want, or maybe try it! Jack says, "If you dream it, you can achieve it!" I think I believe him. Ever since I've been back in my own body, I've been just really happy. I look people in the eye. I have so many friends. I feel more confident, like I can just walk up and talk to anyone and be fine. I'm having a massive all-girl sleepover tonight!

After breakfast, my mom drops me off at the rink. Did you think I was kidding? I walk around the back, open the trunk, and hoist my huge bag up on my shoulder.

"Got it, birthday girl?" my mom calls back, looking over her shoulder.

"Got it!" I say. "Thanks!"

She smiles at me with her usual huge smile. "I'm so proud of you about this hockey thing. I think it's awesome!"

I start walking for the curb, stick in hand, when I hear my mom call out, and I turn and look back.

"I'm going to Lulu's for coffee," she tells me through her open window. "I'll be back in a little while!"

I'm not in a full-on league yet. I mean, indoor soccer just ended. So for an early birthday present, my mom got me all the gear, and she drops me off at the open skate every Saturday morning. I researched it all myself. I signed up. I called and talked to the guy at the rink. I used my life savings to pay for the winter session: one hundred and seventy-five dollars! I'm invested.

Oh my gosh, skating is a lot harder when I'm not in Jack's body! The first time I stepped onto the ice with all the gear, I literally fell down on my face! I ate it. It was actually pretty funny. Like I said, you've got to start someplace!

No biggie, I just got up slowly, one foot at a time. I took little baby steps, like a duck, waddling around the ice. Slowly, I've gotten better and better.

I walk through the rink doors in my soccer hoodie and sweats, my high ponytail, my hockey bag on my shoulder. Inside, I love the smell. The cool air hits your face, and it's like . . .

It's awesome.

I got here a little early. There's a game going on. I look up at the scoreboard hanging over center ice: ten more minutes. There's a lot of people watching, parents cheering. I drop my bag down on the big wooden benches, take my stick, and walk out to stand ice level, right behind the goalie, looking through glass. I see them from behind first, and my mouth seriously just about drops open.

I know it's them.

I can hear their voices.

To my right, like, one foot away, Jett, Stryker, and Gunner are all standing, faces pressed close to the glass. I literally get chills. Man, I want to run up and hug them! I have to stop myself. Because . . . well, they don't know me! They don't know me at all. Even though they kind of do. They'd probably think it was a little bit weird if some thirteen-year-old girl came up to them and threw her arms around their waists, clinging to them like long-lost friends. My heart races, though, I am so excited. If the boys are here, this means I get to watch Jack! Jack and I have become really close. He always cheers me on and gives me good advice. It's really nice to have a good guy friend. We're like brother and sister. I give him tips on him and Mackenzie—even though he swears they're "just friends!" And he's always looking out for me. It's, like, a total tradition that all my friends and all his friends sit together at lunch. And we're not cliquey at all. Anyone who wants to can come sit with us.

I move in to stand beside Jett. I lean on my stick with my hands, the top tucked under my chin, and press my nose to the cold pane of glass.

Jett turns and looks down at me, real quick.

"Hey!" he says warmly. His eyes flash like he knows me.

"Hey," I say, smiling back eagerly.

The other boys all lean forward and look to see who Jett is talking to.

"Nice twig!" Gunner says, checking out my stick. "Is

that an Easton Stealth?"

"Yeah." I nod and shrug and smile like it's all no big deal.

"Dude, that's sick!" echoes Stryker. "Can I see it?"

I proudly hand my stick over. The boys all crowd around it. Stryker takes it and pretends to shoot an invisible puck. "Oh, yeah, this flex is unreal! You obviously know what you're doing," he says, smiling, handing it back.

"Not really," I say, a little shy. "I'm just starting."

"Well, you'll dangle with that!" Gunner winks.

Jett looks at me, grinning through his thick black-framed glasses. "Just keep at it," he tells me. "You'll be sniping in no time."

Two guys come crashing into the glass. It shakes on impact.

"Oh, yeaaaah, bud!" Gunner's face lights up.

I step back.

Jack is one of the guys!

When the whistle blows, the boys go nuts. "Yeah, buddy!" says Gunner. "More of that, bro!"

Stryker turns to Jett. "Yeah, he cranked 'em good. Great shot, great speed, what a shift. Kid's a stud."

Jett pounds the glass with his palms. "That's how it's done, bud!"

At first I don't think he sees us, he's so focused. But then, right before the face-off, to the right of the goalie, Jack coasts in for the draw, quickly looks back at the four of us, and breaks into a huge smile.

* * *

There's more.

After the game, I'm about to step down onto the clean ice. The Zamboni has one more lap. I'm standing at the gate, fully dressed, pads, helmet on, stick in my hand, chewing on my mint-flavored mouth guard. The crowd from Jack's game is emptying out. I look up into stands, and I see her.

My mom.

She's wearing Ugg boots, her yoga pants, and her cozy warm shearling parka. She has on one of those big Russian fur hats, her deep red hair poking out in long, loose waves. *She looks adorable*, I think, and smile up at her, feeling lucky.

I see her smiling too, only she's not smiling at me. She's talking to someone. I almost don't recognize him because he's got this huge grin, and his hair is longer, wavy like Jett's.

Then—

I figure it out.

My eyes linger on the two of them talking and laughing. Jack told me about what happened. How much everything has changed. How his dad's been so much more relaxed, laid-back. How they do fun things together, and they don't have so many rules.

My mom is deep in conversation. She's flipping her hair and leaning forward and laughing. The Captain version 2.0—I'm not gonna lie, he's extremely handsome. The way he carries himself, strong, confident. He's like that good mix of tough and gentle. I'll admit it, as I stand there, about to get on the ice, as the Zamboni drives off into its little garage, the thought enters my mind. Crazier things have happened! I'm far away, but I can tell by the way she's standing. My mom looks so happy. I actually hear her laugh echo through the empty stands. I step onto the ice, smiling at my secret wish, and I dig my skate in and I glide.

3 YEARS LATER

IT'S BEEN THREE YEARS SINCE everything happened. There's so much to catch you up on, and I'll try my best. We sold our place and moved to a beautiful house on the lake—an old cottage that my dad stripped down to the bones and completely rebuilt. We all helped. It took two years. All the wood we used was reclaimed from the old cottage. The joists, the floorboards. It smells like pine. Every room has a view of the water. Every morning I watch the sunrise, and in the summer we take a running jump off our dock and swim all the way straight across lake. Well, no. My brothers, Elle, and I swim. My dad and Summer paddle our canoe, cheering us on. There if we need them.

My life is pretty much perfect. I never thought I'd have a sister, that's for sure. We all love Elle so much. She has four big brothers who would do anything for her. And you should see her play hockey! Man, she's fast! Her stride is almost flawless, her long dark-red hair flowing from the back of her helmet. And I'm her big brother now—by one year—so I can brag.

This spring, she earned the lead role in the high school's production of *Fiddler on the Roof*—as a tenth grader. Pretty badass. She was amazing. We were all there, all six of us, third row back, cheering like crazy. She's only a sophomore, but she's already getting recruited for soccer, hockey, and track. Her dream is Harvard. I'm pretty sure it's gonna happen.

My dad wasn't just saying it. He meant what he said. He changed. He changed more than I could have asked. First of all, he quit his job and works at home. He converted this old barn that was on the land into a wood shop. He makes sculptures now. They're really cool. People buy them for a lot of money. And in the other half of the barn, he built us a space to shoot pucks and mess around. It's better than The Cage. We push the giant sliding barn doors open and it feels like you're outside, even when it's snowing or pouring down rain.

My brothers, me, and my dad decided together that we would only play hockey during the season. It's not a job, it's a passion. We don't touch the ice from May through August. We just lift and swim and eat a lot—anything we want. Summer's even got us all—even my dad—hooked on yoga. Our new less-is-more approach, it's really paying off. Jett and Stryker play for Boston College. Jett is a senior captain and a first-round draft pick for the Los Angeles Kings. Gunner retired from hockey after he had too many concussions. He's playing guitar now, and he has his own band. They practice in the loft up in the barn. They're really pretty decent. They play acoustic country.

I still write down my goals every night. But I am proud to say I got to check one off. This fall I signed a national letter of intent committing to play for Boston College after I graduate high school. Stryker will be a junior, and I'll be a freshman.

I still visualize my dreams, but I've changed. I have a lot less fear. No more panic. My dad's been the biggest role model in my life. He's helped me become the person that I am. The only reason I am where I am is because of him. The discipline he instilled in me. The work ethic. He says, if you want to do something, just do what you love. Do it. And have fun!

My favorite times with my family are the warm, clear summer nights. The seven of us, Summer looking rad as usual with her flaming red hair and her incredible smile; my dad—he has a beard now. They're always holding hands. We all sit around a big bonfire on the lakeshore.

Summer's love and laugh has rubbed off on all of us. Just her presence, her strength. I guess if I had to explain it, she's taught us softness is not the same as weakness.

Gunner brings his guitar, and we sing the Beatles, the Eagles, or James Taylor, the bonfire raging, the lake shimmering under the starry night sky. We laugh so hard. Sometimes we even talk about my mom. We remember her, all the good times.

I still wear the gold chain and pendant around my neck.

I never take it off.

The pendant is engraved with one word in tiny scripted letters. You need a magnifying glass to see—

The word is LOVE.

I love my family more than I could ever say. When I look across the fire at Summer and my dad, Jett, Elle, Gunner, Stryker, I'm so grateful. I feel like the luckiest kid in the world.

And maybe I am.

ACKNOWLEDGMENTS

I live in the house
　　near the corner, which I have named
　　Gratitude.
　　　　—MARY OLIVER

I WOULD LIKE TO THANK Katherine Tegen, Maria Barbo, Kate Morgan Jackson, and everyone at HarperCollins Children's and KT Books who sprinkled so much of their own magic to get this book in your hands and make it beautiful.

A very special thanks to my wonderful literary agent, Margaret Riley King, and the entire team at William Morris Endeavor, expressly—Chelsea Drake, Laura Bonner, Jo Rodgers, Anna DeRoy, Erin Conroy, and Jennifer Rudolph Walsh. What a gift it is to be represented by these smart and gracious women.

I owe tremendous gratitude to Ken Weinrib; he's pretty much a superhero—everyone should be lucky enough to have him on their side.

And finally, to the quiet champs who cheered this story on. This work is a lighthouse shining with your kindness. I am more grateful than I can say.

BORN AND RAISED IN ITHACA, NEW YORK, Megan Shull is the author of several books for kids, including the award-winning young adult novel *Amazing Grace*. Megan holds a doctorate in educational psychology from Cornell University, where she also earned her undergraduate degree. She lives in her hometown, where she feels especially lucky to walk the quiet rolling hills alongside red-tailed hawks and waterfalls.

Connect with Megan online at heymegan.com and find her on Facebook and Twitter @meganshull.